# BAD
# BLOOD

# BAD BLOOD

## E. O. CHIROVICI

First published in Great Britain in 2018 by Serpent's Tail,
an imprint of Profile Books Ltd
3 Holford Yard
Bevin Way
London
WC1X 9HD
www.serpentstail.com

1 3 5 7 9 10 8 6 4 2

Designed and typeset by sue@lambledesign.demon.co.uk

Printed and bound in Great Britain by Clays Ltd, Elcograf S.p.A.

A CIP record for this book can be obtained from the British Library

ISBN: 978 1 78816 063 6
eISBN: 978 1 78283 454 0

Never real and always true

Antonin Artaud


There is no present or future—only the past,
happening over and over again—now.

Eugene O'Neill, *A Moon for the Misbegotten*

# prologue

Paris, France, October 1976

TERMINAL ONE OF PARIS'S Charles de Gaulle Airport was shaped like an octopus: countless arms made up of corridors and annexes spread from the central corpus, connecting the service areas with the other amenities. It was futuristic, packed, and noisy, and arriving in the vast entrance hall, the young man felt an almost irresistible urge to turn on his heel and get out of there.

He'd bought his ticket the evening before, from an agency near the Rue de Rome. There were still four hours until his flight, so he'd have to spend a lot of time in this place where the air was getting thinner by the minute.

He picked up his bag and walked up to the second floor, in search of a place to sit down. Security had been upgraded since June, when an Air France flight had been hijacked by terrorists and diverted to Uganda, with 248 passengers on board. Patrols were everywhere, the agents equipped like they were in a postapocalyptic movie. He tried not to make the mistake of staring at them, which would have drawn their attention.

He found a free table in a coffee shop at the end of the concourse, ordered a double espresso, and placed his bag under his chair. Through the windows, he could see gloomy rainclouds floating across the darkening sky and airplanes lined up in front of the hangars, maintenance crews and buses full of passengers swarming among them. On a small transistor radio nearby, Roberta Flack's "Killing Me Softly" was playing gently—an irony of fate.

He'd been determined not to think much about what had happened two nights before, at least not until he got back to the States. It was possible that her parents might already have raised the alarm, and that the authorities might already be on the alert. In that event, he'd be one of the prime suspects, and the police would make it their priority to prevent him from leaving the country. He had to get out, to reach the safety of home—how precious the word sounded, he thought to himself, home—and to see how well the plan he'd set in motion would work.

It wasn't only the legal problem. The thought that he'd never see her again was agonizing. Whenever that idea rose in his mind, he felt it like a punch in the stomach. He'd always been afraid of the irreversible, of actions that could never be repaired, no matter whether he or somebody else was responsible for them.

When he was six, he'd been given a goldfish as a present, in a bowl that was shaped like half a football. After about a month or so, he'd forgotten to feed it or change the water or both for a couple of days, and the fish had died. He'd found it one morning floating, motionless, like a small gleaming jewel. His mom had told him that goldfish of that species were perhaps too sensitive and that it wouldn't have survived anyway, but he didn't believe her. He knew it had been his fault, even if nobody had scolded him for it. And no matter how sorry he felt, there was nothing that could be done about it.

He was taking a sip of his coffee when a tall, sweaty man asked him if he could sit down at the table. He gave a start and almost spilled his beverage, but nodded to signal that the other chair was free. The man ordered a cappuccino and two croissants, which he began guzzling as soon as the waitress brought them.

"It's the first time I've been to this new airport," the man confessed. He brushed the crumbs from the table and made a sweeping gesture with his hand. "I think they've done a good job, don't you?"

He spoke French with a strange accent, rolling his *r*s and swallowing consonants. The young man muttered something in agreement. He wiped his mouth with a napkin, and immediately realized that the mouth wiping had become something of a compulsive gesture in the last couple of days, as if he were trying to get rid of the stains left by—

"Blood," the man said.

"What?" he blurted, staring at him.

"I think there's a small bloodstain on your jacket," the man explained. "I know about such things. I'm a doctor."

The young man tried to find the spot the guy was talking about, but he couldn't—it was somewhere near his shoulder, and he'd have to take off his jacket to be able to see it.

"Perhaps I cut myself shaving," he said. All of a sudden he felt his throat turn dry and the sweat began trickling down his back.

"Strange. I can't see any trace of a cut on your face. You English?"

"No, American. I'd better get going. It was great meeting you, take care."

The guy looked at him in surprise and muttered something in reply, but he'd already stood up and slipped away among the groups of people looking at the shop windows.

At the other end of the concourse were some toilets, and he walked into a cubicle and bolted the door. The strong smell of odorizer made him nauseous and he was barely able to hold down the espresso that was now rising up his throat. He took his passport out of his pocket, opened it, and looked at the photo, trying to picture his own face. It's alright, he told himself, everything is alright. All I have to do is hold out for another hour or two, and get out of here. Nobody will ever find out.

He left the cubicle and studied his reflection in the mirror as he rinsed his hands. He glimpsed the bloodstain the man at the table had noticed—it was the size of a dime. He took off his coat, soaked a paper towel in soapy water, and began rubbing at it. The towel slowly turned a dull, dirty pink.

Two hours later, he went to the desk, checked his bag, then climbed to the fourth level and walked determinedly to passport control. As he was waiting in line, he took a tissue out of his pocket and wiped his lips. He could still feel the burning sensation when he reached the customs officer, handing his passport through the slot in the glass pane.

# one

"LADIES AND GENTLEMEN, good evening. My name is James Cobb, and as some of you probably already know, for the last few years I've been focusing my research on so-called altered states of consciousness—hypnosis in particular. We have the opportunity to be here together this evening thanks to the generous invitation extended to me by the J. L. Bridgewater Foundation, which I'd like to thank once again.

"I'm not going to talk about my recent book, which deals with the same subject and which I hope you'll find interesting reading, but about the paths I followed in order to reach my conclusions.

"Are there any police detectives, forensics or prosecutors here in the audience? I can see a few raised hands. I'm sure that any one of you would have been happy to replace days and nights of investigation, hundreds of procedures, long hours of interviews, and lab work with one session of hypnosis in which the suspect, having entered a trance, could be asked a single question: Did you do it?

"But things don't work like that. We don't actually have any guarantee that once a person is in a state of hypnosis they'll tell the whole truth and nothing but the truth, and that at least two essential aspects of the communication process have indeed been completely eliminated—dissimulation and fantasy.

"For these same reasons, the lie detector—which in the beginning investigators welcomed as a miracle—is accepted only as circumstantial evidence in court, in some cases, while in others it isn't admissible at all.

"In the eighties, there were psychiatrists who made hay of exposing so-called cases of satanic ritual abuse against children, abuses which were supposed to have come to light during sessions of hypnosis which the alleged victims, having reached adulthood, were subjected to. Today, we know that many lives were destroyed back then on the basis of fantasies as a result of the manipulation of the participants by their so-called objective examiners. In trance, the subjects did not reveal real *memories*, but responded in such a way as to please the hypnotist.

"My research, on the other hand, has confirmed that once under hypnosis, the subject's willpower is dramatically diminished, and his free will is all but abolished. This is why a person in a trance is able to do things that they'd normally refuse to do, if the hypnotist asks them to.

"Now, please, let me give you a simple demonstration. You'll have to answer two questions, one after the other, as quickly as you can. Okay, are you ready? Well, imagine you've been invited to attend a gala dinner in a fancy restaurant. Alright, so the tags with your names on them are placed on each ... Right, on each *table*. Who killed Cain?

"Your answer was *Abel*, although I'm sure you know as well as I do that it's the other way around in the Bible: Cain killed Abel and fled east of Eden, to the Land of Nod. Why did you give the wrong answer? The explanation isn't as simple as you might be tempted to believe at first glance.

"Of course, the word association between *table* and *Abel* is obvious. But why did it have such a strong effect on you, enough to distract you from the answer you knew was correct? We should take into account the fact that it was *I* who asked the question, up here on this podium, whom you have, without argument, endowed with superior knowledge. In such a situation, a *transfer of responsibility* occurs, which is particularly apparent in cases of armed conflict, when large masses of people follow their leaders, regardless of whether their orders might mean death for a significant number of them. The audience automatically endows the person up here with abilities superior to their own, and in such conditions the level of suggestibility increases.

"Or imagine you're in the Amazon rainforest and are being guided by someone to a shelter. The transfer of responsibility/credibility onto the guide is almost total, because you're in a hostile and potential dangerous environment, so your life's under imminent threat.

"I've given you these examples to show to you how things work during hypnosis. The responsibility that the subject transfers onto the examiner is far greater in the cases of states of altered consciousness than in so-called normal states. The mental realm through which the subject is guided is completely alien to him, but the same subject *presumes* that the examiner has a far better grasp of that mental space. And just between you and me, this is often nothing more than that—a presumption.

"Then there's the question of the relativity of what we broadly call *reality*. We 'know' that a subject, an object, a person are *real* because, through our senses, we collect information which, once processed by our brains, leads us to this conclusion. Yes, the auditorium where you're sitting exists, the person talking to you and the PowerPoint projection exist. All these things are *real*, aren't they? We know it because we can *see* them, *hear* them, *and sense* them. Consequently, we *know* that what we're experiencing is 'real.' But a subject under the influence of a powerful substance such as LSD *knows*, *sees*, and *senses* a completely different 'reality,' which is just as convincing to him as this auditorium is to us right now. All that is needed is the intervention of a minuscule alteration in the complex chemistry of our brain in order for us to feel happy or to plunge into depression, for us to be very calm or extremely violent, apathetic or agitated, imaginative or dull, regardless of the 'objective' reality around us and regardless of the past and the knowledge/ information accumulated, which has shaped our seemingly solid convictions, beliefs, and behaviors.

"As a result, I asked myself what kind of *reality* does a subject in a state of hypnosis describe, the reality of that unique and unrepeatable moment, the so-called 'objective' reality? The 'subjective' reality suggested by the examiner? The reality cemented by convictions and beliefs accumulated over a lifetime, the reality that we might call *transcendent*, and which isn't the result of the usual cognitive processes? Does the subject communicate what he *believes*, what he *sees*, or only what he intuits his mental *guide*, the therapist, wants him to communicate?

"Now, let's move on to the second part of our meeting, in which I'll be taking questions from the audience. I've agreed with the organizers that these questions will be limited to five, given the constraints of time. I hope that those of you who wish to ask a question have already written their names on the list at the entrance. At the end there will be a book-signing session at that stand. Thanks for your time and it's been a real honor and a privilege to be here today."

That evening, after the lecture, I'd planned to meet Randolph Jackson, a friend of mine, and Brenda Reuben, my agent, for dinner. But Brenda had a stinking cold, and Randolph had just found out that he had to be in Atlantic City the next morning, so he left in a hurry. I told Brenda to go home to bed, and went outside.

I was looking for a cab when a tall, slim man with a military attitude about him approached me. He looked to be in his sixties and he had a pencil mustache, the kind that was fashionable with lady-killers back in the thirties. He wore a dark suit with a matching raincoat and introduced himself as Joshua Fleischer.

As a rule, I try to avoid contact with people from the audience after a book signing or a lecture. The ones who come up to me are often tiresome and it's always hard to get rid of them. Sometimes, after such meetings, they send me long letters or emails warning me that all my money and fame won't save me from the fires of hell.

He said, "I'd like to invite you to dinner, Dr. Cobb."

We were standing in front of the bookstore and the wind was gusting, lifting the hem of his open coat. Tucked under his arm he had a copy of my book, which he was clenching as if afraid of losing it.

"Thanks, but I've already made plans," I answered and started to descend the steps.

He placed his hand delicately on my shoulder.

"You're probably assailed by all kinds of weirdos after these events, but I assure you I'm not one of them. I have every reason to believe that you'll be very interested in what I have to say to you. I'm very familiar with your work, and I know what I'm talking about. I read your book a month ago, just after it was released, and I knew that you were the person I was looking for."

I thanked him once again, but still turned down his invitation. He didn't insist, but he did wait next to me until a passing cab deigned to stop.

"I'll send you an email," he warned. "Please make sure that it doesn't end up in the spam folder. It's really important, you'll see."

As I was climbing into the car I heard him coughing. It was a deep, exhausting cough, the likes of which I'd only ever come across in people suffering from serious illness.

I forgot about the encounter until the afternoon I received his email, two days later, on a Thursday. It read like this:

Dear James (if I may),

Perhaps I could have chosen a better way to approaching you, but I thought it would be best if we met face to face. I'm not a pest or a wacko. I'm not obsessed with the occult or the paranormal or parallel worlds.

I think I ought to start by telling you a little about myself.

You already know my name. If you caught it that evening, you'll remember that I'm Joshua Fleischer. I was born in New York City and graduated from Princeton in 1976 with an English degree, and in the early eighties I earned a fortune on the stock exchange. I moved to Maine in 1999, after a tragic incident. I'd told myself that I was too tired of living in the big city, and I bought a property near a beautiful wildlife sanctuary. I've never been married, I have no children or next of kin, and I lost both my parents when I was eighteen. I still have some relatives on my mother's side who live in upstate New York, but the last time we spoke on the phone must have been more than thirty years ago.

I hope you haven't already jumped to the conclusion that I'm a loner and a misanthrope, a troglodyte hiding away behind money and the influence it brings. I assure you that I have an extremely active social life. I've never married out of the fear that sooner or later I would have to go through the immense pain of attending the funeral of the woman I loved, and then being condemned to go on living or—even worse—to force her to have to go through it. Maybe I'm just creating complications and perhaps I just haven't met the right person, a person to make me believe that we'll meet again even after death. There have been a couple of women in my life, and some of them have meant a lot

to me. But never so much that I could call it "love,"
apart from one woman, a long time ago. I'll tell you
about her when the time is right, if you agree to my
proposal.

But to move on … I've been a board member of
more than a dozen foundations and charities. For a
time I taught English at a school in Bangor for children
with special needs. I've also volunteered for a home
help program for the needy in Mineral County, where
I live. I've never had the time to feel bored or to ask
myself too many questions.

Two years ago I was diagnosed with a virulent form
of leukemia. They told me it could be genetic—my
paternal grandfather died of the same cause. I didn't
feel sorry for myself and I didn't complain. I've done
everything the doctors have told me to do and signed
all the checks they demanded, but three months ago
they told me I'd lost the battle and that there wasn't
much more they could do. The medicine has done its
job and given me an extra year of life.

I'm not afraid of what is to come and I don't think
it makes any difference whether it happens tomorrow
or ten years from now, as long as my departure causes
nobody any pain.

But there's still one thing I must resolve, and it's a
matter of life and death, to use an expression that might
sound ridiculous given the situation I find myself in.
And I'm convinced that you, James, can help me in this
respect.

I can tell you only face to face what it's all
about, and this is why I hoped that I might have the
opportunity to speak with you that evening. But I
didn't want to insist, lest you think I was intruding
and thereby compromise the chance of you accepting
my proposal. I also think that what I'm going to tell

you will fit in with your scientific interests concerning altered states of consciousness.

If you accept, you'll be my guest here in Maine for a few days. My lawyer's name is Richard Orrin and you'll find his contact information attached below. He'll fill you in on the practical details.

Each day is precious, James. My only hope is that you'll come to a decision quickly and that your decision will be positive.

Until then, I would like to assure you of my esteem and best wishes.

Yours,
Josh

At the end of the message I found the phone number and address of his lawyer.

I spent the whole evening thinking about Fleischer's message.

The style of the letter was fluent and coherent. The information that my online search brought up broadly confirmed its contents. Fleischer was a real patron of the arts in the county where he resided, and the local press was peppered with his praises. He'd helped poor teenagers attend university, battered women build new lives for themselves, ex-convicts integrate back into society, and children with special needs get the best care and education. He'd become an almost legendary figure, a saint and a guru all rolled into one. The "terrible illness" that had lately begun to consume him was alluded to discreetly and with compassion by the local reporters.

Everything he'd written seemed to be true. And a man who had dedicated his life to helping others deserved to receive a helping hand in return.

The release of my book had marked the end of my grant from the J. L. Bridgewater Foundation and I felt like I could use a break. For the last few months I'd been in a relationship with a colleague of mine, Mina Waters, but two months before we'd agreed to stop seeing each other. Neither of us was at an age to harbor any illusions, and it was clear that something just wasn't working. I missed her sometimes, but not enough to break our agreement and call her.

So I had enough time on my hands, even if the few days Joshua Fleischer anticipated were to become a longer stay. I was almost sure that my visit would involve therapy sessions, a kind of preparation for death with a man who, according to his own declarations, didn't believe in God or the afterlife and therefore couldn't find comfort in religion. And this was an even greater reason to appreciate his philanthropy. I've never believed in the charity that springs only from faith, in the philanthropy of those who sign checks for foundations in the same way as they're obligated to pay taxes, of those who put money in the poor box as an offering to a deity they fear rather than out of a feeling of humanity.

# two

ORRIN'S OFFICE WAS ON East 31st Street, in an old eight-story brownstone that was home, as far as I could tell, to a number of healthy businesses.

An assistant met me in the lobby and showed me to the third floor, which was entirely taken up by Orrin, Murdoch & Associates. Just as the clock in the waiting room struck ten, I was ushered into an office with walls upholstered in leather and a floor of exotic wood. Orrin stood up and shook my hand. He was middle-aged, tall, and bald. The wall behind his huge desk was covered with framed diplomas, and some golf trophies were displayed in a glass cabinet.

It all looked exactly as you'd have expected it to look, and this struck me as disappointing rather than reassuring, given that the tone of Joshua Fleischer's message had hinted at mysteries and enigmas waiting to be solved.

Orrin told the assistant that we weren't to be disturbed for half an hour, no matter what, indirectly informing me of the length of our meeting. After I refused the offer of a beverage, we sat down in two armchairs that flanked a coffee table.

"I understand that you have accepted Mr. Fleischer's offer," he began, studying me carefully as he spoke.

"Well, in principle, yes," I said, "but as I don't know what it's all about yet, I hope that our meeting will be enlightening, with a view to my final decision."

The corners of his mouth dropped a bit. "Unfortunately,

Dr. Cobb, I'm not able to offer you any details additional to what you've already discussed with Mr. Fleischer," he said. "My only role in this matter is to assure Mr. Fleischer that from a legal standpoint no information about him or any third parties with whom you may come into contact during the days you're to spend with him will be made public in any form. To put it simply, we're dealing with a non-disclosure agreement. He asked me to handle it because I'm based in New York and he wanted to make sure the matter would be taken care of before you traveled to Maine. I've known Mr. Fleischer for over ten years."

"A strong code of ethics does exist in my profession, as you probably know," I said. "Without the consent of the client, I'm not allowed to make public or use any information I might glean during therapy sessions, not without a warrant."

"I'm aware of that, of course, but we don't even know whether it will be a matter of therapy sessions, do we?"

He opened an elegant leather portfolio and removed a contract, the sheets held together with a paper clip.

"We're a green company and all our contracts are signed electronically," he said. "You'll receive your copy to sign by email later today. This will be the first contract, which deals with the 'medical services' you'll undertake to provide for Mr. Fleischer. I'm afraid it sounds rather vague, but it's the term he chose."

He gave me the pages and I read them carefully. I was to undertake to provide "medical services" of an unspecified nature within a given period of time—six days. Mr. Joshua Fleischer in his turn undertook to pay me a high five-figure sum, in advance. The sum was much larger than what I usually charged and I told the lawyer this.

He shrugged and said, "The sum is Mr. Fleischer's decision, so I have no comment to make. If you believe your services are worth the money, then all the better for you.

Now, here's the non-disclosure agreement."

He handed me the second contract, which was far more complex than the first. It was worded in such a way as to ensure that while I was providing the medical services stipulated in the first contract, not even the smallest detail of any information I might come into contact with would ever travel beyond Fleischer's property.

Nevertheless, one of the clauses stated that in the event that I should consider any item of information to be of sufficiently large scientific importance to be used in a future research paper, I could use it, provided that I change the names of those concerned and never reveal their identities.

It all seemed within the bounds of common sense and professional ethics, so I had no qualms in giving my consent.

Orrin replaced the contract in the portfolio. "This will be good news for Mr. Fleischer," he said. "There are a few more details that need to be taken care of: the bank account where you'd like the money to be paid—I'll be handling that—and the email address at which you'd like to receive the contracts for your electronic signature."

After giving him a business card and my bank details, I thought the meeting had come to an end, but he didn't get up, so I remained seated. He was running his fingers over the case containing the contracts and seemed to be thinking deeply about something, staring into space. On his right wrist he wore a copper bracelet, the kind used to ease rheumatic pains.

"As I mentioned earlier, I first had the pleasure of meeting Mr. Fleischer about ten years ago," he said at last. "In all this time he's never ceased to amaze me with his immense capacity for kindness. There have been people who've taken advantage of him, people he helped and who then hurt him. But he's never seemed to regret even for one moment the things he's done and the way in which he's chosen to live his life. I'm happy, now, to have been able to do him this service, which, given his health, will probably be the last."

I made no comment and let him continue. He went on, "I know that you're highly respected for what you do and that you enjoy the esteem of the scientific community to which you belong, but I won't hide the fact that I carried out a little investigation of my own when Mr. Fleischer informed me of his intentions two weeks ago."

The feeling that somebody has been rummaging through your affairs is always unpleasant, but I had nothing to hide and I told him so. He nodded and said, "I did discover something that—gave me a pause, however, all the more so given that it's been treated with the utmost discretion by the press, to put it euphemistically."

I already knew what he was referring to, but I kept quiet and carried on listening.

"Three years ago, in the summer, to be precise, one of your patients, Miss Julie Mitchell, committed suicide in her apartment in Brooklyn," he said.

"It happened on the evening of June 23rd," I replied. "Miss Mitchell had been diagnosed as bipolar five years previously and had attempted suicide three times before she began therapy sessions with me. One attempt was very severe and she survived only by the skin of her teeth."

"However, her parents sued you for malpractice," he stressed.

"Her parents were crushed by grief. They'd been living a nightmare for years, and they allowed themselves to be played along by an unscrupulous lawyer—please excuse the expression. The DA's office dropped the case. Such things are terrible, but they happen. As a practicing therapist one has to take into account the possibility of such developments in certain cases. I have many years of clinical experience, Mr. Orrin. I didn't just set up practice on the

Upper East Side as soon as I graduated, smoking a pipe and treating rich young widows. I was born and raised in a small town in Kansas, to a working-class family. What are you suggesting?"

"I didn't mean to upset you," he assured me. "It's just that a question mark remains, and—"

"Well, every man's life is full of question marks," I said. "That's why we're human beings and not robots."

"All the same, I think I've managed to upset you."

"Please don't flatter yourself. You haven't done anything of that sort. Probably you tried to convince Mr. Fleischer to abandon his plan in regard to this contract, based on a single tragic incident."

I glimpsed a flash of anger in his eyes. "It's my duty to inform my client about the person with whom he's going to have a contractual relationship," he said. "And I'm not sure whether the phrase 'incident' is the most suitable, given that we're talking about the life of a young woman. Furthermore, from the information I have, things were more complicated than you make them out to be. As far as I'm concerned, it isn't even certain that Miss Mitchell committed suicide, Dr. Cobb. The DA's office investigated the affair, and you were interviewed at a hearing before a commission of peers. The police also questioned you twice."

"It was a standard inquiry, which was absolutely normal given the circumstances. Miss Mitchell had moved out of her parents' home a few months previously, so she was living alone and there were no witnesses. She left no suicide note, in contrast to her previous attempts. But the final conclusion was that she'd voluntarily taken an overdose of sleeping pills, and her death was a result of cardiorespiratory arrest. No accusation of malpractice was upheld after the commission hearing, and the police recommended that the prosecutors dismiss the case, which they did. Is there anything else?"

"I also discovered that, although the concentration of the substance in her blood was twice the lethal dose, no traces were found in her stomach, which suggests that the victim might have been injected with the drug that killed her."

"The second medical examination cleared that up: the first result was, quite simply, a human error."

"You seem like a cynical and harsh man," he concluded, clutching the edges of the portfolio on the table as if he were afraid I might snatch it from him.

I stood up and he quickly did likewise. "I'll be waiting for the contracts," I said. "However, you can consider them as good as signed."

I left without waiting for his assistant to show me out. I heard him mutter something behind me, but I didn't catch the words.

Two hours later, I received the contracts by email. I signed them and sent them back. Toward the evening, Fleischer called me. He began by thanking me for having agreed to the contract.

"I got the distinct feeling that your lawyer was trying to make me change my mind," I told him, and I heard him sigh.

He said, "Well, Dr. Cobb, it seems that sooner or later all wealthy men end up being surrounded by yes-men or idiots or people who are both. I don't know how or why it happens, but I've observed that it does happen, no matter what. In the last few years, Richard has been trying to become more than my attorney, a kind of confidant, an adviser, or whatever you prefer to call him. And now he's seething because I haven't given him any details about what I want from you. Obviously, I didn't take any notice of that story. May I call you James?"

"Sure."

"Thanks, please call me Josh. Well then, James, how will

you be traveling, by car or by plane?"

"By car. If I leave early in the morning, I should be there by evening, allowing some time to stop for lunch."

"You should take Interstate 91 and Interstate 84 and avoid Route 1 along the coast. The traffic is hellish and there's not much to see anyway. You can stop off for lunch in Portland, there's a restaurant just off the turnpike named Susan's Fish and Chips. Try the lobster. When will you set off?"

"The day after tomorrow, so I'll be there on Wednesday evening."

"Do you have any special accommodation requirements, in regard to diet, for example?"

"There's no need for any special preparations," I assured him, "thank you. But I should tell you that the sum stipulated in the contract is much too high, Josh."

"Nobody has ever complained about that before," he laughed. "We'll discuss the details when we see each other. As far as I'm concerned, it's a reasonable sum. If you think it's too large, then why not donate a part of it to a charity?"

"How's your condition?"

"I've given up all treatment except for light painkillers. Fortunately I'm not in much pain, so I only take them rarely and I'm perfectly lucid. I had my last perfusion of cytostatic a month ago. I should mention that I agreed with the doctors that it would be the last. In any case, I'm confident that I'll have enough energy to do what I intend to. You agreeing to this has given me a new lease on life, you know."

"Happy to help."

"We'll see each other on Wednesday. Have a pleasant journey, James. And thanks again for coming."

Before going to bed I thought of Julie.

She was twenty-eight when I first met her, and she was probably the most beautiful woman I'd ever seen. We began her therapy sessions in February, and the next year, in June, she killed herself.

On the three previous occasions she attempted suicide, she'd used sleeping pills twice and slashed her wrists once. It's generally accepted that suicides rarely change their methods. The attempts are either rehearsals for the big sleep or cries for help, which is to say that the suicidal person feels alone and unhappy and craves attention before it's too late.

But Julie wasn't one of those typical cases. Up until the very end I was skeptical about the diagnosis of bipolar disorder. There were days when she seemed like the most balanced person in the world, establishing verbal contact without the slightest difficulty, even taking apparent delight in telling me details about herself. She wasn't a marginalized person—she'd graduated with a degree in Anthropology from Columbia and taken an MA at Cornell. She'd found a job as a copywriter at a major advertising agency, where she earned a good salary and was well liked. She was rarely in a bad mood, and even when she felt sad, she was able to explain the reason to me clearly and to justify it rationally.

She never knew her real parents. On her eighteenth birthday, her adoptive parents, whom she had up until then always believed were her natural parents, revealed that she'd been adopted at the age of one. They stubbornly refused to provide her with any information beyond that, claiming that they themselves didn't know anything more, because of the policy of the orphanage from where she'd been adopted. But they wouldn't even tell her the name of the place.

She was in her sophomore year at university when she managed to save enough money to hire a good private investigator, but he didn't find out much of anything. The detective tried to feed her all kinds of lies just so he could keep tapping her for money. She didn't have a single lead, no name, no address, nothing. Often, when she was alone at her parents' apartment, which was somewhere in Brooklyn

Heights, she used to search the place for clues, but she never discovered any miraculous scraps of paper to point her in the right direction. She even succeeded in discovering the combination to the safe her father had under his desk, but all she found there were property deeds, bonds, and jewelry.

It was then, she told me, that she attempted suicide for the second time. Her mother had insomnia and the doctor had prescribed her some strong sleeping pills. The bottle was in the medicine cabinet in the bathroom, it hadn't occurred to her to hide it. Julie poured the pills into a mug, added milk, and drank the mixture. Then she went to her room and crawled into bed. Her parents didn't raise the alarm until the next morning, when they noticed that she hadn't woken up. When they went to check on her, they found that she was unresponsive and saw she had white foam around her mouth.

Compulsory therapy sessions followed—"a nightmare," in her opinion—and a diagnosis far too severe for what may only have been a temporary postadolescent crisis. Then there was the compassion from everyone who knew her, compassion that smothered her "like a straitjacket," as she put it. She could sense their eyes, full of curiosity, boring into the back of her neck, the slightly alarmed politeness of her colleagues, and the coddling of her increasingly desperate parents.

"Why do you think you did it?" I asked her. "I mean, why did you take those pills? I understand you ingested twenty-eight, enough to send you six feet under if you'd had the slightest cardiac-respiratory issue. It wasn't just a cry for help. You played Russian roulette, Julie."

"Isn't that what you're supposed to find out?" she asked me back, with that smile of hers, which always lit up my practice whenever it appeared. "Isn't that why I'm here?"

"That's right. But I want to know what *you* think."

"What *I want* is never an argument, mister," she said.

"You'll have to explain to me *why* you want to know. You're my therapist, not my master."

And there, stretched out on the couch in the living room, with only the light on the screen of the muted TV, I had a strong premonition that the place that I was to head to the next day had a dark and malignant power, like a damp cellar crammed with old junk and dangerous secrets.

# three

I LEFT EARLY IN THE morning, and half an hour later I was already making good time on Interstate 91, heading for Maine. The weather was fine and the traffic lighter than I'd been expecting. I turned off onto Interstate 84 and onto Interstate 90. In the early afternoon, as I was nearing Portland, the sky darkened and a heavy downpour began to lash the road. The headlights of the cars in the opposite lane were like yellow globes floating in a stream.

I wasn't hungry, so I decided against stopping for lunch and continued to drive along Interstate 95 toward Freeport. I stopped to fill up at a gas station, where I had a coffee and asked some locals about Wolfe's Creek, the region where Fleischer's estate was located.

A dirt road wound through a pine forest that stretched from the edge of the highway to a pair of large wrought-iron gates. I stopped the car, lowered the window, and buzzed the intercom, while two security cameras stared down at me. In a few seconds the gates slowly began to open and I drove into a large courtyard, divided in two by a cobbled lane. To the left there was a tennis court with the netting gathered in, and to the right there was a wooden summer-house by an empty swimming pool.

The house, a three-floor mansion in the colonial style, had its façade half covered with ivy. Josh and another man, who looked to be in his early sixties, were sitting on the

porch. I got out of the car, walked up the stairs, and we
shook hands.

"Walter will take your luggage to your room," Josh said.
A single glance told me that his illness, freed from the
constraints of treatment, had already begun to gnaw at him.
"I'm so glad to see you here, James. Thanks for coming."

We went inside the house, while the man he called Walter
climbed behind the wheel of my car.

We walked down a hallway, with a huge stuffed bison's
head as its sole item of decor, and entered a split-level living
room. The solid oak floorboards were scattered with hand-
woven carpets showing Native American motifs. On the
lower level there were couches, armchairs, and coffee tables.
The upper level opened onto a kitchen with a worktable
in the middle and a large glass door leading to a garden.
Artworks were arranged here and there, mainly tribal
artifacts, but nothing seemed ostentatious or excessive. Josh
motioned for me to sit down on a couch, and he took a seat
in one of the adjacent armchairs.

A butler appeared and asked me what I'd like to drink. I
chose a gin and tonic and my host asked for a manhattan.

"How was the journey?" he asked. "I hope you liked the
restaurant I recommended."

"It was easier than I was expecting as far as the traffic
went, but I drove slowly, so I didn't stop for lunch."

"All the better—I've had a splendid dinner prepared. I
rarely have an appetite, but when I do, like today, it's like
I'm pregnant. I've been craving roast lamb with rosemary
since this morning and I'm certain Mandy will have made
us a first-class meal."

"How many people live here?" I asked him, as our drinks
were being served.

"Now there are five," he replied, tilting his tall-stemmed
glass slightly toward me to signal a toast, "which is to say,
all the necessary staff. There used to be just four, but two

weeks ago I decided to take my doctor's advice and hire a full-time nurse, just in case. Otherwise, the people here have been in my employ for a considerable length of time. I select my employees carefully and pay them well, so they stay with me, which suits me. I'm not a man who likes conflicts, and I don't place exaggerated demands on them."

In his tone of voice, his gestures, his gaze, there was an innate nobility, of the kind usually associated with old money, elite colleges, and a life spared of petty problems.

During the meal, we talked about everything except the reason for my being there. He had an elegant way of conversing, passing pleasantly from one subject to another without dropping names or becoming tedious or self-obsessed. The food was indeed well prepared and the wine was great.

Over coffee he thanked me once again for agreeing to come.

"Your letter intrigued me," I told him, "and naturally, I'm drawn to things that intrigue me."

"Well, things aren't all that complicated, James," he said. "I'm nothing but a dying old man who hopes that his illness won't destroy his last remnants of dignity before it takes him away, and who still hopes that he won't leave unsolved matters behind after he passes. I'm sixty-two years old and I could have lived another two or three decades, but … I believe in fate and perhaps everything happens for a reason which sometimes eludes our understanding. Life has been rather kind to me, except that …" He paused and shuddered slightly, as if suddenly feeling a chill. "Well, let's talk a bit about you. Why aren't you married, James?"

"I'm thirty-five, so I have plenty of time," I said. "My grandpa married when he was only twenty-one, and dad was twenty-seven when my mother said 'I do.' Maybe that's the way things are going these days. Almost all my acquaintances are either unmarried or divorced."

"You said *acquaintances* rather than *friends*," he noted.

"Well, it was just an expression."

"I think it was more than an expression. I know you better than you think, James. And that's why I chose to approach you from all the other psychologists and psychiatrists in the world," he said. "To the consternation of Richard Orrin," he added, and smiled.

After dinner, Walter showed me to the apartment where I'd be staying.

It was on the second floor and consisted of a small living room, a bedroom, and a bathroom. Everything was decorated with the same good taste. I took a shower and climbed into bed, having first placed a paperback mystery novel on the bedside table. But I wasn't in the mood for reading, so I turned off the lights. The silence seemed unreal. The only sounds that filtered through the double windows were the faint calls of night birds.

I'd taken an immediate liking to Josh. He was neither coarse nor pretentious nor full of advice nor eager to shove the story of his business success down my throat. He didn't have that vindictive air the chronically ill so often possess, as if you were partly to blame for their situation or a tiny cog in the universal mechanism that had been set in motion against them.

But at the same time he struck me as the loneliest man I'd ever met.

He dwelled in the midst of his own wealth like an awkward lodger, who likes what he sees but knows that none of it really belongs to him. He was excessively polite to his personnel, but that courtesy placed a barrier between him and others that was more impenetrable than if he'd been boorish or overbearing. Each gesture, each word, and each look seemed studied, making you wonder whether what you saw was nothing but a persona, a mask meticulously fashioned over time, behind which lurked a completely different man.

At one point, I got out of bed, went to the window, and raised the blinds. The sky was full of stars, and a sliver of moon hung in the sky as if left behind. The dark crowns of the trees were silent, enigmatic sentinels, motionless in their endless vigil.

That night I dreamed of Julie.

We were sitting at a table bathed in sunlight, at a garden café. She wore a white dress and dark glasses, which lent her a mysterious air. She reached over the table and grasped my hand. In that instant I felt my whole body being pervaded by a tremendous pleasure, more powerful than the greatest orgasm. "You have to forget," she said, and I told her it wasn't true. "I'll tell you a secret," she added. "I'm not Julie."

As she spoke those words, the café, the sun, and the people around us suddenly vanished, giving way to a dark forest. I awoke in confusion, my heart thudding in my chest, as rays of sunlight glided across the floor.

# four

THE WEATHER WAS UNUSUALLY fine for the time
of year, and after breakfast Josh invited me for a walk in the
surrounding countryside. The butler filled a picnic basket
with sandwiches, small bottles of water, and a thermos of
coffee. Although the sun was already blazing in the sky, Josh
had wrapped himself up in thick clothing. In his condition,
even a common cold could prove fatal.

Behind the mansion there was a fallow field guarded at
the back by a row of tall maple trees that hid a fence swathed
in ivy. Josh took a key out from his pocket and opened the
gate. On the other side of the fence there was another dirt
road. We crossed it and entered a virgin forest, scattered with
fallen tree trunks, wild nut bushes, and the largest ferns I'd
ever seen. Josh seemed to know the place quite well, finding
his way without a path or signpost.

After a ten-minute stroll, we reached a clearing with a
mossy old stone well in the middle, its shaft covered with
a padlocked wooden lid, and we sat down on a bench next
to it. Apart from the chirping of the birds and the muffled
rustle of dead leaves, there was no sound to be heard. We'd
only walked about three hundred yards, but Josh was already
breathing with difficulty.

I was very curious to find out what he wanted from me,
but I had to let him choose the moment to bring up the
subject. He asked me whether I wanted some coffee, then

poured the dark, piping hot liquid into plastic cups, two twin minuscule ghosts of steam rising up in the air.

"This spot is called Claire's Spring," he told me. "They say that the well was dug in the late eighteenth century by a French adventurer named Roger, who was involved in the fur trade with the Algonquians. Claire was his secret lover, the sixteen-year-old daughter of an Acadian merchant. Legend has it that Roger was killed during the French and Indian War, when the Acadians were thrown out of this region by the English. Claire refused to leave and came here searching for her lover. She starved to death right here, next to the well that now bears her name."

He took a sip of coffee.

"Now, I guess I should start telling you a couple of things about myself. I was born and raised in New York City, into a wealthy family. My father, Salem Fleischer, was a valedictorian at Harvard and a decorated hero of World War Two. In the fifties, he became one of the most respected lawyers of the New York City bar. My mother came from the Rutherford family, who made their fortune in railroads.

"I went to Columbia Grammar School, and when I was just eighteen both my parents died in a car crash in Florida. They were healthy, relatively young, and the suddenness of that event left me petrified for months. I suddenly found myself completely alone, the sole heir to an important fortune, which, according to my father's will, I was to receive at twenty-one.

"I broke with family tradition and went not to Harvard, but to Princeton, which struck me as being a more open, liberal place. Like many other young men in those years, I was a hothead, a radical, and had the feeling that we were experiencing something crucial, a new millennium. I took part in a few marches, but I quickly realized that all the things that had probably been interesting in the sixties had already disintegrated, leaving behind mostly a kind of perverse snobbery, promiscuity, and congenital laziness skillfully disguised as a rejection of society.

"It's fashionable nowadays to accuse the baby-boomers of naïveté and wastefulness, but we just felt good in our halls of residence, our campuses, our fancy cars, and we didn't want anybody to threaten our well-being and send us off to die in the rice paddies of Asia before we could enjoy the prosperity that had landed in America.

"Of course, I'm telling you what I thought.

"Others thought they could change things, whatever those things might have been, by writing petitions and causing social unrest. I wasn't one of them, I must admit, being probably too rich, lazy, and contemplative. I was too much of a success with the girls to get carried away by extreme radicalism, which, I think, always conceals a certain amount of individual frustration. In those days, you wore your prosperity almost like a thing of guilt, trying to hide it. It was fashionable to be working-class, to shove hard-earned bills in the pockets of your worn-out Levis.

"Abraham Hale, whom I met in my senior year, was one such person.

"His father was from Portland, Oregon, and his mother was a Cajun from Atchafalaya, Louisiana. She died when he was only seven or so. They lived in a small town about twenty miles from Baton Rouge and were very poor. Abe told me that he was around ten when his father bought their first TV set.

"We shared a two-room apartment in Penns Neck, a quiet and nice neighborhood. I majored in English, and Abe majored in Philosophy."

We'd been sitting on the bench for ten minutes, surrounded by the mysterious, dizzying woods, and it was only then that he started to recover his breath, and a vague hint of color returned to his cheeks.

\*

"I'm telling you all this, James, because it's connected to the reason why I asked you here. The introduction will be long, but important, and I hope that you'll have the patience to listen carefully."

"In my profession it's more important to listen than to speak," I told him. "The key to understanding is often concealed in seemingly banal remarks, a description of a shopping ride or a favorite sweater."

"That's right. See, it was with my friend Abe, in Paris after graduation, that I experienced the event which, in a way, was to change my entire life."

He fell silent and his expression became tense, as if the mere mention of that event had frightened him. He'd uttered the name of his friend with a kind of horror, as if to pronounce it was to invoke a sort of demon.

"My years at Princeton brought me no closer to discovering what I really wanted to do. In a way, looking back now, I think I used to float above it all, living each day as if I were immortal and had enough time to guide my existence in whatever direction I wanted, whenever I wanted. I had no financial concerns, as I'd already come into my inheritance. I'd had a few articles accepted by a couple of small magazines, and this supplied a kind of alibi for my chronic idleness, nurturing at the same time my hope that sooner or later I'd write something that would bring me the public recognition I secretly craved. So, what was the use in hurrying? At that age, appearances are often more important than reality.

"I used to fall in love about once a month, and I think that I broke a great many hearts in those days. Not because the suffering I caused flattered my pride or brought me any perverse satisfaction, but quite simply because I didn't care much. I was seen as a bohemian, a wasted genius craving for salvation, and this attracted the girls like a magnet.

"Abe was, in many ways, my opposite.

"He was poor, as I've told you, and as a result very deter-mined to do something important and to build for himself a different life than the one his father led. A lot of the time he lied and told people he was an orphan, to avoid questions about his family. That's what he told me when I first moved into the house on Alcott Street, in December, just before Christmas. I'd been renting another apartment in Princeton Junction, but the landlord had lost the job for which he'd moved to Philly and on his return to town, he gave me notice to find another rental urgently. I found a place through the classifieds, and that was how I came to meet Abe, who had been living there for over three years. The two-bed apartment was on the ground floor of a colonial mansion that was almost in ruins—something was always falling into disrepair. Abe had been living alone up until then, but he'd lost his scholarship and had to save some money.

"A month after I moved in, I met his dad, who turned up to visit unannounced. Abe wasn't at home, so I was the one who opened the door to a gloomy, skinny middle-aged man, who smelled of sweat and alcohol. When he told me his name was John Hale I realized that Abe had been lying to me, so I was able to avoid making some terrible gaffe. Abe didn't come home until two hours later, which meant that I had to make conversation with his father in the meantime.

"He was coarse and poorly spoken, with airs of being the Good American Worker and an embarrassingly superior attitude, which I think came from a strong feeling of infer-iority. In his eyes we were nothing but snot-nosed brats, idling away our time instead of working. He intended to leave his son one hundred dollars before he left, and he informed me of this with a lofty air. He was convinced that students did nothing but get high and have orgies. He'd been too young to enlist during World War Two and too old to get sent to Vietnam, but he gave me a long patriotic speech and described the freedom riders as crypto-Bolshe-viks who made a mockery of their great country, and who had managed to eliminate the best American president of all times, Richard Nixon. With difficulty, I refrained from arguing with him until Abe came back.

"Abe's face turned white when he saw his father, and he invited him out for a coffee. The guy had arrived with a furniture van, which he wouldn't be returning until the next day. I insisted that we go to a restaurant together, and in the end Hale senior agreed, as if he were doing me a great and undeserved favor. During dinner, he constantly chastised Abe for all kinds of things.

"That evening, the guy left, but not before solemnly handing his son five twenty-dollar bills, along with a pathetic speech. Abe looked very embarrassed and apologized to me afterwards. I assured him that there was nothing to worry about, although I wondered how many other lies he'd told me. But ultimately it was none of my business.

"He was very happy that evening. A girl from New York he'd known for a couple of years, and whom he was secretly in love with, had come to Princeton to visit some friends and she'd invited him to a party. He asked me to go with him, eager to introduce her to me. On the way to the party he talked a lot about how wonderful she was. Her name was Lucy Sandler, and she'd gone to high school in England, which in Abe's eyes made her mysterious and somewhat aristocratic. Reading between the lines, I realized that he intended to confess his love to her that evening and was firmly convinced that she shared his feelings. Abe was a small-town boy and those were the seventies, so that was the way things worked for young people who still followed the same mating rituals as their parents.

"I found myself in an apartment full of guys I didn't know, parting dense clouds of tobacco and weed smoke and stumbling over people sprawled on the carpets. Abe was overdressed and looked lost, while Lucy barely gave him a second glance. I got myself a drink and took shelter in a corner. About five minutes later, she came up to me and asked me to dance. I looked around for Abe, but he was nowhere to be seen.

"To be honest, I can't really remember how one thing led to another, because I'd been drinking a lot. At one point, Lucy told me that she knew where the spare room was, so I followed her into a dusty attic where the only piece of furniture was a ratty davenport. She jumped on me and kissed me. I mentioned Abe and she gave me an offended look.

"'Are you really going to spoil this?' she asked. 'Abe's just a friend.'

"'I don't think he'll take this too well,' I said as she began to undress.

"'The important thing is that we're here now,' she answered. 'Come on, don't make me wait.'

"For the rest of the evening she acted like she was in love with me, kissing me on the sly and trying to hold my hand. She told me about her parents, about her life in Europe, about visiting the exotic destinations she dreamed of. People had begun to leave and I looked around for Abe, but I still couldn't find him. Lucy had come with some friends, and she ended up leaving with them, after telling me a dozen times that she would call me.

"When I got home, Abe was sitting at the living room table, stone drunk. He said that Lucy was a slut, a junkie, and a filthy manipulator. After a time, his insults became almost poetic, like the Song of Songs in reverse, with her breasts as suspenders, her butt as a baseball pitch, and her face as a scarecrow in a cornfield in Kentucky. For the first time since I met him, he seemed truly alive and full of verve. See, hatred can be as energizing as love. In those moments, I got the feeling that not only did he hate Lucy, but he was also capable of harming her."

*

Josh put the empty cups back inside the picnic basket and asked me whether I wanted a sandwich. I declined.

It grew warm, and tendrils of steam were rising from the carpet of dead leaves. The crowns of the trees and the closely spaced trunks had turned the clearing into a kind of greenhouse and I was sweating. Josh took his coat off and laid it beside him on the bench, carefully folded. Everything he did seemed pedantically precise, and I noted that the passing years had left little trace of the erstwhile bohemian.

"In the end he fell asleep there, at the table, and I helped him to bed," he went on. "I threw a blanket over him and made myself a coffee. I felt sorry, but not guilty. Things became more complicated the next morning, when Lucy turned up at the door. Casually, she announced that she'd decided to stay with me for a few days, tossed her bag in a corner, undressed, and climbed into the shower. When she emerged, stark naked, Abe was coming out of his room and for a few moments I thought he might have a heart attack. He said nothing, took his coat, and left. He didn't come back for five days, by which time she was already gone. I tried to bring her up, but he always avoided the subject. I spoke to her on the phone a couple of times, but after that she stopped calling me and I didn't seek her out.

"I think it must have been about two months after the incident with Lucy that Abe told me he was going to Paris.

"His situation was even more tangled than mine. He'd probably thought that once he got a scholarship and left his hometown his problems would resolve themselves in some natural way. That the professors would quickly pick up on his intelligence and cultivation, and so he would get good grades and meet influential people. He believed that he was gifted with a talent for research, and he thought it was as good as certain that he would be offered a job on the university staff. But things didn't turn out that way at all.

"He'd been more intelligent and cultured than the majority of the people in his hometown, and he'd been treated as such by his teachers. But at Princeton he found himself among some of the most intelligent new adults in America. In his freshman year he pushed himself hard to prove his worth, but without much success. Among the rich kids it was fashionable to slum it—there was a lot of hypocrisy out there, believe me—but that didn't mean they accepted real paupers. Abe was the silent type, steeped in provincial habits and prejudices he wasn't even aware of. More often than not you would see him dressed formally, and he was always eager to show off his genuine culture at the most inappropriate moments, probably in order to compensate for the sense of inferiority that came from his poverty. The worst thing was that he lived every day knowing he only had four years to change his life, which made him tense and surly.

"So he was rejected by that environment, just like the immune system rejects an alien form of life that penetrates the organism. His reaction wasn't to change the way he was, but to blame the others. So he retreated even further into himself and became bitter and critical of everything he saw. His grades were mediocre at best.

"He was neither the interesting, brilliant rebel, secretly envied by the nerds, nor the outlaw fighting against the rules, swathed in the dark smoke of revolt. At the end of the day, he was nothing but a tormented, increasingly lonely small-town boy.

"In other words, all his dreams had come to naught, and the clock was ticking. When I met him, he had less than a year to go before graduation. He didn't know which way to go and he was becoming more and more depressed. He'd lost his scholarship and was forced to take up all kinds of odd jobs in order to make enough money to live on until he finished his degree.

"The only person who took a liking to him was a lady by the name of Elisabeth Gregory. She was in her mid-thirties, if I remember correctly, and the owner of a small translations company that worked closely with the university. Abe had taken an internship there during a summer. She was considered one of the most beautiful women in the area and there were many students who dreamed of playing Mrs. Robinson with her, but she seemed as cold and distant as she was beautiful.

"I can't recall where I found out details about her private life, but the campus grapevine probably proved as infallible as always.

"She was married to a depraved drunk named John Gregory, who had taught at Princeton a couple of years previously and been sacked from his chair following a couple of sordid affairs. Back then, cases of sexual harassment didn't necessarily become public, as they were seen as damaging to the renown of the institution, so everything used to be dealt with behind the scenes and buried in the secret crypt of the board.

"It seemed that at the time Abe met Elisabeth, John Gregory had moved to New York City, where he claimed to be writing scripts, but actually was just a barroom brawler.

"Abe bumped into Mrs. Gregory one day and she questioned him about his plans after graduation. She noticed his embarrassment and asked him whether he'd be interested in working in Europe. You can imagine what that meant to Abe! She was the long-awaited ray of sunshine in an existence that had become darker and darker.

"Although his conversation with her had been vague and she hadn't made any definite promises, Abe was already in seventh heaven. In the end, I advised him to buy a bouquet of flowers and take them to her at home. He hesitated for a few days, but then he did as I suggested. I don't know what happened that evening, because Abe refused to utter a single word.

"What's for sure is that a couple of weeks later he received a letter from a French foundation, called L'Etoile. They offered him a yearlong contract, with a three-month probation period and the opportunity to extend the contract for a further three more years. That evening we celebrated, and Abe was genuinely happy. After his finals he left for Paris immediately, asking me to promise to follow him a few weeks later."

We stood up and walked down a path almost hidden beneath the ferns and dead leaves. For a while he said nothing, lost in thought. We came to a stop near a spring that ran lazily between the rocks and we sat down on a fallen pine trunk. We'd come less than fifty yards, but it took him a good few seconds to catch his breath.

"To be honest, it's hard for me to say *why* I kept my promise and followed him to Paris," he resumed his story. "Honestly, I didn't regard him as a friend, but more as a chance acquaintance. I cared about him, but not enough to give up my own habits or plans. I think that I quite simply didn't have anything better to do that fall.

"So, at the middle of August, when I received a letter from Abe—in those days friends still used to send each other letters written down on paper—I packed my luggage and went to France. He described his life there in very enthusiastic terms and said that everything was more alive, more interesting than back home.

"The myth of those brilliant Parisian expats—Hemingway, Fitzgerald, Dos Passos, Hughes, and the rest—it was still alive for my generation. Paris was a shiny Babel full of inspiration and mystery, while New York seemed to fall apart back in the mid-seventies. I imagined that all Parisians wore painter's berets, ate four-foot-long sticks of bread, and drank absinthe, surrounded by tender-hearted loose ladies. The ideas of genius floated through the air like raindrops, so all you had to do was take off your painter's beret for a few seconds and you could fill it to the brim. Here, in the States, the atmosphere was rather gloomy—the side effects of the Vietnam War, political scandals, social restlessness, and the racial issue.

"I arrived in Paris in late August, when the city was still boiling because of the heat. Abe picked me up from the airport, and I barely recognized him, although it had been less than two months since I last saw him. He was bearded and had let his hair grow. He'd given up his sober brown and gray formal clothes and now was wearing a pair of bellbottom jeans, a linen shirt, and a black leather jacket. He looked happy and carefree. I felt like Paris was really capable of working miracles.

"He lived in an old building on the Rue de Rome, not far from the Champs-Élysées. The rooms were like matchboxes and you had to be careful not to bang your head on the wall when you hit the sack. Here we worship the big: big houses, big beds, big Cokes, and big bags of popcorn. In Paris, size didn't matter as much as location. The apartment was in downtown, and the foundation rented it to him for a modest sum of money.

"I quickly got over the inconveniences—adaptability is one of the gifts of youth—and I let Abe show me around. I didn't feel like making plans, and let myself be carried along by chance. But he'd written a lengthy list of places I had to visit, and for about a week I wore out my shoes traipsing around Montmartre, Montparnasse, Faubourg Saint-Germain, and Faubourg Saint-Honoré. I've always loved arts and the Louvre took my breath away. I found it strange when Abe declared that the place that impressed him the most was the Dôme des Invalides, that insipid monument in which Napoleon is interred.

"He didn't mention Simone to me at first.

"Sometimes he would enter a phone booth and linger there for ten minutes or so, but I presumed he was talking to the people at the foundation. He would always emerge with that giddy, happy air that lovers have, but I'd assumed that the city itself was the object of his adoration. In the evening we would drink Pernod in backstreet cafés, or while away the time in small clubs, where they played jazz and performed sketches of which I couldn't understand a word. I barely spoke a dozen words of French, but Abe was fluent. I mentioned that his mother was a Cajun from Louisiana, so French was almost his maternal tongue. Anyway, I remember that first week being like an enchanted dream. I was seriously thinking about trying to find a job there. What's more, there were quite a lot of American expats working in Paris and it was easy to make friends.

"One evening, Abe dressed up more than usual and, without giving me any details, took me to a restaurant near the Palais des Congrès. It was a nice place called Chez Clément, far too expensive for his pocket. Ten minutes after we sat down at our table and ordered our drinks, Simone arrived.

"I think I fell in love with her at first sight. At that age, you could fall for a frog, but I could immediately tell that it was much more than just a late adolescent crush.

"She had blonde hair and looked as if she'd been carved in ivory, delicate and gracile, completely different from the young women in America at the time. The fashion for many girls back then was to burn their bras and try to look masculine and self-assured, as femininity was thought to be an odious means of manipulation, concocted by men in order to turn women into mere sex objects.

"Simone was glamorous and mysterious, exuding not

only beauty but also angelic goodness. To me, it was almost as if she was from another planet. My conversation with her proved that she was very cultivated and had studied extensively. She loved literature and knew Sartre personally. We spent the whole evening talking about the existentialism, the political involvement of artists, and other such things.

"I finally realized what the explanation was for Abe's transformation. I'd ascribed it to the miraculous effect of Paris, but he was head over heels in love. In her presence he was shy and uneasy, but not lacking in a certain clumsy charm, the kind that usually bowls women over. He kept his eyes fixed on her the whole time, either trying to anticipate her wishes or merely contemplating her like a work of art.

"Simone spoke fluent English, albeit with an accent. She'd been working at Abe's foundation for two years and had been assigned to help him settle in. She'd been the one who picked out the apartment on the Rue de Rome for him, the perfect location for a newcomer unfamiliar with the labyrinthine layout of Paris.

"I couldn't tell whether she was in love with him or whether she was just trying to be polite. In any case, Abe's advances were platonic, and I was convinced that they hadn't slept together. But knowing Abe, I was sure that he didn't see this as being important. Shall we?"

# five

WE WALKED BACK TO the mansion for lunch. A nurse wearing a white uniform, who introduced herself as Lisa Bedeck, handed Josh a glass of orange juice and a small plastic receptacle half full of pills.

He was trying to keep a brave face, but the walk and our conversation had obviously tired him. He interrupted his story about Paris, and during the meal he asked me how I'd come to choose psychology as a profession.

"I think it started with a conversation I had with a doctor, when I was like ten," I told him. "My grandma from my dad's side suffered from a nervous breakdown. I was in love with sci-fi novels and I'd read a book by Philip K. Dick, if I'm not mistaken, about a man who was able to heal everybody by entering a parallel world while he dreamed. Well, one day a psychiatrist visited us to speak to grandma and I asked him to explain to me what dreams are, why we dream, whether dreams have any meaning or not, and so on. He was very kind, so we chatted about the subject for over an hour, but my conclusion was that he didn't know very much about it, and that seemed to me more fascinating than any potential précis answer. The next day I went to the public library and borrowed a book about sleep and dreams. From there, a couple of years later, I went on to study anthropology and from anthropology to psychology and psychiatry. In my last year at medical school, during my clinical experience, I met Professor George Atkins, who trained me for a few months in the hypnosis techniques he employed at Bellevue Hospital in New York. We're still in touch. You may have noticed he wrote the foreword of my book."

"What about your grandmother?"

"She recovered well."

"I'm glad to hear that, James. Well, it's great to know early on what you want to do in life and to have the strength to persevere," he remarked, as we were brought our salads. "That way you don't waste time and energy on things you later think of as utterly pointless. On the other hand, you risk carrying curiosities, regrets, and sorrows around with you—what might've happened if I'd opened that door, if I'd followed that impulse, if I'd answered that invitation. Kierkegaard wrote that one would be better off killing a baby in the cradle than leaving behind a wish unfulfilled, with the condition that the wish does nobody any harm. Have you always been sure you chose what was best for you?"

He'd barely touched his salad, but he poured himself a glass of red wine from a carafe and drank it in one go.

I shrugged. "No, never. As a scientist, I refuse to ask myself questions for which I can never find the answers. I don't know what would have happened if I'd chosen to be an explorer, for example, or if I'd gotten married in my senior year at university to a girl from California named Jessica Fulton and moved to the West Coast, like I almost did."

"I think you're wrong," he said. "I think the things we *haven't* done define us just as much as the things we have. I think it's no coincidence when we find ourselves in front of a door at a given moment, even if we choose to never open it. The doors we never open are just as important as the ones we walk through. People are tempted to forget, and at the hour of reckoning, nobody counts the doors that stayed closed, but only the few doors they chose to open."

"Forgetting is an important part of our mental immune

system, Josh," I replied. "Our brains erase the files considered to be useless or even damaging, just like a computer eliminates viruses, old documents, and useless icons. Then there are other disturbing memories that are faked, airbrushed or spruced up, in an attempt to save parts of them, for one reason or another. Freud supposed that a sort of recycling bin does exist, the *subconscious*, which can be accessed by the psychoanalyst—that is, a place where all the erased memories end up, the memories the patient isn't even conscious of. He believed that psychologists only need to comb through them to reach the real causes of the mental impasse the subjects finds themselves in. Jung, his brilliant apprentice, took it even further and believed that all individual recycling bins are somehow connected in an invisible network he called the *collective unconscious*."

"By your tone, I take it you don't agree with these famous gentlemen," he said as we were brought the main course.

"Well, psychoanalysis has always had its limits, and an extremely speculative side. Human knowledge seemed omniscient in those days of scientific enthusiasm," I said. "Scholars were looking for unifying, all-encompassing theories, that's how Einstein came up with the theory of relativity, a theory that can encapsulate the whole universe, an equation by which you can explain almost everything, a scientific philosopher's stone. In the spirit of the times, that was what Freud attempted to do, with his theories about the libido, Jung, with his concepts of individuation and archetype, and Adler with his notion of complex. All these are very seductive from the intellectual standpoint, but the main aim of the medical act is ultimately to cure, isn't it? The psychoanalytical method is more often than not exhausting for the patient as well as for the therapist because it takes a lot of time, and it's also very costly. It's a luxury of the modern world, which replaced the old confessional with a fancy leather couch in a downtown medical practice."

"Do you really think it will ever be possible to measure the human mind using figures, formulas, and equations?" he asked.

"If I didn't believe it, I wouldn't be a scientist," I stressed.

He shook his head. "Allow me to be skeptical," he said. "Maybe you can get inside a man's mind, dissect it, rummage around, and then sew it back up. But there's still that thing commonly known as the *soul*, which isn't tucked away in the brain, as we like to think nowadays, or in the heart, as people in the Middle Ages believed." He sighed and looked down. "I think we're getting closer to the reason I asked you here, James ..."

We were alone. The nurse had not come back, and the butler had left a tray with coffee, a sugar bowl, and a milk jug on the small table by the armchairs.

"In your book you argue that there's no guarantee that a subject in a state of hypnosis will communicate ... let's call it *reality*," he said. "I don't like to use this word. It suggests that there's an objective truth, beyond the appearances in which we're shackled by our senses, our perceptions, our convictions, and our taboos, as you underlined in your lecture. But nonetheless I would like to try the method."

So that was what this whole thing was about. "Josh, it appears that you've studied the subject thoroughly enough to know that hypnosis involves a series of risks," I said.

"I've read a lot on the subject, yes. I know those risks and I'm prepared to take them. In my condition, I don't think I've got very much to lose."

"I'm not just talking about physical risks."

I'd lost my appetite, and he hadn't touched his plate. We got up and went over to the coffee table, where we sat down in the armchairs.

"The experiences of a subject in trance are just as strong as if he were really living through the episode he reproduces or imagines in that state," I said. "Sometimes they're even stronger, especially during a regression. I don't know whether it's the best idea for someone in your state, especially if it's a question of a very traumatic event, as you've led me to believe. If you've forgotten it, even only apparently, it was because your mind decided that was the way things had to be. Forcing it to come back up to the surface might create serious and uncontrollable consequences.

"What's more," I went on, "I'm skeptical about the practical results, as I've told you before. It's not a question of lying ... In fact, the patients don't lie under hypnosis, not in the same way they use lies in a waking state, as a weapon from our natural arsenal of self-defense. The problem is that the 'truth' a subject communicates doesn't necessarily correspond to reality."

He bent over the table and looked me straight in the eye. "James, I've spent forty years obsessed with what happened that night and I don't want to pass away without trying everything possible to discover the truth." His voice was harsh. "I chose you precisely because you're a skeptic and there's no risk of you manipulating the session, of using me as a lab rat in one of your experiments. If we don't succeed in shedding some light on what happened back then, that's that, but I'm determined to try, if you'll agree to help me."

He was very sad, as if he'd just received an overwhelmingly bad piece of news.

"Have you ever heard about the Book of the Dead, the ancient Egyptian funerary text?" he asked. "Well, the manuscript says that in front of their judges, the dead have to swear that they haven't committed during their life any sin from a list of forty-two. After that, their hearts are weighed on a pair of scales. If the scales balance, it means that the deceased told the truth: He led a good life, so he's admitted into paradise. But if he lied and his heart is out of balance, then a beast named He Who Lives on Snakes,

or the Devourer, eats his heart and sends him into hell for
eternity …

"Now it's time I tell you what all this is about. One night,
Simone was murdered, and Abe vanished for good without
a trace. We'd been together that night, all three of us …"

# six

"THAT NIGHT WAS THE climax of a tragedy that began the moment I first met Simone at that restaurant, Chez Clément," he said.

"I've already mentioned that she didn't seem to be in love with Abe, treating him with a kind of touching friendship, the way a gentle person treats somebody in pain, who's begging for attention. Behind his appearance of having adapted to Parisian life, I quickly realized that Abe had remained the same young man full of inhibitions and complexes. But Simone was the scion of an aristocratic family, heir to a considerable fortune, and the bearer of a name that opened many doors out there. She didn't make a show of such things, but it was clear that she belonged to a sophisticated world as far away from Abe's as a planet in another galaxy.

"Put simply, we fell in love with each other. At that age, I guess, things either happen straightaway or they don't happen at all.

"In a way, it was a repeat of the story with Lucy, but this time, things were much more serious for both of us. At first, Abe merely looked on in amazement, avoiding the subject. Simone didn't change her behavior toward him, showing him the same friendship, but he was smart enough to guess how things were developing. She didn't seem to care that the way she acted when we were together might hurt him.

"As for me, I was discovering feelings I'd never experienced before. The small mole on her right wrist, the way her eyes changed color depending on the light, a lock of hair tumbling across the nape of her neck, the way she moved her shoulders when she walked in high heels, all these things seemed extraordinary to me and they became the center of my universe the instant I noticed them. When we weren't together, not even a minute passed without me thinking of her.

"Once, when we were alone together—Abe had to go to the foundation, and I'd offered to walk her home—I brought up my fears regarding the strange triangle that we'd unwittingly brought into being. Simone told me that she shared my concern and didn't want to hurt Abe. But she also told me that she wanted us to be together, and that was the most important thing for her.

"So, after three weeks or so, we started seeing each other, just the two of us, although our relationship was still platonic. One night, we went to a party with Abe, somewhere in Montmartre, and that was where we kissed for the first time. On the way home, I tried to work out whether Abe had noticed anything, but he was drunk and gloomy, and it was impossible to talk to him. The next day I didn't have the guts to broach the subject.

"But the worst blow for Abe came a few days after that party—the foundation withdrew the offer of a job just a few days before it would have become permanent. He was completely bewildered and not even capable of explaining to me coherently what had happened. All he said was that L'Etoile had cancelled the offer, and then he sat for a while on the couch, staring into empty space, before dashing out of the building. At first, I didn't believe him—I called the foundation to check for myself, pretending to be one of his relatives from America. A secretary confirmed that it was true—Mr. Abraham Hale's offer of employment had been withdrawn for reasons that were to be communicated to him, in writing, in the near future.

"I didn't see Abe for a couple of days. He didn't even come back to change his clothes. I was the one who received the envelope from the foundation and signed for it in his name. I didn't open it. I placed it on the phone table in the hall and asked myself what to do next, given the new circumstances.

"I knew that it was likely that Abe would have to go back to America, because he'd already blown through all his savings. If that were the situation, I would have to decide whether I would help him with money to prolong his stay or not. The rent agreement for the apartment on the Rue de Rome depended on the foundation, so we would be losing it either way.

"By that evening, I'd made my decision: I would stay in Paris, whether Abe left or not. If he agreed to stay and let me help him, I had enough money for us to live comfortably until we found jobs. I kept telling myself that things weren't as dire as they seemed. I knew that Abe had a kind of stubborn pride, but I still hoped that he would accept some friendly help.

"Abe was absent for the rest of the week, and I was on tenterhooks the entire time. Simone was away visiting her parents in Lyon and we spoke on the phone. She knew that Abe's job offer had been withdrawn and she seemed very upset by it. She invited us to go to Lyon, to meet her parents and forget about our problems for a couple of days.

"When he got back home—it was a Sunday—Abe seemed completely changed. It was obvious he'd been drinking heavily. He was unshaven, he'd lost weight, and his clothes were in disarray. He was furious, even though he was trying to look calm and self-assured, and had an expression on his face that I'd never seen before: he was showing his fangs, literally, his face twisted into a kind of grimace that thrust his lower jaw forward and bared his teeth.

"I tried to encourage him, telling him that we had enough money to live on until we found jobs, but that we had to start looking for another apartment first thing. He opened the envelope from the foundation, cast a brief glance at the letter inside, and then crumpled it up and set fire to it in an ashtray.

"'You don't think I'm going to live on *your* handouts, do you?' he said at one point. 'That would be the limit. Don't worry. I'll manage. I know some people who are going to pull some strings and everything will be alright.'

"Given his condition, I was worried about the kind of people he'd met, but it wasn't the time for such a discussion. I told him that Simone had invited us to Lyon to meet her parents.

"'You mean that she invited *you*,' he bitterly pointed out. 'You're the dream of every mother who wants to see her precious daughter married off—handsome, well dressed, rich, and successful. I'm poor and with no prospects. And if Simone were in love with anybody, it would be you, pal.'

"He continued to feel sorry for himself for another hour or so. Though he hadn't done anything wrong, he seemed to take a real pleasure in punishing himself. He kept repeating that his father was right: the poor man's sacrifices had turned out to be for nothing.

"There was a bottle of cognac in the apartment and he drank most of it by himself, after which he fell asleep fully clothed, with a lit cigarette between his fingers. I helped him to bed and threw a blanket over him.

"In the morning he was somewhat more coherent. He still seemed depressed and as taut as a spring about to snap, but at least he'd given up on his endless monologue about his faults. He took a shower, shaved, and put on clean clothes. We went to a café and had breakfast. I mentioned Simone's invitation again.

"'There's no question of my going,' he said categorically. 'But you should go. I can see how much you want to. I'll be fine, don't worry.'

"There wasn't much else to say. I knew that I shouldn't leave him by himself, that my going there wasn't the right thing to do, but I was twenty-two and I was in love, and so I packed my bag and Abe came to see me off at the Gare de Lyon. I can still remember, even today, how he stood at the end of the platform and watched as the train departed, his hands thrust in his pockets and the collar of his coat turned up. October had arrived with cold, gloomy rains. For a moment I thought I should get off the train again and stay in Paris with him, that I should just wait for Simone to come back to town, but then the train picked up speed and the opportunity was lost. I left him there alone."

The memory of that scene must've been painful for him, because for a few moments he said nothing more, sitting back in the armchair with his eyes half-closed.

For a few moments, it seemed that he'd even stopped breathing. "Almost inevitably, the days I spent in Lyon were catastrophic," he eventually went on. "Simone's mother, Claudia, was a kind and gentle woman, but completely dominated by her husband, Lucas, who was hostile to anything that wasn't French. I learned that he wasn't Simone's real father, but he'd adopted Simone and her younger sister, Laura, when they were just toddlers.

"To him—he was very tall and slim, somewhat reminiscent of General de Gaulle—Americans were Neanderthals who posed a threat to European culture. It was unthinkable that his daughter might leave the country in the company of such a barbarian. He barely spoke two words to me. He'd been a member of the French Resistance against the Nazis during World War Two and had been arrested and tortured by the Gestapo. For one reason or another, his experience at the hands of the Nazis had recently come back in the spotlight, because his name was all over the newspapers during that time.

"I asked Simone if she knew why Abe's job offer had been withdrawn. She told me that she'd had a phone conversation with someone from the board, who had mentioned a letter about Abe sent from America.

"I didn't stay at their house, although they had a two-story mansion, but took a room at a nearby hotel. Simone visited me in secret, as if we were teenagers, and it was there where we made love for the first time. I told her that I'd decided to stay in Paris for a while. Hearing this, her father stressed that France had become a magnet for bums from all over the world.

"As I mentioned, Simone had a sister, Laura, who was a year younger than her. She was studying English and lived in Paris too, but I hadn't met her up until then. By chance, she was at her parents' house and we all got together a few times. She adored America and could hardly wait to one day visit New York City. The three of us went for walks around Lyon and spent our evenings in interminable conversations, swathed in cigarette smoke and the scent of coffee.

"When I returned, the concierge told me that he hadn't seen Abe during the entire time I'd been away. Some of his belongings were missing. He hadn't left a note, but quite simply vanished, and I wondered whether he might have gone back to the States.

"A clerk from the foundation visited me at the apartment and we came to an agreement that I could keep it until the end of October. I had plenty of time to find a new place to stay.

"Abe turned up out of the blue a few days later. I think it must have been around midnight when I heard the key in the lock. He looked bad and was drunk and incoherent. All

I could gather was that he had a girlfriend somewhere in Montmartre and that her ex was causing them trouble.

"When I woke up the next morning, he was already gone. Not only was some cash missing from my wallet, but I also discovered a gold wristwatch and an expensive Dupont lighter were missing. I didn't have any clue where to find him. The same thing happened a couple of times after that. When he came, I took care to leave some cash in a visible place, which he would disappear with after showering, shaving, and changing his clothes. He was like a ghost, arriving at midnight and vanishing at the third crow of the cock, taking away the offerings left for him by humble mortals. It didn't bother me, but I was worried about him, and kept intending to have a serious talk with him.

"Simone came back to Paris and we began to spend almost all our time together. She shared an apartment with another girl, so we preferred to meet at my place. Once, she'd fallen asleep there, when Abe showed up at around three o'clock in the morning, drunk as usual. I told him that Simone was in the bedroom and he looked at me with an idiotic grin on his face. What he did then left me speechless—he went into the bedroom and gently lifted the blanket, gazing for a long while at the sleeping naked woman.

"'You're a lucky man,' he murmured, and then let the blanket drop. He quickly turned on his heel and left, forgoing his usual ritual of showering and changing.

"Shortly after that was the night everything went wrong, the night I told you about … But we'll talk about it later, I'd like to rest for a little while now."

He took a small device out of his pocket and pressed a button on it. The nurse appeared and helped him leave the room.

Walter came in and said to me, "If you'd like to go fishing, I'll accompany you. I've prepared everything we need. The creek is less than a mile's walk from here."

I told him that I wasn't keen on fishing and also turned down his invitation to accompany me on a stroll around Freeport. I went back to my suite, read for a few minutes, and fell asleep.

I dreamed of Julie again. She was standing in front of me, heavily made-up, wearing kinky clothes, and her double stood next to her.

"I didn't know you had a twin sister," I said.

We were in an empty room. I was sitting on a sort of throne with a carved wooden back, and the two women were standing, their long shadows covering me like a shroud.

"I don't have a twin sister," said one of the two, "and I'm not Julie. I'm Simone."

I woke up panting in fear. I knew she was in love with me even before she told me. These things can happen during therapy, especially when the psychologist is male and the patient is female or the other way around, and it's called "transference." There are patients who have a huge affective need, which they project onto the person they associate with safety, responsibility, and attention.

When I explained this to her, Julie tried to convince me that, in her case, it wasn't anything of the sort.

"I like you a lot," she told me, "I admit it, but I don't see what the problem would be."

"A therapist–client relationship"—I avoided the words *doctor* and *patient*—"in this situation would be not only immoral and unprofessional, but also highly risky," I told her.

"Every relationship is risky, James. When people are in love, they open up their souls and more often than not they end up getting hurt, maybe even maimed for the rest of their lives. Not because their partners are bad people, but because they can be cold or fearful or both. Have you read *The Divine Comedy*?"

"One of my professors considered it compulsory reading for any future psychoanalyst," I told her. "According to him, Dante's work best reflects the way in which people imagine their inner hell."

"Well, in Canto 3, there are some mysterious lines. In that no-man's-land before hell begins, which is neither damnation nor life, the poet sees a character of whom he says, 'When some among them there I'd recognized / I looked, and I beheld the shadow of him / Who made by cowardice the great refusal.'"

"Yes, I know them. Dante was referring to Pope Celestine the Fifth, who had abandoned his throne in the late thirteenth century."

"I don't care who he was referring to and I'm not interested in history. I'm too fond of dreaming to destroy my fantasies with stupid games about truth and reality. The supreme truth is always in the belly of the woman who gives birth, and not in books. The primitives knew this very well when they fashioned their goddesses."

I remember that she got up from her armchair, her eyes half-closed, as if in a trance. She took off her clothes with slow movements and stood naked in front of me, her legs slightly apart and her arms by her sides.

"Nothing more than this exists," she told me, "life is right here, running through my body. Beyond this, there's only nothingness."

I didn't say a word. I made no movement. She was extraordinarily beautiful. The seams of her lingerie had left light marks on her skin, like old scars.

"'The great refusal,'" she said and moved toward me, walking around the desk. "It seems that all of us must choose between the nothingness of limbo, and the pain of hell. Which do you choose, James?"

# seven

I TOOK A SHOWER, lingering for long minutes under the hot water, trying to pull myself together. The memory of Julie left me with a feeling of profound, harrowing sadness, which I felt physically, in every cell of my body. At the same time, I tried to weigh the risks that Josh would be exposed to during hypnosis.

He was waiting for me in the living room, sitting in an armchair in front of the coffee table. The room seemed very familiar to me, as if I'd been there for months. Just as I sat down, he began to narrate the story. His tone was different, stronger, and the words rapped out like bullets, as if he were eager to rid himself of the burden of recounting the events as quickly as he could.

"Simone told me that she'd met with Abe. He'd come looking for her at the foundation and insisted on talking to her in private, so they'd gone to a nearby café.

"For two hours, Abe had done nothing but talk about me behind my back, inventing all kinds of awful things about me. He told her that I wasn't at all what I seemed to be and that my real intention was to make a fool of her, to drag her down into one of the perverse games I apparently liked playing with women. That when we'd come back from Lyon, for example, I'd told him that I'd fallen in love with her younger sister, Laura, and that I planned to invite her to New York in order to seduce her.

"Obviously, he didn't use these exact words but the most

vulgar language conceivable. He told her that I was a lecher, that at university I'd raped a friend of his, whose silence I'd then bought with money. He confessed to Simone that he was thinking of going to Mexico to hide from me, but that he wanted to leave Paris with a clear conscience and not to have to live with the thought that her life had been destroyed because he'd introduced her to me.

"Simone told him she didn't believe a word of it and asked him why he hadn't said anything to her before then, if that was really the way things stood when it came to me. Because he didn't know how serious things were, Abe explained to her. It hadn't been until we got back from Lyon and I'd mentioned the word *marriage* that he realized my game was getting out of hand.

"And if she could bear to face the truth, he promised he would supply her with all the evidence to prove that what he was saying was true. That evening, all she had to do was visit him at the suite where he lived, somewhere in the 18th district. He told her that he had letters and photographs that he'd stashed there and which he had no intention of taking out of the building.

"After Simone finished her story, I was lost for words, trying to comprehend what exactly had caused Abe to come up with such a pack of lies about me. I tried to persuade her not to go to him. But she was already determined to do it, not because she believed for one second that Abe was telling the truth, regardless of what 'proof' he was going to show her, but because she felt sorry for him. She was convinced that he'd suffered a nervous breakdown and was rapidly descending into madness. Gradually, with patience and kindness, she hoped to pull him out of it and convince him of the unreality of the world he'd created in his mind.

"I told her not to play with fire. Neither of us was a psychiatrist. I remembered a former acquaintance at college, a guy named Green, whose psychosis had erupted during our freshman year. He built in his room on campus a kind of altar around a TV set, adorned with empty toothpaste tubes and remains he'd picked out of the garbage. When the ambulance eventually came to take him to the hospital, the paramedics had a real battle on their hands with him, even though he was short and puny.

"I asked her whether she'd considered even for a second the fact that her life—or our lives, if she would agree to let me go with her—might well be in danger if Abe took the final step toward outright insanity."

As he approached the end of his story, I noticed that he was becoming more and more agitated and disturbed. At first he'd seemed quite sure of himself, even if he was visibly anguished by all those memories. Having reached this part, he was like a balloon from which the air was slowly draining, his face as pale as a corpse.

His breathing was becoming quicker, and he kept fidgeting with his hands, smoothing an imaginary crease in the corduroys he was wearing or fiddling with the things on the coffee table. It grew dark, but he didn't seem to notice, and we continued to sit in the gloom with the lights off.

"In the end we reached a compromise—she'd meet with Abe, but I'd be there, hiding somewhere. And the meeting wouldn't take place in Abe's room, which was probably in some trash hole full of drunks and junkies, but in a decent hotel.

"She agreed to it.

"The next day, I rented a suite for two nights at the Hotel Le Meridien, paying cash in advance. It wasn't far from the restaurant where we'd first met. I packed a couple of things and moved in there. Meanwhile, Simone called Abe and told him that she'd meet him, but only at the address she indicated. Abe replied that he'd be there the next day, at nine p.m.

"At eight o'clock in the evening, Simone arrived at

the hotel. I desired her—we made love whenever we were together—but the rooms of the suite already seemed haunted by Abe's spirit and it would have felt like he was there looking at us, so we contented ourselves with smoking a joint. Simone only took a few drags, but I think I overdid it, and also downed a few glasses of brandy. At nine on the dot, when Abe arrived, I was already feeling potted. I hid in the bedroom."

The room was in almost complete darkness, with only a faint glimmer from a full moon seeping through the window to cast a wan light.

"I could only faintly hear what they were saying in the living room, because they were both talking in low voices. But I realized that Abe was still telling lies about me, and that Simone was contradicting him. At one point I thought I heard Simone calling for help, so I opened the door and rushed into the room.

"Nothing had happened. I'd probably only imagined I heard that cry. As I told you, I was quite stoned. Simone was sitting in an armchair by the window, the cherry-red curtains closed. Abe was sitting on a small settee in front of her and had his hands under his thighs, as if trying to warm them. He looked at me in shock and reproached Simone for having betrayed him.

"I can't remember clearly what happened over the next hour or so, until the film reel broke entirely, as it were.

"Abe continued to utter monstrous lies, starting from the moment we met and finishing with my arrival in Paris. He claimed that I'd painstakingly woven a conspiracy aimed at tarnishing him in Simone's eyes, so that I could destroy their relationship. He used the most vulgar expressions imaginable and punctuated his speech with gestures as obscene as his words.

"Simone and I said almost nothing at all; we merely let him spill out his venom. I poured brandy into some glasses and sat on the rug in the living room. Except for Abe's words, anybody who had seen us would have thought we were three friends having a drink together, smoking, and reminiscing.

"There was a large wall clock in the living room, above the TV. I remember that it was midnight when I looked at it for the last time. I was confused and couldn't be bothered to argue with Abe. I repeatedly asked myself what we were doing there. I remember that at one point Simone went to the bathroom and I was left alone with Abe, who had stretched out on the floor.

"He told me he hated me and that he wished I were dead. I had a strange, disconnected feeling, as if everything he was saying referred to a completely different person, someone I didn't even know and about whom I didn't care at all, so his words couldn't hurt me. I was still sitting on the rug, leaning against an armchair with my arms folded around my knees. It might seem weird, but I fell asleep.

"When I woke up, I was no longer on the rug but on the couch. My whole body was aching, and my head felt like it was about to burst. The clock read eleven minutes past two in the morning. A couple of bottles of brandy lay empty on the floor. There was nobody else in the room.

"I went into the bedroom, then into the bathroom, and it was there that I found Simone.

"She was lying in the tub, her hands folded over her chest in a macabre funeral posture, her eyes closed, her face horribly damaged and covered in blood. Her head had been smashed in with a marble lamp stand, which was on the floor under the sink. Abe was nowhere to be seen."

He paused, as if groping for the words.

"Not even to this day do I know why I did what I did next. The most plausible explanation was that, after I'd fallen asleep, Abe grabbed the marble lamp stand, went to the bathroom—I remembered that she'd gone in there before I fell asleep or passed out, I don't know which—killed her, and then fled.

"But I was still too stoned to understand how that tied in with the fact that I hadn't heard anything and that there was a trail of bloodstains from the bathroom to the living room.

"I thought that maybe I'd collapsed on the couch after I'd tried to stop Abe. Or might I have killed her while under the influence? But why would I have done such a horrible thing? What exactly had Abe said to me, before I passed out?

"Until morning, I cleaned the room. I polished everything to remove all fingerprints and I cleaned up the bloodstains as best I could. I was trembling violently and all I could think about was how to escape from the trap I suspected Abe of having laid for me, in order to destroy me forever. I vomited a few times, and then I began to think about how to get Simone's body out of the hotel.

"In the morning, I hung up the DO NOT DISTURB sign on the door and went to the shopping center across the street, where I bought the biggest suitcase I could find and some new clothes for myself. Simone had been small, so I was able to stuff her body into the suitcase along with the clothes I'd been wearing that night. I still had one more joint left and I found a number of small bottles of whiskey and vodka in the minibar, which I drank one after the other until I plucked up the courage to call the reception and ask them to help me carry my suitcase outside to a cab. I had this permanent feeling that the whole thing was nothing but a nightmare, that I wasn't really in a taxi, in Paris, and that Simone's body wasn't in the suitcase in the trunk.

"When I got back to the Rue de Rome, the concierge asked me how my trip had been and I told him it had been wonderful. I asked him whether he'd seen Abe and he answered that Monsieur Abe hadn't set foot there the whole time I'd been away. I lugged the suitcase up the stairs to my apartment and stretched out on the bed.

"I realized that I was rapidly passing from one extreme mental state to another, each worse than the last. In a situation like that, first comes the initial shock, which paralyzes you, roots you to the spot. Once you get over that, there comes a second state, which prompts you to feverish action—you have to do something, straightaway, to escape from the dangerous situation. Tiredness vanishes as if by magic, you discover unsuspected reserves of strength, make swift decisions, and act accordingly. Your mind works with a speed you'd never have thought yourself capable of. But after that, the payback comes: exhaustion and an awareness of what has happened, which punches you right on the jaw. Each minute, I was reliving the moment when I'd found Simone's body in the tub and realized that she was dead. Each time, I felt the shock in the pit of my stomach.

"Not only had I lost Simone, but it was also possible that I might have been the one who had ended her life. I was in a foreign country and it was highly likely that I'd be made a patsy even if I were innocent. It would have been a piece of cake for the prosecution to convince a jury of my guilt, whether the accusation was grounded in truth or not. And Abe was nowhere to be found. I didn't even have his address.

"I couldn't tear my eyes away from the door of the closet where I'd stashed the suitcase. I kept thinking it would open at any second, like in a horror film, and that Simone would step out, her face disfigured, her arm pointing at me accusingly. I had some brandy in the apartment and I drank it, but the only effect was that it made me sick and I vomited again. Finally, I remembered that I had some sleeping pills somewhere. I found the bottle in a drawer and I swallowed a few. I fell asleep fully clothed and didn't wake up until the next morning, when day was already breaking outside. I'd slept for eight hours.

"The first thing I did was go to the closet and open

the door—it was empty. My legs almost collapsed. When I pulled myself together, I discovered that Abe's things had disappeared too. I supposed that he must have come and taken them away. Looking for a suitcase, he'd found the one in which Simone's body was hidden. Why he'd still taken it, I was unable to fathom.

"I took a shower, changed my clothes, and went to the concierge. I asked him whether he'd seen Abe, but he said he hadn't. He had only just come on duty and the night concierge had already gone home.

"Later that evening, the police came to my door. I must have chain-smoked a pack of cigarettes, so my hands were shaking and I was barely able to stand up.

"There were two of them, uniformed, one of them in his late fifties, and the other about the same age as me. When I opened the door, the first thing I saw was the vanished suitcase between them. Strangely, I felt almost relieved: I was going to pay for what I'd done, if I'd really done it, but things would at least be over one way or another. I invited them inside and confirmed that I was indeed Joshua Fleischer, an American citizen.

"They began by asking me whether the suitcase belonged to me. I confirmed that it did. They asked me why I'd abandoned it at three in the morning, near the intersection of Rue Duplessis and Rue de Plone, five minutes' walk from my building. A tramp who was sleeping there had recognized me—the American from Rue de Rome.

"I told them that I had nothing to do with leaving it there and that the tramp had probably seen Abraham Hale, my former roommate, who had come during the night, while I was asleep, and who was about the same height and weight as me.

"They asked me whether I owned a pair of green corduroys and a navy blue jacket. They were the new clothes I'd bought near the Hotel Le Meridien. I acknowledged that I owned the clothes and that I'd worn them the day before, but it was still a case of mistaken identity: I'd taken a powerful sleeping pill and been fast asleep all night. But I had reasons to believe that Abraham Hale had been there. Who knows, maybe he'd been wearing my clothes, he sometimes did that.

"I lit a cigarette, wondering whether it was possible that they might not have looked inside the suitcase, weren't aware that it contained a woman's corpse. Or maybe it was all a morbid game, Simone's body was already at the morgue, on the autopsy table, and the building was surrounded by officers waiting for the signal to burst into my apartment and take me in.

"The older one asked me whether I was aware of the fact that the suitcase could be searched without a warrant if it had been abandoned. *It's starting*, I thought. I told him that I was aware of that, and he thrust his hands inside his trouser pockets. I saw a gun in its holster and a pair of steel handcuffs attached to his belt. The young officer bent over and opened the suitcase.

"It was full of clothes, which looked as if they'd been stuffed inside in a hurry. Abe's clothes, to be exact, the ones that had vanished from the flat during the night. Not a trace of the body. They asked me why I'd thrown all those things away.

"I couldn't understand any of it. Why had Abe abandoned the incriminating suitcase in such a visible place after having somehow gotten rid of the body?

"'Were you in conflict with … Mr. Hale?' the questions continued. 'Where is Mr. Hale now?' 'When and where did you see him last time?'

"I told them that Abe had been behaving oddly, but conflict wasn't the right word to describe relations between us. Abe had moved to somewhere in the 18th district, that was all I knew. I'd never visited him. The last time I'd seen him was when we met at a café about a week previously.

"Finally they left. After I closed the door behind them, I sat down in an armchair and tried to make sense of what was happening. After a few minutes, I gave up. My head was aching so badly that I almost passed out again.

"I looked through the clothes in the suitcase, in the mad hope of finding a clue. In a drawer I found Abe's passport and a small gold pendant with the Statue of Liberty on it that I'd given to Laura, Simone's sister, although I had no idea how it had come to be in Abe's possession. And there, below the stacks of clothes, I found a note on which was written a single word in capital letters: RUN!

"I acted out of instinct—I obeyed the note to the letter and fled. I bought a one-way plane ticket to New York, packed, and went to the airport the very next day. I used Abe's passport, because mine had disappeared and I was too scared to go to the consulate and ask for a duplicate. I needed to get home as soon as possible.

"After I got past the border control and made it back to the States, I sat down on a bench outside the airport and cried. A few people asked me whether they could help, but I was unable to utter a word.

"The rest doesn't really have anything to do with why I called you here. I spent a few months in Mexico and then I gradually resumed my life. The fear that the police would knock on my door gradually faded and finally disappeared.

"I had only sporadic and superficial relations with women after that and it never entered my head to marry. If I had turned into a murderer that night, it meant that it could happen again, so I had to remove any possibility of that horrible thing repeating itself.

"I never heard anything about Simone or Abe. For many years, I tried to forget everything, and for a while I thought I'd succeeded. But then, a few weeks ago, something happened—the details aren't important—and I realized that those memories have always been there, locked up in a secret room of my mind, biding their time. I've never forgiven myself for what happened that night, for the fact that I was there, whether I was the murderer or not. I fled like a coward instead of staying to clear matters up and take responsibility.

"I tried to compensate for the remorse by dedicating most of my life to charity. I wish I could turn back the clock. I can't do that, but I don't want to leave this world without knowing whether I am a criminal or not."

I felt just as exhausted as he looked as we sat there in the dark. I could no longer make out his features. He was nothing but a deep shadow, a vague outline dissolved in the black water in which we were submerged, making us prisoners of the mystery he'd finally shared with me.

He got up slowly and turned on the lights before sitting down in the armchair once again.

"Now you know what this is all about," he told me, looking at me somehow defiantly. "And tomorrow, if you agree, we shall begin our task."

"It's not quite that simple," I told him. "First, I need your medical records. Second, I also need you to sign a statement confirming that you understand the risks involved with such therapy and that you accept full responsibility for any eventual consequences. Depending on the medication that is being administered to you, it remains to be seen whether such a statement will have legal validity, given the possible ground of diminished responsibility."

"I know all that. You'll find a copy of my medical record in your room. I've already been advised by my lawyer in regard to the statement—the painkillers I've been taking and the doses don't diminish my mental faculties."

"I see you've thought of everything."

"I've had months and years to think about this, and I'm a man who likes to have things in order."

"We could try a word association test," I said. "It would only take me a day or two to devise it. Sometimes the results are truly spectacular, and a lot more certain than those of hypnotic regression."

He shook his head. "I'd like to stick to the hypnosis. We'll see after that whether further tests are required."

"Josh, did you keep a diary during that time?"

"No, I didn't keep a diary. Why do you ask?"

"Sometimes our memory can play terrible tricks on us … How someone put it a long time ago, remembrance of things that happened isn't necessarily the remembrance of things exactly as they were."

"I have a very good memory, James. I've always had. And over the past few days, before you came here, I wrote everything down on paper, trying to remember precisely every detail."

"I understand that and I've noticed that you can remember a lot of details, but our memory isn't a camera that simply registers images and sounds; it has an incredible capacity to cosmeticize and even falsify its recollections."

"I know what you're suggesting, but I can assure you it's not the case. Now, if you'll excuse me, I have to get some rest. See you tomorrow morning."

I found the medical record on the coffee table in my suite. Next to it, in an envelope carrying the logo of one of Joshua Fleischer's foundations, was a waiver of liability in the event of any eventual unpleasant consequences arising from the therapy sessions he'd agreed to, along with a doctor's certificate attesting that his current medication didn't affect his mental capacity.

The leukemia had been detected in its late stage, had gone into remission after treatment with cytostatic drugs, and had then erupted and spread. It was almost a miracle that he was still alive and that his suffering wasn't more acute. But all in all, it was a typical case, without any special connotations.

Before going to bed, I took out a notebook and fountain pen and jotted down an outline of the session. I also wrote down a plan B, in case the first didn't work.

# eight

I PRESERVED THE NOTES I made during the two sessions of hypnosis that took place successively on the following day. I reproduce them here verbatim.

## Session 1

Patient: Joshua Fleischer, male, sixty-four, suffering from leukemia, no other known conditions.

The subject is slightly agitated, has an elevated heart rate and blood pressure, dilated pupils. He's in a state of emotional alertness and wants to make sure that I've taken care of all the details. He states repeatedly that he has complete trust in me.

Before starting the session, he spoke on the phone with his attorney in New York for a couple of minutes. He checked that Walter and the nurse were on standby and tested the panic button. At my request, the curtains were drawn in the room. He made sure that we wouldn't be disturbed by the medics or the house staff on duty.

The session is being recorded on an audio-video digital device, with the magnetic disk to remain in the patient's possession. No copies have been authorized.

I commence the procedure for inducing a trance via verbal suggestion.

Patient is very tense. He reacts significantly only when I suggest he pictures himself on an empty beach. His level

of suggestibility begins to increase. I proceed to induce the
trance. The reaction is positive. Level-two state successfully
induced.

To begin with, I attempt the method of objective
induction. The subject's definite identity is annulled with
a view to diminishing the anxiety attendant upon abandon-
ment of the repressive filters.

"Joshua Fleischer is now four years old. He's calm and
safe. You're his only connection with other people. Can you
ask him to describe for you what he sees?"

"There's a lawn. He's afraid of a bumblebee. It's flying
close to him. Mrs. Michaelson ... Yes, he ... The grass is wet.
He might be invisible. Maybe he has vanished in the grass.
Water ... Debbie ought to have come out, to be with him.
She's wearing red stockings and white sandals."

"Who's Debbie?"

"She's his babysitter. She talks on the phone for hours
and her hair smells bad. She has a big, brown mole under
her nose."

He's uneasy, he groans.

"An old man was hit by a car. The road was gray. He
saw him when they pulled his body out of the highway. His
face was red. He doesn't know where everybody is. Debbie
should be with him. He hears her voice, but he can't see her.
Ants, they are all over the place."

"Everything's fine. Many years have passed since then
and Joshua is now sixteen. You're standing just beside him.
Tell me where he is and what he sees."

He has an expression of fear on his face. He turns his
head as if he's trying to work out where he is. He gnaws on
the fingernails of his left hand. With his fingers, he twists an
imaginary lock of hair above his ear.

All of a sudden he leans forward, as if he's been hit
across the back of the neck, and he lets out a deep groan.
He clutches his face in both hands, covering his mouth,

as if he's stifling a scream. He opens his eyes and looks at me without seeing me. Saliva trickles down his chin. He is breathing rapidly.

"Where's Joshua?"

"He ... enough ..." he says and makes a gesture with his right arm, as if to say something is over. "Please ... for ... give ... him ..."

His voice is that of a teenager, choking on his tears. He's weeping. But there's something in that tone, as if he's under anesthesia and his larynx is stopping him from articulating his sentences properly. The words are gelatinous. His eyes are now half-closed. He's rocking back and forth in his chair, groping around him with his hands, like a blind man.

"He had no business being there," he says, in a different voice, that of a grownup, bitter and harsh. "What the hell was *he* doing there, with that girl? Of all the boys, it had to be *him*! Who gave him alcohol, for God's sake?"

He's suddenly thrust backwards, hitting his shoulders against the back of the armchair. He lifts both hands to his left clavicle. The sounds he emits are suggestive of intense pain.

"The red room," he says. "That room ... I don't want to go back in there ever again ..."

I pause for ten seconds and then take the state of relaxation deeper, to the third level. His breathing is now regular. His expression relaxes.

"Ten years have passed and Josh has graduated from college. How does he celebrate on the day of his graduation?"

He looks preoccupied. He laughs, keeps running his tongue over his lips, he's swallowing as if he's salivating strongly. He says something in a low voice, but I can't make it out. He seems to be searching for an object near him. He keeps looking at his left wrist, as if trying to find out the time.

"I don't think she's coming," he says and mimes lighting a cigarette. He "smokes" angrily, increasingly agitated. "Hey, Phil, how have you been doing? No, man, I don't think so, I'll wait a little longer, and maybe … Somebody has to … It's not a question of cowardice, just that …"

He doesn't say anything else. He's concentrating, as if trying to remember something. His lips are moving silently. His facial expression keeps changing every few seconds. Then he takes a deep breath and enters an almost catatonic state, his arms outstretched in front of him, palms facing upwards, as if releasing a captive bird.

"Joshua is in Paris, France, in a suite at a hotel named Le Meridien. Abe Hale, his friend, should be arriving in a few minutes. Joshua and Simone are already there."

He seems to be concentrating hard, and nods quickly as if trying unsuccessfully to grasp what is expected of him.

"Joshua thinks it's a mistake," he says with sadness in his voice. "He likes it there and he wants to stay. He can't believe Simone agreed to it. He knows it may be dangerous, but … Maybe it's not the only way …"

"Was it Josh's idea that they meet there?"

"No, it was hers … Who cares, anyway? Abe shouldn't have come."

"Why are they in that hotel suite?"

"She said that she wanted to … Abe's trying to persuade her to change her mind, but she doesn't want to. He's a lunatic. She says that she would rather die than tell him what …"

His voice is low, weary. Then he gives a start, twists his head around as if he's heard a noise somewhere to his right. His lips are moving, but he makes no sound for a number of seconds.

"That's room service. They ask for another bottle," he says, looking at somebody invisible on his right. "Hey, where … No, he doesn't think so …"

He looks all around him, blinking rapidly, like a man who has found himself in the dark and is trying to work out where he is. Suddenly, he opens his mouth wide and freezes with a look of terror on his face, with his eyes wide open, staring into space. He's sweating profusely.

"There's a clock on the wall. Look at it and tell me what time it is now."

He slowly turns his head to the left, like a mechanical doll. He mutters something unintelligible.

"What time is it now?"

"No," he says, and shakes his head adamantly. "He can't do it. He doesn't think it's the right thing to do. Not now, not ever. They should …"

He lifts his legs up and hugs his knees, as if he's sitting on the floor.

"Must … It's a mistake … No, he won't say anything. Each of them must choose what to do."

He keeps shaking his head, and from time to time it seems like he's watching somebody moving around within a confined space. He seems to be holding a book, which he leafs through, shaking his head.

"Now … "

"He can see her now … Oh, my God, this can't be true! What have they done? Oh, no …"

His scream is so loud that I'm sure it must have been heard all through the house. He leans forward, places his feet on the floor and clutches his knees tightly. He freezes, catatonic once again.

He no longer responds to questions, he rejects two successive suggestions at regression. I decide against taking the trance to level four. I proceed to gradually bring him back to a waking state.

He breathes deeply, looks in every direction, glances at the clock on the table.

"Only twelve minutes have passed," he says.

"We reached an impasse," I explain. "There was no point in trying any further."

"So, what have we found out?"

He's impatient, his habitual mask of composure seems to have slipped, and he doesn't attempt to adjust it.

"Nothing significant," I tell him, and he can't conceal his disappointment. "You were there, in the hotel room, most likely with Simone and Abe, just like you said. One of you tried to make the others change their minds about something. Abe arrived later, but it seems that you were both waiting for him in the room. I don't think you were hiding when he arrived, unlike what you told me. I think your memory's guarding those recollections extremely well, as I expected. You kept repeating that you weren't going to say anything."

"Is that all?" he asks. He shifts his gaze from me to the video recorder, which is still running, as if he suspects I might be hiding something.

I tell him that the first session is exploratory and that in the second I won't be using the objectification method. I explain to him what this method has entailed—it's suggested to the subject that he's a different person witnessing the scene he's about to relate, in order to eliminate blockages and inhibitions. The description of a scene from a neutral perspective on the subject's part greatly enhances the accuracy of his account. In the following session, I'll be using his real identity.

He doesn't seem very convinced, but then he agrees and tells me that the second session should take place immediately. I suggest that he should rest for a couple of hours, in order to be able to relax as deeply as possible. Maybe he should listen to music while trying to empty his mind of thoughts.

He rejects my suggestion and invites me to go for a ride instead.

He asks me to drive. Walter brings the car out and we set off. Josh tells me the way. We stop somewhere near the turnoff to Interstate 95, twenty miles down the highway, at a place named Nancy's Diner. We order two portions of lobster, but he barely touches his. He talks to me about fishing techniques and tells me that during the season he used to go fishing with a friend. His thoughts seem to be elsewhere, his attitude has changed. He seems half absent, somewhat hostile. The fact that I'm taking notes seems to bother him.

I ask him whether he's remembered something and he avoids giving me a straight answer.

I point out to him that any detail might prove vital in a psychological investigation of this kind.

He hesitates for a few moments and then tells me, "I think I killed her, James. I remembered some things … Different things, bad things … They just came to me. I can see them in front of my eyes even now, but in a neutral way, as if it wasn't me, as if I were watching it in a movie or something."

"You don't realize it now," I tell him, "but a real storm has taken place in your brain. Allow things to settle before jumping to conclusions. Our memory not only has hiatus, but there are plenty of false memories. Eyewitnesses to a car accident, for example, often describe things completely differently than what in fact happened. What is stored in our memory isn't what has been recorded by the retina, because we aren't robots. Our consciousness operates like a director, cutting scenes from his film however he pleases and weaving bits together to give them a certain meaning and significance. We don't actually record *facts*, but *meanings* and *emotions*, which differ from one individual to the next, even if the facts might be the same."

"I know all this," he says wearily. "But I'm more convinced than ever that I was the one who murdered her. I don't know why I'd have done something like that, but I did it."

He's reacting as if he'd never seriously believed that he was the one who committed the murder and that all of a sudden he's had an overwhelming revelation, which leaves little room for doubt.

We return to his estate.

His blood pressure, heart rate, pulse, and blood sugar level are checked once more. He is administered his current medication, without the painkillers. We go into the living room and turn on the recording device. We change the seating arrangement. He lies down on the couch and I sit in the armchair. The second session commences.

## Session 2

The patient goes into the trance more easily this time. He's breathing deeply, suggesting a state of deep sleep.

He reacts positively to my suggestion that he's four years old and tells me about buying his first pair of sandals. He's very cooperative. He again mentions the troubling presence of nearby water.

I ask him how he ended up in Paris after graduating from college. He frowns.

"He suggested that I should leave. I don't know why. I don't want to go there. But after the scandal, nothing was the same again."

"What scandal are you referring to?"

Silence.

I repeat the question, "What scandal are you referring to?"

"That story with her husband. Who cares? Everybody knows. He was killed and I went to Paris, but things got worse. With *him*, things always get worse. And everybody has to let him have his own way. He's never to blame for the things that happen to him, is he?"

"Are you referring to Abe?"

"He was … If he'd just listened to me, the whole scandal would never have happened."

"Are you referring to Abe?"

"The guy who … I'm not allowed to say anything."

His tone of voice shifts. He's "looking" carefully all around him.

"We shouldn't be talking about this … If he finds out … Better let things lie … I don't know what to do … Neither of us knows."

He doesn't say anything else. He's whispering something unintelligible and shaking his head.

"How do you feel about Simone?"

With no hesitation, he says, "She's different. I don't want to do her any harm. I'm certain he's going to hurt her if … I love her, I think."

"Is there someone who wants to harm her?"

"He does … That's the way he is, the way he's been taught to be. He's a bad person. 'And each man kills the thing he loves … The coward does it with a kiss … The brave man with a sword.'"

There's a long pause.

"She doesn't love him. He should leave the country."

"And what does *he* want to do to Simone?"

He sighs, runs his right hand through his hair, and turns his head. His eyes are closed but I can see his eyeballs moving rapidly beneath the closed eyelids.

"My stupid kindness … He always tells me he's going to … Although I'd demonstrated to him then that …"

"Is Abe the one who wants to hurt Simone?"

He gives me a nasty grin. His voice has changed. "No, it's fuckin' Santa."

"I want you to listen to me carefully. How did you arrive at the Hotel Le Meridien, with Simone and Abe? Did you arrive later? What time does the clock on the wall show when you enter the apartment?"

He looks frightened, his face is contorted. "Who told you that?" he whispers. "Nobody can know. It's very important that nobody knows. He stole my passport, the crazy bastard!"

"You told me, because you have complete trust in me. And I want you to continue telling me what happened."

He shakes his head and keeps trying to get up from the couch. "I'm afraid," he says.

"There's no point in being afraid," I assure him. "You're safe now and nobody can hurt you."

"You don't get it, do you?" he asks me irritably. "It's very important that nobody know anything. He would kill her."

"Why?"

"Because people wouldn't understand … She suffered greatly because of …"

"But now they're far away, safe, and they can't do you any harm. They can't harm you or anybody else. They have gone away for good. You don't need to be afraid of them anymore."

He shakes his head as if he's not at all convinced that I'm telling the truth.

"What happened that night?"

"There was a fight."

"Are you talking about Simone?"

"Yes."

"Did you arrive at the hotel first? I mean, before him? Was Simone with you?"

"I got there first. I had a lot to drink. I was upset. At one point, I walked out and thought about leaving, but then I came back. I told him to stop hurting people."

"What exactly are you talking about?"

"About him, about what he did to us."

"Name the thing you're referring to."

"I can't, nobody would understand …"

"And did he do that thing?"

"I was frightened, I don't know ..."

He stops. His agitation increases. He's clenching his right hand into a fist and miming the striking of blows with his arm.

"Blood," he whispers, and the tears begin to flow down his face. "Blood like on the highway. The highway is gray and all of them are dead. I can see her. There's blood in her eyes. She's crying blood."

All of a sudden his entire body begins to quake, as if he's just been administrated an electric shock. Flecks of white foam appear at the corners of his mouth. His hands are flexed, as if he were trying to push away a weight crushing his chest. His fingers are clenched like claws.

I end the session and bring him out of the trance, but he remains frozen in that position. I press the panic button and the nurse arrives immediately.

I lingered there for two more days, but never got the opportunity to speak with him again.

He had suffered a nervous breakdown, even though the tests found no significant change in the parameters of his health. His general condition was severely altered. He wasn't even curious to find out if the second session had revealed something new.

I wrote a report that was locked away in a safe, waiting for the moment when he'd ask to see it.

I avoided drawing any firm conclusions, but I was sure that at the very least he'd been an active accomplice in the woman's murder, if not the sole perpetrator.

From the data I had, neither Josh nor Abraham Hale seemed to fit the psychological profile of a potential murderer. But there are people who should never meet, like Bonnie and Clyde. It's like a chemical reaction—two innocuous substances can produce an explosion once they are mixed together. When he rang the doorbell of that apartment in

New Jersey and met Abraham, his life changed for good.

Apart from that, there were a large number of things that didn't fit, and whose sequence and real significance I hadn't been able to unravel. But I told myself that, given the circumstances, it was of no importance.

When I went to say goodbye, while Walter was taking my luggage to the car, he tried to tell me something, but was unable to articulate the words. He was lying in bed and his hands and face were as white as the sheets. Then he gestured in disgust and turned his face to the wall.

I was certain that I'd never see him again. But I also got the feeling that the story wasn't over.

Before I climbed into my car, Walter handed me an envelope with my name on it. "From Mr. Fleischer," he told me. "I'd ask you not to open it until you get back to New York."

I thanked him, put the envelope in the glove compartment, and drove away. He remained standing on the porch and waved to me, following me with his gaze.

When the iron gates closed behind me, I breathed a sigh of relief. I felt as if I'd been shut up in a musty room for days and somebody had thrown the windows open wide at last, and let the air in.

Of all the patients I'd had over the years, Joshua Fleischer had been the closest to death. And that death, his death, was almost a palpable presence, hidden in a corner, waiting for the right moment.

I don't recall much about the journey back. The highway was more crowded than on the way there and a heavy gray rain dogged my progress for hours. I stopped at a gas station to fill up and drank a coffee, trying to decide what I should do the next day. I couldn't get Josh's story out of my head, and I was sure I wouldn't succeed in doing so for a very long time.

# nine

I ARRIVED HOME EXHAUSTED, took a shower, and went straight to bed. First thing in the morning, a colleague of mine from LA called and told me about a conference in Switzerland which was being held in three days. Professor Atkins had a cold and wouldn't be able to attend, although he was one of the speakers. Even though the invitation caught me by surprise, I agreed to stand in for him—it would force me to occupy my mind with something other than Josh's story.

I'd put the envelope from Josh on my desk at home and, after I got back from the conference, I glanced at it from time to time while I read my emails and wrote the outline of my report for UCLA, but I didn't have the courage to open it. I suspected it was a farewell letter and I didn't feel up to reading it yet.

I'd liked him. He was almost a romantic character, torn between good and evil, but he'd nonetheless found the strength to do so much good. Had he killed Simone in Paris long ago? If so, why had he done it? Probably nobody would ever know for certain.

One evening, I decided it was time to read the letter.

I'd been watching an old movie on TCM and had made myself a cup of coffee. I went to my desk and sat down to draw up my schedule for the coming days. The envelope was there, between the pencil holder and the laptop. It crossed my mind that it might contain some last wish on my former client's part, and that I shouldn't ignore it. I opened it.

I found another, smaller envelope inside. The larger one also contained two sheets of paper with my name written on them. It was a letter from Josh as I'd presumed.

Dear James,

When you read these lines, your job will be over. I don't know whether we'll ever manage to solve the mystery, and now I don't even know anymore whether I ever really wanted to. But I do know that you came over to help me and that you didn't do so for the money, and for that I thank you one more time.

I chose you not only for your proven competence and your renown in the academic world. My preliminary investigation also recommended you for another reason—in a way you have experienced a similar tragedy. I'm referring, of course, to Julie Mitchell. I suspect that you understand all too well the true sense of guilt and remorse.

You shouldn't feel embarrassed at my researching your past. I did it only with the intention of knowing you better, before I entrusted you with the darkest secret of my life. And also, perhaps, because I listened to a certain type of intuition I've believed in all my life and which has rarely let me down.

Money is often looked down upon, and its power is unjustly considered overrated. I think this happens because wealth has always been the privilege of a tiny minority. This is why people who never get rich will never know about the almost mystical power concealed within true wealth. Believe me, its power is huge.

So my money has allowed me to obtain a copy of a certain document. It's in the enclosed envelope. I must confess, I've read it. Its contents will, I believe, help you clear up a dilemma. It's what I can do for you.

Why have its contents not come to light until now?
Because two parents overwhelmed by grief chose to
hide this letter from you. They were convinced that you
indirectly caused the death of their daughter. Maybe
a part of you believed the same thing. I don't know
whether you still believe it today, but I am more or less
convinced that you do.

I lied to you when I said that I'm not afraid of death.
When I think of the moment when I'll be standing
on the threshold, I feel the most terrifying dread I've
ever experienced, even though I'm exhausted by my
fight against this illness. I have the same feeling as I
did then, in Paris, the terrifying sensation of facing
something irreversible, fully conscious of the fact that
what has happened and what's about to happen to me
can never be repaired, at least not in this world. And in
the last few days I realized that, regardless of what really
happened in Paris, whether or not it was my fault, I also
died that night.

Now that I'm so close to death, I recognize the same
sensations, the same tastes, and the same smells. My
memory has perhaps deceived me in many things, but
all those sensations have remained intact somewhere
in a corner of my mind. Perhaps we won't ever know
what happened in Paris that night, but I know without
question that I was in the presence of death.

We should never idealize youth. There's no age in life
more banal, and young people easily fall prey to clichés
of every sort. They go to school only because they have
to, and learn pointless things that they'll quickly forget.
They harbor naïve ambitions, fall in love, hate with
reckless ease, because they have no idea of the meaning
of love and desire and passion, nor what consequences
extreme feelings have on a person's life.

In fact, it's the age at which many people destroy their lives and fall into traps from which they'll never escape. It's the age at which future alcoholics, murderers, thieves, torturers, swindlers, the silent accomplices of evil, construct their personalities.

At such an age, it's believed that even the worst mistakes can be redeemed, forgiven, and forgotten. I don't agree. I think we're more likely to err irrevocably in our youth, when our true being is still intact, than later, when society has already made sure of enveloping us in a cocoon of fears and weariness and inhibitions, which anesthetize our senses and dampen our genuine impulses. No adult will ever be as villainous as a villainous youth. Fate willed that I met such a man, and perhaps at the time I was one of them too. Abe, Simone, and I should never have met each other. It would be easy for me to put the blame on them, but something inside me accepted and even loved the evil that surrounded us, and followed it into the room where the murder took place.

Most likely, I'll never see you again. I'm sorry that we didn't meet earlier, under different circumstances. Take care of yourself. You're a good man.

Your friend,
Josh

P.S. Please don't try to dig deeper, because things are much more complicated than I've been able to tell you. I realized something during our discussions: Some events should never come to light, because once they do, they shrivel up like flowers pulled up by the root, and their shapes become meaningless. They're merely abstract designs, senseless occurrences, ink splotches in which everyone is free to see whatever they want to see, because regardless of what each person might see, the initial meanings have long since vanished, even for those who experienced them at the time. All of us have the right to forget and be forgotten. So let the dead sleep in peace, James. It's better this way.

I realized that he must have written the letter on the morning of the day when we'd carried out our sessions, or the evening before. Once again, I felt dreadfully sorry that I hadn't been able to give him the peace he sought.

I examined the second envelope.

Julie had always seemed detached and confident during our relationship, as if it was all just a game. It wasn't even a relationship in the proper sense, all it boiled down to were a few sexual encounters in places and circumstances bizarre enough to make me feel like I was nothing but an experimental prop, like one of those crash-test dummies.

I told her so once, and she more or less confirmed it.

She said, "I think that men sometimes look at the reverse situation as being normal, with women as sex objects. For centuries you've imagined women as creatures subject to your pleasures, without it ever entering your heads that the reverse might be the case. Maybe there's always been a conspiracy of women, who knows?"

"Even as recently as the beginning of the twentieth century, women were still regarded as nymphomaniacs if they had too strong orgasms, and they risked being locked up in psychiatric clinics," I told her. "A man who frequented brothels three times a week on average—that's what the statistics from the Victorian era tell us—was regarded as normal, but a woman who cheated on her husband for pleasure was at risk of being declared insane and shut up in a mental hospital for the rest of her life."

"That's because men are afraid of the terra incognita of

the female body. Do you know what I think sex means to most men?"

"I suspect you're about to tell me."

"It's your way of reconciling yourselves with the idea that you're going to die."

"Isn't it the same for women?"

"I've long since reconciled myself with the idea that I'm going to die, and I've decided to choose for myself when it's going to happen."

"So what does sex mean to you?"

"It's the best way of seeing someone as he really is."

I opened the envelope.

It contained the copy of a hastily written note on two pages torn from a spiral notepad, in ballpoint pen.

Dearest,

As soon as you decide to die, living becomes incredibly easy. From that moment on, you can enjoy it beyond strings, fear or shame. I made the decision a long time before meeting you. Our encounter was merely an accident. It didn't change my commitment, because nothing could do that, but it did make me delay it for a while. Perhaps you'll never realize what wonderful moments you gave me in my last year on this world.

Whatever I write now would sound false, but I don't want to depart before saying goodbye. I couldn't do it if I were looking in your eyes. You'll allow me this one small act of cowardice, I think.

Over the course of our relationship you've asked me questions about myself, and I did the same. I lied to you many times, not because I was afraid of the truth or for the sake of some perverse game, but quite simply because I didn't know what to say to you. I've avoided

answers and the truth all my life, ever since I was five
and somebody tried to explain to me that Santa didn't
exist. It was then that I knew that the truth has no value
and that imagination means everything. The so-called
truth is nothing but a graveyard, a sum of things that
have died because people have stopped dreaming of
them. For thousands and thousands of years, millions
of lovers dreamed of the moon, until Neil Armstrong
went there and proved that it's nothing but an insipid
lump of dust, a barren, hostile place.

I think I must have been like twelve when my
parents planned a trip to the Grand Canyon. They
showed me photos, they'd bought brochures and glossy
illustrated books about it. I tried not to look at them,
I wanted to open my eyes and find myself faced with
a wonder I could never have imagined. I wanted it to
take my breath away, to leave me speechless. It wasn't
so—my parents had taken good care of that. But that
was exactly how it felt when I met you. Thank you so
much for everything you've done for me and for trying
to save me. In a way, you did.

I remember a quote from that book you love so
much: "I'm not one and simple, but complex and
many." Now is the time to pull myself together and
leave. I'm impatient to do what I have to do. I feel like
I'm about to set out on a journey to a miraculous place
and rejoice that I'm the lucky one who's been chosen.

Julie

It was her writing, there was no doubt. Her parents had
probably hidden the letter, although it might have proved
that Julie and I had had an affair.

I think I must have sat at my desk for over an hour, looking
at the pieces of paper spread over its surface, making an

effort to tie my thoughts together. I tried to remember the last time I saw her and I couldn't. What was she wearing? Did she say goodbye? Did we kiss? Did I try to call her after that? Did she answer or try to call me back?

"You always complicate things," she'd once told me.

We were in my apartment, lying in bed. I was talking to her about the book I intended to write regarding my clinical experiments.

"I hope you're not going to turn me into 'The Case of Miss X' or 'File no. 2343VM.' Do you think that people always know, on some level, why they do a certain thing? You're looking for events and facts that have no special meaning, combing through your patients' minds like a mechanic under the hood of a car, but sometimes I get the feeling that you miss what's essential. What do you hope to find? I think the most wonderful things are those which cannot be explained."

I gathered together the pieces of paper, put them in the small safe behind my desk, got dressed, and went out. It was raining and the city was shivering beneath a thick layer of gray clouds. The wet pavement glistened like the dark surface of a river.

I came to Sixth Avenue, which was still seething with people and all of them seemed as alien to me as if they were from another planet. I stopped at Joe's Pizza and got a slice, and then I walked into a bar and ordered a drink.

Somewhere, hundreds of miles away, a man was in agony, surrounded by ghosts, in the midst of a fortune that no longer had the power to defend him from anybody or anything. Not only had he taken me by the hand and ushered me into his haunted house, but he'd also reawakened my own nightmares.

I think it was then, in that instant, as the gray rain stared at me through the bar window, that I decided I had to find out what happened in Paris that night—if not for Josh's peace of mind, then at least for my own.

The following day I called Kenneth Mallory. He'd been an NYPD detective for ten years, before deciding to open his own agency. He was a favorite of the talent agencies on Broadway when they needed to find out about their clients' past. It was risky to invest millions in marketing and then have some scandal rag blow it all away by writing about drugs and orgies and stolen cars. So he specialized in investigating past lives and became one of New York's spooks, a man with access to the well-guarded secrets of the rich and famous, discreet, tenacious, and efficient, a flesh-and-blood shadow on the streets of the city.

I'd first met him four years earlier, when the police suspected that one of my patients had paid a hitman to kill his wife. Shortly before she was shot dead in her home in Fort Greene, Brooklyn, she'd signed a life insurance policy for a high six-figure sum, so the company had hired Mallory to carry out an inquiry. In the end, the real murderer had been caught, and there proved to be no connection between him and the victim's husband.

I wouldn't say we became friends, because I doubted that any such notion existed in Mallory's vocabulary, but we'd remained in touch and met for dinner two or three times a year.

He agreed to take on the case and I sent him an email with all the details I knew about Josh, Abraham Hale, and Simone Duchamp. I suggested to him that he begin his investigation in the archives of the Paris police, because unsolved murders are put on ice and kept in the files for decades. He told me he had a contact who worked in the French police and that he'd let me know as soon as he found out anything.

The investigation was going to cost me some time and

money, but the check Josh had given me was certainly big enough to cover all the potential expenses, and I had enough spare time before starting my next project.

On the other hand, I'd signed a non-disclosure agreement, which I'd already broken by giving Mallory real names and details about the whole affair. But he made his living by being a reliable secret-keeper, and so there was zero risk of finding the story in the press someday. More than that, at the end of the day Josh had paid me to bring him the truth about that night. I hadn't been able to do it on my own, but with a hand from Mallory, I might still be able to do so.

I didn't hear from him for a week, and then he called me just as I was leaving the gym one Thursday evening. I stopped by my parked car, got inside, and answered my cellphone.

His voice was as gruff as always. "Hi, can you talk?" he said. "Okay, now listen: There's no murder case with a victim named Simone Duchamp in the archives of the French police. Not in 1976 or in any other year."

I was more than surprised.

"That's impossible! Maybe the file went missing. Back in those days—"

"Yes, sure, I've heard the tune," he said. "They didn't have electronic archives back then, and so on … But don't think that before computers the detectives kept records in cheap spiral notebooks and then threw them away. My man out there checked in all the possible files and I assure you they're kept meticulously. There's no cold case about a woman named Simone Duchamp, aged twenty-something. They checked the whole period from 1970 to 1979. Maybe your friend got the name wrong, or the timeline might be wrong. Anyway, there are a few homicide cold cases in Paris that fit her age. I'll send you a list by email."

"What about trying Missing Persons? My client told me that the body disappeared. Maybe it was never found, so it might have been investigated as a missing person case rather than a homicide."

"Well, I'll do that, but in the meantime try to find out whether your man gave you the wrong name. After over four decades, your man might have gotten her name wrong. You're too young to know that, but a part of growing old is that you start remembering everything you've gone through in a different way. However, in most countries, after a few years, depending on the legislation, a missing person is automatically considered deceased and registered as such. But I'll check one more time, just in case."

"Thanks, Ken. I don't think I can get in touch again with the guy."

He cleared his throat. "Can I ask you something?"

"Please."

"Are you sure you want to be involved in this story? I mean that patient of yours is a big shot. I know from experience that these long-gone messes always have a lot of undergrowth when very rich guys are involved in them."

"I know what you mean, but I'm sure."

"Do you really trust him? You guys have spent just a few days together, so you can't say you know him well, with all due respect for your profession. Maybe he just jumbled up a story for one reason or another."

"Ken …"

"Okay, it's your money. I'll call you if I get something."

Four days after Thanksgiving, I received a letter from Josh's attorney, along with an old black-and-white photograph and a small gold pendant embossed with an image of the Statue of Liberty.

Mr. Cobb,

I'm writing to inform you that Mr. Fleischer passed away on Thursday, at about three p.m. It was a miracle he hung on for so many days after your visit. He didn't suffer and died in his sleep. I'm very happy that things turned out in such a way that we, his friends, could be with him in his final hours and keep watch over his departure. It was the least we could do after everything he did for us.

Sincerely,
Richard Orrin

PS: The enclosed photograph and the pendant are gifts from Mr. Fleischer. I understand that the photograph was taken in Paris, in the mid-seventies. He kept it on his night stand in his final days.

The locket pendant was plain, oval-shaped, and encrusted with the Statue of Liberty. I opened it; its interior was empty.

The photo showed a young woman wearing a white dress and a sunhat with a wide brim that cast a shadow over her face, sitting with two men at a table between some trees.

Their outlines seemed to melt into the large splotches of light, like in an Impressionist painting. One of the men was sitting in front of the woman, leaning cross-legged against the back of his chair. His flared trouser bottoms were hitched up to reveal half of his left calf. His right hand rested in his lap, while his left was placed on his hip, in a cavalier attitude. He had a proud look, heightened by his thirties-style pencil mustache. The other man, probably Abraham Hale, was seated at the head of the table, between the other two, leaning toward the woman, although his gaze was fixed on the other man, who had surprised him with a gesture or word and to whom he was about to reply.

The picture was overexposed, causing the figures to dissolve into a kind of milky mist, and it was impossible to see them any more clearly.

I turned it over. In old-fashioned calligraphy, the following words were written in the bottom right-hand corner: *A memory of Paris: Abe, Josh, and Simone, September 29, 1976.* I put it on my desk and I looked at it for a while.

So, there was no farewell. I brought to my mind Josh's eyes, his withered hands, his breathing, his features furrowed with the trenches of a battle I didn't know whether he'd lost or just won.

It was the first time that I'd interacted so intimately with a man so close to death and I was sure that I'd never forget those days we spent together, that I'd always remember every detail, each expression on his face, each word and gesture, and each moan of the wind against the windows.

Mallory called a couple of months later, after the winter holidays. He told me that he'd found something interesting, and we met the following evening at the Gramercy, in Union Square. After we ordered our sides, he handed me a notebook over the table. It was bound in black leather, old and worn.

"You might find this helpful," he said. "I'm not sure, but … Well, it's a very tangled story, you'll see, but those guys' names are mentioned in there. Officially, the diary belonged to a man named Jack Bertrand, who died in a mental hospital fifteen years ago. He was arrested in the late nineties, charged with second degree murder, found guilty but insane, and committed to Kirby Forensic Hospital Center. Don't ask me how I got this, you don't want to know. Take your time reading it, and then we'll talk."

I put the notebook in my briefcase and changed the subject, but I could scarcely wait to glance over the notes. After getting home, I made myself a cup of coffee and studied the pages, which were covered in a loopy handwriting. But the text was almost unintelligible, so the next day I asked a tech-savvy I knew to scan the pages and run them through a handwriting re-composition program. The final result was an almost clean 25,000-word document, which I started reading that same evening.

# ten

IT ALL STARTED WITH A woman looking for a man who wasn't me.

But I should tell you the story from the beginning, because what I'm trying to do is to turn random, meaning-less slices of reality into a story that might help you under-stand why I wound up in a hospital for the criminally insane, accused of a murder I didn't commit.

About two months ago, on October 11th, a woman called 911 to report that something seemed to be amiss with one of her neighbors. The man, named Abraham Hale, had failed to move his car from one side of the street to the other, in accordance with parking regulations, and so he'd wound up with a ticket under the wiper of his Toyota. It was something that had never happened before, the woman stressed. She'd tried to get in touch with Hale, but he hadn't answered when she'd rung his doorbell and he wasn't picking up the phone. She'd last seen him on Thursday afternoon.

They lived in a pre-war four-story brownstone in Jackson Heights, Queens, near Travers Park. Ms. Jenkins worked for the DA's office, so her call was taken seriously and twenty minutes later two patrol officers arrived at the door of apartment 8, accompanied by the super. They rang the doorbell for a couple of minutes, with no reply. Eventually, the super produced the key from his pocket and tried to open the door, but the latch chain was on, so they broke it and entered the apartment.

A man was lying naked on the living room floor, by the couch. He was tall, slim, and his skin was bone-white. There was no congealed blood, no signs of violence or burglary. None of the things in the room seemed to have been disturbed, but the man lying on the carpet was obviously dead. An officer checked for a pulse and found none, so his colleague called the medical examiner's office. The super confirmed that the dead man was indeed the apartment's current tenant, Mr. Abraham Hale. The door and windows didn't show any signs of forced entry, but the officers noted the presence of two glasses on the coffee table, one of them smeared with red lipstick. They waited in silence, as if the slightest noise might disturb the corpse.

After an initial examination of the body, the assistant medical examiner established that, at a glance, there was no evidence that any criminal act had been committed, and he officially pronounced the man dead. The paramedics zipped up the body bag and drove the corpse to the morgue at Queens Hospital Center, on Jamaica Avenue.

Neither the super nor any of the neighbors knew anything about the guy's next of kin: he wasn't married, didn't have a partner, children, or any known relatives, which complicated matters, because legally it meant there was nobody to officially identify the body at the morgue. He'd moved into the building about four years previously, renting the apartment through a real-estate agency.

The medical examiner took his fingerprints and sent them to the law enforcement agencies, but nothing came up. An autopsy was carried out, and the lab confirmed that there didn't seem to have been any foul play. The man had died about twenty-four hours before the police found his body, and the cause of death was ingestion of a lethal

cocktail of pills: antidepressants, lithium, and benzodiaz-
epines. The guy's body was like a mobile drug-testing lab,
the coroner remarked.

Had Hale committed suicide? It was difficult to tell for
sure, but he probably hadn't. He'd been taking pills for a
good few years, so there had to be a prescription somewhere
in his apartment, signed by a doctor who should be able
to provide more information about his late patient. Most
likely, he'd mixed up the doses, the prescriptions, or both,
and it had turned out to be fatal. Could somebody have
slipped him the pills, dissolving them in his drink without
him noticing? Very unlikely: That volume of pills would have
drastically altered the taste of any drink, strongly enough for
anyone to realize, and the guy hadn't consumed any alcohol
in the forty-eight hours prior to his death, so he couldn't
have been too drunk to notice. The body revealed no signs
of violence, not so much as a small contusion or scratch.

Five days later, the medical examiner reported the death
to the office of the Queens County Public Administrator,
the institution temporarily in charge of disposing of the
guy's estate, and an investigator entered the scene, while
the police were still carrying out their inquiries. Sometimes,
winding up an estate can take a year or even longer—lost
papers, a nephew from Utah who didn't pick up the phone,
two cousins fighting over an old car.

Purely by chance, that investigator was me, Jack Bertrand,
yours truly.

At the time, there were four of us working as investigators
for the Queens County Public Administrator. The others
were Ralph Mendoza, a former police officer in his fifties,
tall, sad, and divorced; Linda Martino, who had been a stay-
at-home mom of three for the last seventeen years, before
her husband suddenly died of a stroke, leaving her broke;
and a twenty-something guy named Alan Cole, hired just a

couple of weeks before, and whom I knew almost nothing about, except that he was from Missouri.

We worked in pairs, as a means of discouraging theft, but Linda and the new guy were already on an inquiry elsewhere and Ralph was off work to attend the funeral of a relative in upstate. So I took the bus to Jackson Heights by myself, and eventually tracked down the super, a short man with a strong Slavic accent. He showed me to the apartment on the second floor, removed the police tape from the door, opened it and left, after leaving a set of keys on the coffee table in the living room.

It was a seven-hundred-square-foot apartment with a Murphy bed and a small bathroom, a clean, decent home for a middle-aged single. My task as an investigator was to ransack the apartment in search of cash, rocks, gold, artworks, and any other valuables, which had to be kept secured until the next of kin were legally able to get their claws on them.

I knew that the detectives had already searched every nook and cranny for clues, but as they hadn't found anything useful to their inquiry, except for some papers, all of the guy's belongings still had to be there. I opened the window and sat on the couch for a while, trying to figure out where I should begin. Did he have any cash or gold stashed somewhere? You don't have to be rich to hide things under the floorboards, especially when you live alone. Folks with deep pockets keep their valuables in concealed wall safes or bank deposit boxes. But this guy had no safe, so he probably had a stash.

The furniture was old and the items didn't match; they'd probably been picked up from garage sales or second-hand stores. There was a small cream-colored rug on the floor, under the coffee table, with a pale, brownish stain in the middle, and five bookshelves by the window, with about fifty cheap paperbacks covered with dust, and a pile of old magazines. A strong smell of tobacco lingered in the air, but I didn't notice any ashtrays or cigarettes. I stood up, moved the table into a corner, rolled up the rug, and put it by the door. Outside the window, I could hear a woman laughing loudly.

An hour later, I was sitting in an armchair, contemplating the shabby haul of items that were lying on the floor before me like the last remains of a vanished planet. A vintage, solid gold Hamilton wristwatch with a black leather strap, still working; twenty-one old American silver coins (nickels, dimes, quarters, halves, and dollars), stowed in a brain-tanned leather pouch; a Japanese etching, depicting a landscape viewed from above, set in a tiny plain frame; a St. Christopher-Pray-for-Us pendant on a chain, probably silver or silver plated, but without any hallmarks; another wristwatch, a gold Omega, not working; an expensive Ghurka Marley Hodgson old duffle bag, made of leather and canvas; a stag-handled Case XX folding penknife; a Zippo lighter, dry and with no flint, emblazoned with a golden Hawaii ad.

The keepsakes and family heirlooms left behind by those who die don't lose their meaning, but in the absence of their former possessor, they just obscure their true significance, turning themselves into puzzle pieces. Every little object—a toothbrush in the bathroom, an empty prescription bottle forgotten in the medicine cabinet, a pair of old shoes in the cupboard, a pile of correspondence lying unopened on the dining table in the living room, a mysterious key that doesn't fit any lock, some old photos—all these become small parts of the same riddle, and one has to fumble for each little piece until, suddenly, they reveal the real story of the one who once owned them. What kind of a person was he? Did he live a happy life? Did he know he was going to die soon and have time to prepare himself for the big jump, or was it something completely unexpected? What about that gold watch? Was it a gift from his parents? Were they still alive, wondering why wasn't he calling them? Did he kill himself or was it just an accident?

That's what I like more about my job: the riddles, each of them different than the others, each of them telling a completely different story.

I checked the clothes in the mirrored wardrobe by the bedroom window one more time, carefully searching every pocket and feeling each seam, but I didn't find anything else. Just as I was about to go back into the living room, I spotted a Cole Haan shoebox, which I'd missed during my first sweep. I opened it. There were three spiral notebooks inside, filled with writing. I rifled through the pages for cash, but found nothing, so I put the box back in the wardrobe and went into the living room.

I'd noticed that there were no personal photos or letters in the apartment and I thought that the police must have taken them away, even though they usually didn't do that.

After finishing the inventory, I put the items in the standard bag I'd brought with me from the office and sealed it. I made myself a coffee and drank it by the open window while smoking two cigarettes, one after the other. Usually in such cases, the super notifies the utilities suppliers right away, so that they can disconnect the phone, electricity, water, and gas. But all the utilities were still on and I wondered whether somebody else had already rented it.

I closed the window, washed the mug, put it back in the cupboard, and left, taking the belongings with me. I tried to find the super, but he wasn't in his office on the ground floor, so I held on to the keys.

That was on a Tuesday. The woman showed up three days later, on Friday, at around six p.m.

\*

Over the next two days I thought of Abraham Hale every now and then, the man who had become just another case number in the computer system at our office. His belongings were down in the underbelly of the building, in the property room, so for all intents and purposes my work on the case was basically over. I hadn't mentioned to anybody that I still had the keys to his apartment. No one asked me about them, anyway, and the super didn't call me to retrieve them.

On the third day, I couldn't resist asking my boss, Larry Salvo, whether the police had dug up any information on Hale. But he just shrugged and sent me to another address, somewhere in College Point, on 127th Street. This time, I went there with Linda Martino, so on the way I had to listen to her endless stories about her kids, bad schools, and groping bankers.

After we'd finished, I lied to Linda about having to meet somebody in the area, so she dropped me off near a subway station. I took the train to Jackson Heights and got off at Roosevelt Avenue. I'm not sure what I was thinking. Maybe I just wanted to give the keys back to the super. But then, as I was walking down the street, I remembered the notebooks and got curious. I told myself that it wouldn't do any harm to take a closer look at them. What if they had sentimental value and I'd left them there, for someone to throw away?

I used the brass key to enter the building, and it was then that I first noticed the mailboxes on the left of the lobby. After you die, your mail keeps on growing, like your hair and nails. People continue to send you letters, because either they don't know or they don't care that you're gone, as if they were playing some macabre prank on you. I used another key to open the mailbox with his name on it and took with me the wad of envelopes and fliers that were inside. The building was silent and still.

I let myself into the apartment and closed the door behind me. I noticed a mug on the table, which hadn't been there three days ago. The police must have come back and one of the officers had made coffee. I checked the lights and the faucets: the electricity and water were still on, and the phone hadn't been disconnected either, which was unusual.

I sat down on the couch and looked through Hale's mail, discarding the fliers and ads. There was a letter from a bank, in a white envelope, and an invoice from Time Warner Cable.

I opened the window and smoked a cigarette, using a saucer as an ashtray. I asked myself what I was doing there. If I were caught in the apartment, I'd be in deep trouble. I took the notebooks from the wardrobe and began looking through them.

Two were old spiral Rhodia notebooks, and the third was an elegant Clairfountaine, with a black cover. The notes looked as if they'd been written at different periods, but there was nothing that could have helped me put an exact date on them. They didn't look like diary entries, but rather like random, occasional jottings. I didn't know which of the notebooks to start with, so I picked one of the Rhodias at random, opened it, and read:

When you really want to rob someone, you destroy not his future, but his past. The future is by definition a nebulous uncertainty, a sum of blurry hopes that often won't come to pass, and if they do—usually either too late or too soon— they'll be rather disappointing, because our expectations are always too high.

Our past is the sole certainty, the only real shelter we have, even though our memory has in the meantime poured the long-gone important facts and the not so important facts into a completely different mold. The past is unique and unrepeatable, and unlike the future, it's all yours; good or bad, significant or insignificant, wasted or fruitful, nobody else can have it.

This is what he took from me.

I carried on reading for another two hours or so, walking now and then to the open window to take a few drags on a cigarette. A couple of times, I thought I heard light footfalls outside, but nobody rang the doorbell. The lights were off and the apartment was growing dim.

In his notebooks, Hale had written about an unspecified period of time in the mid-seventies, when he'd been in Paris with two friends of about the same age: Joshua Fleischer, his former roommate at Princeton University, and a French woman by the name of Simone Duchamp, his lover. Later, things had gone south, although he didn't provide very many details in his notes about why that had happened, and he'd returned to the States. It looked like his friend had seduced Simone, and she'd broken up with him, despite their having been very happy together up until then. In a couple of places he went on about how unscrupulous Fleischer used to be when it came to getting what he wanted. Now, Hale was hell-bent on revenge and hatched all kinds of plans for how to get even. It was clear that he'd kept a close watch on Fleischer, who had also returned to New York by then.

Suddenly, the phone rang. It was a clunky old model, perched on a small stand by the couch. I started violently enough to drop the notebook on the rug.

For a couple of seconds, I tried to figure out what to do. Finally, I decided to answer, thinking I might come by some useful information for the ongoing investigation. Whoever was calling probably knew Hale, but hadn't yet heard about his death. I reached over and picked up the phone.

There was a woman on the other end of the line. Without introducing herself or even saying hello, she asked me whether I would like her to come over in half an hour, as previously agreed. It somehow felt inappropriate to tell her that I wasn't the man she was looking for or to give her the bad news over the phone, so I just told her to come right over. She said goodbye and hung up before I had time to change my mind. Everything happened very quickly, while I was still deeply immersed in the story I was reading.

I emptied my improvised ashtray into the trashcan, closed the window, and put the notebooks back in the wardrobe. I decided to tell her (one of Hale's relatives? his lover? an acquaintance?) that there was still some paperwork that needed to be done and that's why I was there. It crossed my mind that I could also tell her that I'd met the man before by chance, which was how I knew a couple of things about him and his life. No, we hadn't been pals, I wouldn't go that far, but he'd once told me that he'd lived in Paris for a short while, in the mid-seventies. Then I thought better of it: if she asked me something I couldn't answer, she would end up calling the cops. I considered that she might be able to give me some information about him: occupation, place of work, tastes and inclinations, what motives for suicide he may have had, if he'd ever mentioned the idea of killing himself.

Hale had written in his notebook

People like talking about the dead. It's as if they conjure them back to life. Everything to do with the deceased already belongs to the past. It's all carefully stored away in closets, trunks, and boxes, and the timeline has been settled once and for all and it has that definite clarity which comes only with the ending, once all potentialities, uncertainties, reversals or disappointments have been eliminated, and nothing can be misunderstood or reinterpreted anymore. It's all there, as solid and silent as a gravestone.

I was still thinking about his words when the woman knocked, ignoring the bell. I turned on the lights in the living room and opened the door.

She was around my age, maybe a bit younger, and had the uneasy air of somebody who really wanted to be somewhere else, even though she did greet me with an attempt at a smile. I stepped aside to let her in, and she looked around the place, paying careful attention.

"I know it isn't exactly the Four Seasons," I said.

She stopped in the middle of the room, under the light fitting. She didn't ask me my name or what I was doing there or where Hale was, and I didn't know what to say. Without waiting for an invitation, she put her shoulder bag on the floor by the couch and sat down in an armchair. She lit a cigarette and glanced around for an ashtray. I went to the kitchen and fetched a saucer, which I put on the coffee table. She crossed her legs and thanked me.

"You're welcome. Would you like some coffee or tea?"

"No, I'm good, thank you."

She wasn't quite beautiful, but she was delicate, had great legs, very nice eyes, and elegant gestures. She was wearing a dark gray two-piece suit with matching shoes. Given the nature of my job, I'd learned to pay attention to apparently insignificant details: the purple polish on her fingernails, the delicate string of pearls round her neck, the minuscule gold earrings, and the small mole by the right corner of her upper lip. She had dark circles under her eyes, which she was unable to fully conceal beneath her makeup.

I lit a cigarette, and for a couple of minutes we just smoked, looking at each other from the corners of our eyes, each waiting for the other to say something. I found the silence embarrassing, so I decided to take the plunge.

"I take it you don't know what happened ..." I said.

She raised her eyebrows. "No, I don't. What are you talking about?"

"Well, I'm very sorry, but your friend, Abraham Hale, passed away three days ago. His body is at the Queens Hospital Center, on Jamaica Avenue. Do you know where that is? The police are still looking for someone who can formally identify him."

For a couple of minutes, she made no comment, as if weighing how she should react. Then, she stubbed out her cigarette and said, "Well, I'm very sorry to hear that," and lit another one. Her gaze drifted around the room, almost absently. After a while, she asked, "How did it happen?"

I shrugged. "Nobody knows for sure yet. But it looks like he swallowed too many sleeping pills."

"You mean he took his own life?"

"Well, it's possible, but the police think it was most likely an accident."

"I see ..."

I sat down on the couch, next to her. I had a strong feeling that the whole situation was somehow absurd and disconnected from reality, like some random scene from a movie that would be meaningless to anybody who had missed the opening.

"Maybe you're wondering who I am and what I'm doing here," I said.

"I don't think it's any of my business, but please go on," she stressed. "May I use the bathroom first?"

"Please, do. It's on the left."

"I know where it is."

She left her cigarette in the ashtray, stood up, and walked to the bathroom, her high heels clicking on the floor. I finished smoking and swallowed a Tylenol, sensing a migraine was closing in on me. She came back, took off her jacket, and hung it on the hook by the door.

"Were you close friends?" I asked her.

"You might say that."

She took her cigarette, walked up to the window, and gazed outside. She held her back rigidly straight, in that slightly stiff posture typical of women who attended ballet classes in childhood.

"I knew him a little," I said. "He told me he lived in Paris for a while. But I didn't know he was on medication."

"Sure," she confirmed, without turning her face toward me. "He really loved talking about those years ... I didn't know about the medication either. I wasn't aware that he was ill, I mean."

"Do you know what he did for a living?"

"I never ask personal questions, Mr. ..."

I realized that we hadn't introduced ourselves. I told her my name, but she didn't tell me hers.

"So, Mr. Bertrand—"

"Please, call me Jack."

"Okay, Jack ... And what did you say you were doing here?"

"I'm thinking of renting this apartment. Do you live in this area?"

"No, I have a place in Woodhaven. Before that, I lived in the Bronx. I'm not from here. I moved to New York ten years ago."

"I noticed your accent. Is it French?"

"Yes, it's French. And when do you intend to move in, Jack?"

"Soon, maybe next week. I haven't finished the paperwork yet."

Suddenly, she looked uneasy. She nervously crashed the cigarette butt in the ashtray, took a cellphone out of her bag, and walked to the kitchen. I caught only a few snatches of her conversation: "No, he didn't ... Why do you talk to me like that? ... Yes, I'm going there straightaway, don't worry ..." She came back into the living room and said, "I've really got to be going now, I'm sorry. Are you alright? You look pale."

"I've had a lot of work to do today and I skipped lunch, but I'm fine."

"Okay then, take care. See you later."

She put on her jacket, picked up her bag, and walked to the door. Bracing myself, I asked for her phone number. "How about I call you next week? Maybe we could get together for a cup of coffee or something."

She cast me an intrigued glance, shrugged, and jotted down her number on a yellow Post-it. "Here's my number."

"Thanks. I'll call you."

Before she left, she did something very weird: she came closer and whispered a single word in my ear, as if she were afraid that someone might overhear us, and then she walked out before I had the chance to reply. That word was: *Run!*

# eleven

### Jack Bertrand's diary (2)

THE NEXT MORNING, I woke up early and had breakfast at a nearby café. I was tired and confused, as if I had a hangover. Without questioning what I was doing, I went home, stuffed a few things in a bag, and came back to Hale's apartment. I spent the rest of the day stretched out on the couch in the living room, drinking coffee and reading the notebooks.

I felt an odd affection for Hale, whose life had ended so soon and in such a tragic way. What I'd read of his notes so far showed that he was a kind and sensitive person, even though his heart had been broken by those tragic events that had taken place in France. He'd met that man, Joshua Fleischer, at university, when they were in their senior year, and the guy had been his nemesis: from that moment on, everything had slowly gone downhill. After that he'd merely struggled to hold on and get by. He'd seen himself as a victim of the dramatic circumstances triggered by Fleischer because of his frustrations and his leaning for doing evil. From Hale's writing, he'd clearly been in love with Simone and she'd been in love with him, but events had taken a different course because of his so-called friend.

At one point, something very bad must have happened on a specific night spent in a Parisian hotel with Fleischer and

Simone. He didn't describe exactly what, all he'd written was, "That night, I lost everything." Referring to Fleischer, he'd added, "He destroyed her and me along with her. Why did he do it? Because he could, and because that's who he is, like a scorpion stinging the being who's trying to help it get across the stream."

I went to the nearest corner store and bought some groceries, and then spent the entire weekend reading the notebooks. On Monday morning, I woke up early and it took me a while to realize where I was. The place seemed shady and unfriendly, and I felt kind of relieved when I left, leaving the notebooks on the coffee table by the couch. I got the bus on Elmer Avenue and headed to my office. I walked into the building feeling guilty, like I'd done something wrong and they were about to catch me out. I couldn't afford to lose my job. Despite my efforts to put something into my change jar, I was flat broke.

It was one of those days: we were assigned to two apartments in the Heights, and a small house near Queens Boulevard. In one of the apartments, an old lady had died a week before the neighbors called the police, so the stench was still terrible when we got there. Somebody scratched our car in the parking lot nearby, and Linda almost sprained her ankle climbing the stairs to the attic.

Before heading back to the office, we stopped off for lunch in a café on 99th Street, in Forest Hill.

"Hear anything new about that guy from Jackson Heights, Abraham Hale?" I asked her, as the waitress brought our coffees and bagels.

"What guy? Sweetie, what's this? I didn't want extra cream cheese, but extra lox."

"Want me to take it back?"

"No, I don't have time for that. So, what's up with that guy? Is there something wrong?"

"I was just curious, that's all."

"Why?"

"I remembered you know a guy at the 115th Precinct, and—"

"Yeah, his name's Torres, Miguel Torres."

"I was wondering if you could ask him if they've got anything new on Hale."

"And why would I do that?"

"I told you, I'm curious."

"I don't remember you ever being this curious before. Did you find something at his place without telling them back at the office? Like a lottery ticket?"

"Come on, Linda, don't be like that ..."

"Like what? I've got plenty of troubles as it is, Jack, I don't need to go looking for more. Fine, when we get back to the office, I'll call Torres. What was his name?"

"Abraham, Abraham Hale. Thanks, I owe you one."

"You're welcome. Now eat your bagel, we've got to go. You okay? You don't look okay. Maybe you should quit smoking."

"These days we don't talk about pollution or gangs or shitty food, but only about how bad cigarettes are. Take a look at these bagels ... Do you remember how big and tasty they used to be when we were kids? Do you remember how tasty everything used to be when we were kids? Forget it. I haven't been sleeping well, that's all. I'm not hungry and this stuff sucks."

"I know you're single, but do you live with someone?"

"No, why?"

"Because I know how difficult it is to live alone. Did you hear what happened to Ralph?"

"What?"

"His uncle from upstate died, so he came into a small fortune, a five-acre farm in Mayville County, by the lake. He's going to quit his job and move out there."

"Good for him."

"Yep … Now, cough up and let's get moving."

I spent the next couple of nights in Hale's apartment, leafing through the notebooks time and again. I was no longer afraid of being caught there, because nobody had come by to cut off the utilities, and nobody had called.

Reading those notes, I'd taken an instant dislike to Fleischer. I wanted to understand why a good man like Hale had ended his life in that miserable way—alone, poor, and defeated—while Fleischer, a manipulative douchebag, was so successful. It was like a fairy tale turned upside down. Was it just a case of luck? Is there a moment in your life when a decision, once taken, influences the rest of your existence, no matter what happens after that? All those questions were rolling over and over again into my mind, even in my sleep.

But there was still a man who had to have the answers. The very next week, I began tailing Fleischer.

# twelve

### Jack Bertrand's diary (3)

TRACKING HIM DOWN WAS easy, because he was sitting in the catbird seat.

I walked over to the Public Library on 42nd Street and discovered from some old newspapers that he'd become famous in the mid-seventies: he'd donated his entire inheritance—thought to be worth over twenty million dollars at the time—to a foundation called the White Rose. After that, he'd lived abroad for a while, and then he'd struck it rich on Wall Street in the early eighties. He'd lost almost everything on Black Monday, in '87, but made a spectacular comeback a couple of years later, when the *Wall Street Journal* dubbed him "the gentle sniper."

That morning, I called my boss and took a few days off. I went to the Upper East Side and staked out the entrance of the tower where Fleischer lived: a luxury thirty-six-floor apartment building on East 58th Street and First Avenue.

Abraham Hale's car, an old black four-cylinder Toyota Celica, had still been parked in the lot across the street from his building. I found the keys in a drawer, so I borrowed it to follow Fleischer when he went out the next morning. He didn't use his car, but took a cab instead and stopped off at an elegant café on Greenwich Street, close to the financial district.

He walked inside, and a few minutes later, I followed. The

place was almost empty, but even so, the maître d' asked me if I had a reservation. I told him I didn't, and he ushered me to a table by the door, after casting me a skeptical glance. I ordered an espresso and a waiter brought me my coffee.

Fleischer was sitting at a table by the counter, in the company of an elegant woman in her thirties and a man of about the same age, both very well dressed. They looked relaxed, eating their croissants and chatting. It didn't look like a business meeting to me.

He was tall and slim, had pleasant features, dark hair, and a tiny mustache. He looked younger than his years. If I hadn't already known his age, I would have guessed he was around thirty-five. He wore a tailor-made suit, and his wristwatch was probably much more valuable than all my possessions put together.

I pictured Hale lying on the floor, naked, shrouded up in silence and loneliness, the life slowly draining from his body. And I wondered whether the woman I'd met in his apartment, that elegant lady with the soft strange accent, was the same one he'd mentioned in his notes, Simone. Was it possible that she might have followed them back to the States? If so, were they still in touch? I recalled how she knew where the bathroom was in the apartment, and I realized that she must have been there before. But was she still in touch with Fleischer too? Was it all some sort of perverted game, a possible explanation for why Hale had eventually taken his own life? She hadn't seemed at all distressed by his death.

Before I knew it, he was at the entrance, helping the woman put on her raincoat. I left a five on the table and went to the door, but the waiter stopped me and told me that the coffee was $5.99. I raked through my pockets, gave him another buck, and headed for the exit, but it was too late: Fleischer and his companions had vanished.

*

On that same day, at about five p.m., Linda, my colleague, called me on my cellphone while I was smoking by the window, wondering what might have happened that night in Paris. She told me that the police inquiry was still ongoing, and so her friend had refused to leak any information about Abraham Hale. She asked me why I hadn't come to work. I told her that I'd taken a couple of days off and hung up.

In his notes, Hale provided a lot of details about himself and about Fleischer. Why didn't he just say what really happened in that hotel? A couple of times he'd stressed that his entire life had been ruined because of that night, but he wouldn't take the bull by the horns and confess how that happened.

I took a blank sheet of paper and a pencil and drew a sort of diagram of boxes joined together by arrows and lines. I wrote Abraham Hale in one box, and then I connected it with another one, in which I wrote Joshua Fleischer. Everything seemed to come down to that night in Paris, so I wrote in another box, Simone Duchamp, Hotel Suite, Fall 1976.

Either one of them or both of them had done something terrible that night. That much was clear. After that, they'd come back to the States. What about Simone? Hale had stopped mentioning her after that incident; he'd written only about himself and Fleischer. All his recollections of Simone related solely to that period of time spent in Paris. But if she was really the woman I'd met at his place, they must have kept in touch after she moved to New York, ten years ago, as she'd mentioned.

Beneath the box with Simone's name I traced another one and wrote, The Facts. She'd been seeing one of those men, but had then dumped him and begun a relationship with the other. Why? Hale had presumed that Fleischer knew how to manipulate people and make them do his bidding. Hale had probably been hurt and furious when she left him for Fleischer, especially given that he was sure that Fleischer wasn't really in love with her, but had just wanted to hurt him. And he'd succeeded. But what happened next?

I knew that the question was rhetorical. There were only two people in the world that could provide me with some answers: Simone, if she really was the woman I'd met, or Fleischer, if he'd agree to have a talk with me.

An hour later, at about seven, the apartment's phone rang and I answered. It was the same woman who had come to the apartment. Her voice sounded as if she were speaking from the bottom of a well.

"I'm sorry, but I'm not feeling well," she told me and sighed. "Would you mind coming over? I've got something important to tell you."

I was surprised. We barely knew each other, and now she was inviting me to her place in the most natural way.

"Sure ... Has something happened?"

"What do you mean? I told you, we need to talk. Do you want to come over or not?"

"Okay, sorry, sure. Can I have your address and your phone number?"

"What? You have my address and phone number, remember?"

"I think I lost them."

I jotted down her information on the pad of paper with my diagram and hung up. I put on my jacket and went out, wondering whether it would be appropriate to buy her some flowers, but then I realized that I should probably get there as quickly as possible, since she was ill. I climbed into the car and set off for Woodhaven. It was already dark and it took me a couple of minutes to realize that the headlights were off. I came to a halt on Grand Central and bought a cellphone, a small Ericsson with an expanding antenna that looked like a big black bug. The clerk, a guy barely out of his teens with a red dragon tattoo on his right forearm, showed me how to save her phone number into the device's memory.

When I got onto Jackie Robinson, I knew that I was really taking this way too far. I was living in Hale's apartment, using his car, his phone, his electricity, even some of his clothes. It was no longer a question of losing my job. I could get arrested for trespassing, burglary, theft, false identity, and probably on half a dozen other grounds. Sooner or later, the super or the neighbors would notice me hanging around the place and call the cops.

I turned left onto 87th Street and the address led me to an old two-story redbrick building that lay behind a derelict yard. I parked the car next to a lighting pole and crossed the turd-studded yard to the porch. There was an intercom to the right of the door with three call buttons, but the plastic slots for names were blank. A copy of a free newspaper and a few flyers were lying on the welcome rug, their pages curling. I lingered for a few moments, and then I called her on the phone to tell her I was there. A couple of seconds later I heard the buzz and went inside.

A strong smell of food was hanging in the air and the wooden floorboards creaked. I couldn't find the light switch, so I climbed the stairs groping like a blind man. At the top there was a yellow door and I knocked.

She was almost naked, dressed only in a sheer nightgown, with no bra or underwear. Her hair was tied back in a short ponytail and she looked older than I remembered. She invited me in and headed toward the living room, swaying her hips. I closed the door behind me and followed her.

The apartment was small, dark, and almost dilapidated, rank with the smell of cheap perfume and tobacco. A few items of clothing were lying on the floor. There were no lamps in the room, just a bare bulb hanging from the ceiling like a gigantic firefly.

"Mind if I smoke?" I asked.

"Go ahead, there's an ashtray in the kitchen. Gee, I'm so tired … Did you bring something to drink?"

"No, sorry, but I could go and get something."

"There are no liquor stores around here. Forget it."

She sat down on a couch and I went to the kitchen to fetch the ashtray. She asked me for a cigarette and we smoked in silence. The couch was shabby, like the rest of the furniture: a pair of decrepit armchairs, a couple of almost empty bookshelves, and a dining table with four chairs by the window. The carpet on the floor was threadbare and I spotted a couple of holes.

"Thanks for inviting me," I said to her. "I like your place."

"You're being nice, it's nothing but a shithole, but at the moment I can't afford anything better," she replied in a bitter voice. "How are you? I guess I've got the flu, I feel like hell. Maybe you shouldn't have come."

"Don't worry, I'll be fine. Can I ask you a question?"

"Sure."

"You're Simone, right? Simone Duchamp? I'm not sure I'm pronouncing it correctly, I speak very little French."

For a few seconds she didn't reply, and then she said, "Yes, of course I'm Simone, I thought you knew that. Why?"

"Your late friend, Abraham, told me about you: about how you guys met in Paris and fell in love and about the other guy, Fleischer, who tried to—"

"I don't remember that period of my life very well, and anyway, I don't feel like talking about my past tonight. Why don't you make yourself at home?"

The hem of her nightgown had slipped aside, baring her thighs. She had a big greenish bruise above her right knee.

I tried not to stare at her legs and shaved pubis. "When did you come here, to New York?" I asked and she yawned. "About ten years ago," she said. "Listen, do you want some coffee?"

"No, I'm good, thanks. Why didn't you follow them here straightaway, back then?"

"Follow who?"

"Those guys you met in France, Hale and Fleischer. They were both in love with you, as far as I know and—"

"I told you, I don't like talking about my past. What are you, a shrink or something?"

She stood up, went to the kitchen, and I heard the sound of water flowing down the sink. I took a closer look at the room: the corners of the wallpaper were peeling and in a few places the floorboards had been mended by some guy who had botched the job. There was a pile of porn magazines by the side of the couch and the curtains were grubby.

She came back after a couple of minutes with two mugs of coffee and handed me one. Her nightgown was now completely open, but she didn't seem to care.

"You shouldn't smoke. You told me you're not well," I said, feeling that my words were feeble and out of place.

"Who gives a damn?" she said, and sat down in an armchair, her legs curled up beneath her. "Look, do you want anything else from me tonight or are you going just to sit there and ask me weird questions? I told you we need to talk."

"What do you do for a living, Simone?"

"What? Well, I'm a musician, isn't it obvious? I play the clarinet. Isn't it clear what I do? What's wrong with you?"

I felt really stung. I remembered the way Abraham Hale had described her in his diary: a beautiful young lady, cultured, highly educated, and brought up in a wealthy French family. I also noticed that her accent had grown much fuzzier, as if her exposing of her occupation had lent her a new mask, one completely devoid of her former elegance, charm, and even beauty.

I couldn't help but asking, "How did you get into this life, Simone? Why didn't they do anything to help you?"

She cast me a snotty glance above the mug, which she was crushing between her palms as if trying to shatter it.

"When you're down, everybody wants a piece of you. And I don't like asking for help. I'm no cripple and can manage my own life, good or bad, whatever. Stop looking at me like that! You don't have a clue what it feels like to be something and then … Listen, are we going to do this or not? Or would you prefer to sit there and watch?"

"Abraham told me lots of things about you and he kept a diary. I just wanted to talk to you about some of the things he'd written—"

"What kind of diary? Is it about me?"

"Yes, he mentioned you many times. I think he really loved you."

She became angry.

"Look, this isn't funny anymore … Why would someone write about me in his goddamn diary? Can I see it? What does it say about me?"

"Please relax, it's not exactly a diary, just some notes, and actually I'm not sure that—"

"I want to see them, whatever they are, do you hear me?"

"Okay, next time you come over I'll show them to you, don't worry."

That seemed to calm her down a bit. She stood up, took her nightgown off, and started touching her breasts.

"Are we going to the bedroom or not?"

To be honest, I was petrified. I stood up, gave her all the cash I had on me and my pack of cigarettes, and left. When I closed the door behind me, I heard her laughing.

# thirteen

## Jack Bertrand's diary (4)

I FOLLOWED FLEISCHER FOR the whole week. Every day he left his apartment early in the morning and got back late in the evening, spending most of his time at his office in the financial district.

He used to go out for lunch at one p.m. sharp, always at the same place, a small restaurant on East 1st Street, near the Marble Cemetery. A well-built guy in his thirties—always dressed in black, chauffeur, bodyguard, and right-hand man all rolled into one—would do his groceries and laundry. Every Friday, at around eight p.m., he would pick up the lady I'd seen him with at the café and, after dinner, they would spend a couple of hours together in her apartment, not far from his own home, on East 76th Street.

I tried not to think of Simone too much. I had a very vivid image of her sitting in that shabby place, naked, angry, probably a bit drunk, inviting me to sleep with her. Did Abraham Hale have any idea what she had become? Was this one of the reasons he'd committed suicide? If he'd known, why hadn't he done anything to help her? He wasn't healthy, but he might have been able to help her get out of that kind of life. I'd solved one mystery only to stumble upon another. Thinking of the whole story, I had the sensation you sometimes have in nightmares: you try to move on, straining your muscles, but can't make any ground.

One evening, at around ten, someone buzzed the intercom. It was Linda, my colleague. I opened the door and waited for her at the end of the corridor. I was very upset because while I'd been out following Fleischer, all of the notebooks had vanished. I'd left them on the coffee table by the couch, as usual, but when I'd come home, they were nowhere to be found. I was sure that Simone had come over in my absence and took them, which meant that Abraham Hale had given her a key.

"I knew you'd be here," Linda said, out of breath after climbing the stairs. "Where's the money, Lebowski? Have you seen that new movie? You should, it's great."

I invited her in and headed to the kitchen to make coffee.

"You're going to get fired, Jack," she said, leaning against the doorframe. "Come to the office tomorrow and talk to Larry. He's a good guy, you know that. Tell him you've been sick or something."

I poured the coffee and brought the mugs into the living room. The lights were off, except for a small floor lamp in one corner of the room. The atmosphere was somber, like in some noir movie. I opened the window and lit a cigarette.

"He was okay with me taking a few days off," I said. "I talked to him on the phone about a week ago."

"He says you never called and you haven't been returning his calls either."

"He's lying."

She put her mug on the coffee table, walked up to me, placed her hands on my shoulders, and looked me straight in the eye.

"Jack, what's wrong, baby? Please tell me. You're scaring the hell out of me. This old lady really cares about you and wants to help you."

"There's nothing wrong with me, Linda. Thanks anyway. I just wanted to—"

I stopped in the middle of the sentence, realizing that I

didn't quite know how to put it. What was it that I wanted, really? I finished my cigarette and stubbed the butt out.

"Linda, I don't mean to be rude, but I think you should go now," I said. "I have some work to do."

"What kind of work? Have you found another job?"

"With all due respect, that's none of your business."

"Why are you talking to me like that? I'm just trying to help you."

"I know. But I'm fine, believe me."

She went to the door. I'd been mean to her and I immediately felt sorry for that. I asked her, "Please don't tell anybody you found me here. In this apartment, I mean."

She opened the door, turned to look at me, and said: "Take care of yourself, Jack. You know how to find me if you need me. If I were you, I'd come to the office tomorrow and speak to Larry. It's not too late. Bye now. Be good."

I watched her cross the street. She looked up at me for a moment, and then she got into her car and drove away. I had a shower, got dressed, and went to find Fleischer. It was twenty to seven, and I knew I didn't have much time. If Linda let slip at the office that she'd found me in Hale's apartment, they'd be coming for me very soon.

I bought a tuna bagel from a bodega by the parking lot and ate it while scanning my surroundings: a J. Crew store; a few people standing in line at an ATM; an expensive-looking restaurant called The Living Room; a guy dressed like the Cookie Monster handing out flyers; a toddler hanging onto his mom's arm, trying to get her attention; an elderly man wearing a silly fedora, staring straight ahead of him, as if hypnotized by something invisible. On the other side of the street, the upper stories of Fleischer's tower were flaming in the sunset.

I was just finishing my bagel when I saw Fleischer's car approaching. I positioned myself by the pedestrian crossing, and when the driver stopped at a red light, I leaned forward, knocked on the window, and yelled loud enough so he could hear me from inside, "Mr. Fleischer, one moment, please!"

The chauffeur cracked the window and asked, "What do you want?"

"I'd like to talk to Mr. Fleischer. Is he in the car?"

I heard a voice from the womb of the limousine: "What's going on, Walter?"

"Good evening, sir," I shouted. "I need to talk to you about Simone, Simone Duchamp!"

The traffic lights turned green and a couple of drivers honked. The car moved forward about ten yards, pulled over to the side, and came to a halt. Fleischer got out, waved at me, and I waved back. The car turned right, disappearing into the underground parking, and he walked up to me.

"Did you say Simone Duchamp?" he asked me, carefully searching my face. "Who are you?"

"My name is Jack Bertrand. We haven't met before, but I know a lot of things about you."

How much time had I spent in that shabby apartment imagining what it would be like to talk to him … But now, lost in that endless stream of people flowing down the street, I didn't have a clue about how I should begin. A man bumped into me and walked off without apologizing. Standing there, staring at Fleischer, I felt my heart broken and my mind empty.

"Are you alright?" he asked. "You don't look well. Sorry for insisting, but did you mention the name Simone Duchamp?"

Over his shoulder, I saw the chauffeur, Walter, coming toward us, sliding through the crowd like a big cat, his eyes glued to mine. I wondered whether he was carrying a gun.

"Yes," I said. "I did."

"What about her?" he asked me. The chauffeur reached us and asked, "Everything okay, sir?"

"It would appear to be," Fleischer said. "I'm going to have a word with this gentleman, Mr. Jack—"

"Bertrand."

"—Mr. Jack Bertrand. Well, Mr. Bertrand, shall we? I don't think this is the best place to talk. There's a bar around the corner."

"Sure."

We walked down the street, and Walter followed at a distance. The bar was a nice place with solid wood floorboards, paneled walls, and a couple of old black-and-white Irish photos. Walter stayed outside and we found a table for two and ordered coffees.

"I'm listening," he said, pouring some sugar in the tiny cup. "What do you know about Simone Duchamp?"

I couldn't help but ask, "Do you really care about her?"

He looked at me in surprise.

"What kind of a question is that? Of course I do, that's why I'm here, talking to you! Mr. Bertrand, look ... I'm a busy man. You were the one who approached me. I was kind enough to invite you here and give you the chance to tell me what it is you want from me, even though I don't know who you are. If you're just using that name to—"

"I know her," I said. "She lives in Woodhaven. In case you didn't know already, she came here from France about ten years ago."

His jaw dropped an inch. He looked truly shocked.

"You mean she's alive? She lives here, in New York?"

"Should she be dead?"

He moved his cup of coffee to one side and rested his elbows on the table, leaning toward me.

"Okay, who are you and what do you want from me? Money? Are you trying to blackmail me? Why should I believe you? No offense, but you look like a lunatic. How did you get to meet her?"

"It doesn't matter who I am or how I met her. You really

think that everybody is after your money, don't you? You and your damn money—"

Making an effort to keep his cool, he interrupted, "You said she lives in Queens. Do you have an address? I'd be willing to pay just to find out where she is, but only if I can verify that you're not making this up."

I sipped my coffee and grinned. I suddenly felt powerful and full of confidence. He wore the expression of a man ready to go to any lengths to have what I had in my pocket. All his cool poise had vanished, and I was getting a kick out of making him sweat.

"Like I told you, I know a couple of things about her," I said, toying with a paper napkin.

"Like what?"

"Well, for example, she's a hooker."

His face really contorted when I said that. He mumbled to himself, "What?" Then he repeated aloud, "What?"

"Yes, a prostitute. Surprised? Call her and check it out, if you like. I have her number and her address."

"Who are you? You look familiar. Have we met before? Have you been following me?"

"I told you it doesn't matter who I am. Are you going to call the cops or set that pit bull outside on me? Do you want me to give you her address or not?"

"How much do you want for it?"

"Keep your money, asshole!"

I took a pen from my pocket, scrolled through the contacts on my new cellphone, and wrote her number down on a napkin along with her address. As I handed it to him, his eyes continued to bore into mine.

"I don't need your money. I came across your story and found out about your past because of a man who died a couple of weeks ago. His body is still in the morgue, there's nobody to claim it. He probably killed himself with an overdose. He died lonely, miserable, and brokenhearted.

But you don't care, do you? If you did, you'd have done something to help him, you son of a bitch!"

"What are you talking about?"

"You know what I'm talking about! I'm talking about that man, Abraham Hale, whose life you destroyed!"

My whole body was shivering, as if I were freezing cold. I stood up and walked out, almost bumping into Walter, who was waiting by the entrance. As I was leaving, I caught sight of Fleischer's reflection in the café's window. He was just sitting there staring into space, his elbows leaning on the table, his chin resting on his clasped hands. He was shocked, as if he'd seen a ghost.

As far as I can remember, I ended up wandering aimlessly for the rest of that evening. I walked the streets, took the subway from the station on East 77th Street, got out at Times Square, and headed for the Lower East Side. I sat on a bench and chain-smoked, while looking at the cars moving on the bridge in the distance like toys on tracks.

I replayed the conversation with Fleischer in my mind and realized that I'd been stupid. I'd fantasized about avenging Abraham Hale, but instead I'd wound up giving his greatest enemy Simone's phone number and address. His surprise seemed genuine, which meant that they hadn't kept in touch and he hadn't know she was in the country. She probably had strong reasons for avoiding him. Had she wanted to track him down, it would have been a piece of cake. After all, it hadn't been difficult for me. He was a dangerous man, as Abraham Hale's notebooks suggested. But if she was afraid of him, why had she come to New York? She could have chosen anywhere else in the world. If she hadn't come here for those two men, what other reason could she have had for moving here all the way from France? I was angry with myself: I'd had a great opportunity to get some answers, but I'd wasted it.

I didn't feel up to going back to Jackson Heights or to my place. Since I'd run out of cigarettes, I went looking for a store, heading in the opposite direction, toward Midtown, and I stopped at a twenty-four-hour bodega. I bought two packs of smokes and ate a sandwich. By then it was almost midnight.

Suddenly, I felt that Simone might be in danger. What if Fleischer would call her or go to her place? She was just a middle-aged prostitute, one tiny speck in the immensity of the city's underside. To cover up her disappearance would have been easy for a guy like him.

At the same time, the police hadn't concluded their investigation and it was reasonable to presume that Fleischer might have been involved, directly or indirectly, in Hale's death. If Fleischer were guilty, he'd have done everything in his power to maintain the cover-up. Hale and Simone had been the only eyewitnesses to what Fleischer had done in France back in the seventies. He'd done something bad, that much was clear. I didn't know precisely what, but it must have been something evil. Now Hale was dead, under strange circumstances, and it dawned on me that Simone could be Fleischer's next target, now that he knew she was alive and could talk.

Before heading for Woodhaven, I tried calling her a couple of times, but her cellphone was switched off. Finally, I hailed a cab and went to her place. I paid over forty dollars, almost all the cash I had on me, and wondered how I'd get home later. I couldn't remember where I'd left the car: maybe in Jackson Heights, or else I might have left it in a parking lot near Fleischer's apartment on the Upper East Side.

Standing in front of the building, I realized that I couldn't remember her apartment number either. I thought of calling her again, but my phone was dead; I'd forgotten to charge it.

I pressed a call button at random and I heard the sleepy voice of an elderly woman. I apologized, introduced myself, and told her that I was looking for Ms. Simone Duchamp.

"I don't know anybody called Simon," she said.

"Not Simon, Simone, with an e at the end, like in French. It's a lady's name. She lives on the first floor."

"Oh, you mean Maggie. Pretty, chestnut hair?"

It occurred to me that Simone probably used a different name while on the job, so I said, "Yes, that's her. Simone was her nickname at school, and—"

"Is she expecting you, sweetheart?"

"Of course, she invited me."

"Alright, come on in."

She buzzed me in and I walked inside. The smell of food still lingered, as if it had seeped into the walls. I groped my way up the stairs in the dark. A door on the second floor opened, flooding the place with light. The same voice I'd heard on the intercom asked me, "Find it, mister?" I looked up toward the landing overhead and saw an old lady wearing a white dressing gown leaning over the bannister.

"Yes, thanks," I said. The light went out and the woman vanished. Using my Zippo, I found the yellow door and rang the bell. After a while, I heard her footfalls and she shouted from behind the door, "Who's there?"

I felt relieved knowing that nothing had happened to her. I told her it was me and she opened the door.

"What the hell do you think you're doing?" she asked, but stepped aside to let me in. "You should have called me before coming here. What time is it?"

"It's late. Feeling any better? You had a cold the last time I saw you."

"Did you come here in the middle of the night to ask me how I feel?"

She was stark naked, except for a pair of slippers, and her hair was mussed. But in a strange way, she looked more natural and appealing without the makeup and the cheap lingerie.

"I'm really sorry," I said. "I tried calling you, but your cellphone was off, and then mine went dead. You okay? Did Fleischer try to get in touch with you?"

She rubbed the sleep out of her eyes and asked me, "What are you talking about? Who's Fleischer?"

"What do you mean, who's Fleischer? I was worried sick about you!"

We went into the living room and she pulled on a T-shirt. She invited me to sit on the couch and sat down cross-legged on the floor in front of me. "Oh, yes, Fleischer," she said, "the French guy, right? Got any cigarettes?"

"How can you not remember him?" I asked her. "He's not French, he's American, but you met him in France. What's wrong with you tonight?"

"Why would I remember him? And what if I hadn't been alone? You can't just come barging in like this whenever you want … I thought I'd made that clear."

"Yes, you did, but under the circumstances—"

"What circumstances?"

"A couple of hours ago I gave your number to Fleischer, and I was—"

"What are you talking about?"

"I'm very sorry, I shouldn't have, but he said something, I lost my temper—"

"You did what?"

And it was right then, as she was yelling at me and cursing me, that I realized what I'd actually wanted from that story ever since I stumbled upon it. It had nothing to do with avenging Hale, because he was dead anyway, and it wasn't about punishing Fleischer, who was much too powerful for a guy like me. If I'd really wanted to hurt him, physically I mean, I'd probably have tried to do it right there and then, in the bar, when we were face to face. Maybe in the beginning I wanted to, but later it morphed into something else.

It was all about her, about Simone, from the very beginning. All that time I just wanted to figure out why she'd chosen Fleischer, back then in Paris. Okay, he was rich, but she was hardly the starving little match girl, pressing her nose against a frozen windowpane. So why did such a woman, beautiful, smart, educated, choose a dangerous predator like Fleischer, instead of a decent young man like Hale, who was head over heels in love with her? Why did she go for the bad guy? Why do women let the villains go on spreading their seed all over the world, while the good guys die lonely, defeated, and miserable? And she herself ended up rotting away in a shithole, poor and desperate, trading her body for money. I thought that maybe I could turn the clock back and make her admit that she'd made a huge mistake back then, that she'd chosen the wrong guy, and in the process destroyed the man who had loved her so much.

But she went crazy. It wasn't just her language, but she also tried to hurt me. She bit and scratched at me, like a mad cat, and attacked me with a knife she'd grabbed from the kitchen. I tried to calm her down. At one point, I guess, I held her wrists and immobilized her. Finally, she stopped screaming at me and asked me to leave. I wanted to listen to her, and I'd have left, but, as weird as it sounds, I didn't know how to get home from there. I was in Woodhaven, a place I didn't know at all, and it would have taken me two hours to get home on foot. I'd run out of money and I didn't even have bus fare. I didn't think it would do any harm if I stayed there for another few hours and left in the morning.

I tried to explain it to her, but she started yelling again and asked me to leave immediately. She told me she would call the cops if I didn't. So I tied her up with the telephone cord, trying not to hurt her, and put her in the bathtub. I was as gentle as possible. She stopped struggling. She just cried quietly and before I gagged her, she asked me not to kill her. I tried to calm her down, told her that I wasn't going to hurt her, and that I just really needed to take a nap, because I was exhausted and confused. So I left her in the bathtub, and slept like a log on the couch until morning.

When I woke up, at around six o'clock, she was dead.

The first thing I noticed was the blood. It was all over my face, hands, and jacket, and shirt—big, red, sticky stains. My whole body ached, as if I had the flu. I needed to go to the toilet, so I went into the bathroom and found her lying in the tub in a pool of congealing blood. I checked for a pulse and realized she must have been dead for quite a while, because her skin was ice-cold.

I washed her body with the shower, then carried her out to the living room and laid her face up on the floor. I removed the gag, untied her, and examined her. There were four or five deep wounds to her chest. They looked like parted ruby-red lips. I went back into the bathroom and discovered a carving knife by the toilet. The blade and handle were covered in blood. After I fell asleep, somebody must have got inside, killed her, and then vanished. She'd been tied up and gagged, so she couldn't defend herself or cry for help.

I was in trouble. The old lady who lived on the second floor had seen my face, and she could also recognize my voice: "Number Four, step forward!" "Oh, my God, yes, it's him, I'm sure of it." "Thanks, ma'am, you've been a great help." The neighbors must have heard her screaming during our argument, too.

It was an easy enough task for the police to re-enact the circumstances of the killing. A guy had arrived late at night, they'd had an argument, probably about money, because he was broke, and the guy had flown off the handle, grabbed a knife from the kitchen, and stabbed her to death. But I didn't do it, sir. You know, Jack, that's what they all say. I mean, even when they're caught at the scene, they still claim they're innocent, all of them. Can you afford an attorney? I see ... In that case, you'll have a court-appointed one. Well, he won't exactly be Johnnie Cochran, if you catch my drift, but at least you'll have a lawyer. Listen, I don't think you planned any of it, Jack. Let me guess, heat of the moment, right? Want a smoke? Here it goes ... Maybe she said something funny and you just lost your temper. I can understand that, I'm a man too, and sometimes women know exactly how to make you crazy ..."

Over the next two hours, I washed, scrubbed the blood out of my clothes, and then searched her apartment, rummaging through her kinky lingerie, dildos, cosmetics, wigs, other bits and pieces, looking for the notebooks. In a purse, I found a Kentucky driver's license in the name of Margaret Lucas, five-six, brown eyes. It was her face in the picture, there was no doubt about that. She'd probably changed her name after she got to the States. To Margaret Lucas, the same name the old lady upstairs had used. I didn't find Hale's diary and I told myself that she'd destroyed it.

I'm not sure what I did for the next few hours, but at one point I noticed that the ashtray on the coffee table was overflowing with butts and my second pack of cigarettes was almost finished. It got dark, and a light rain was lashing at the window. I'd been sitting there for the entire day, naked, two paces from her dead body.

I unpegged my clothes from the washing line over the tub and got dressed. I got that weird feeling that I was seeing everything from above, like I was floating next to the ceiling. Every single detail became dazzlingly clear. As if through a huge magnifying glass, I saw a splotch on the wall and below it a Japanese rose in a ceramic pot; I saw the red tattoo of a heart on her shaved pubis, a cigarette burn on the back of the couch, a single green shoe lying upside down by the closed door to the balcony, a bumblebee lost above the surface of that strange new planet, gingerly swishing its antennae.

The guy sitting in the middle of the room wasn't me anymore. He was nothing but a stranger I vaguely knew, and the dead woman on the floor wasn't Simone, but a middle-aged hooker I'd never met. That guy was in trouble, and soon he was going to be the prime suspect in a murder case, but that was none of my business. Even the story about Paris had gradually vanished from my mind, piece by piece, like props from a theatre set being dismantled and carried offstage once the show is over. I was far away from all of it, and nothing mattered.

Now the guy in trouble goes into the bathroom, turns on the lights and shaves carefully, using the double-blade razor he found on the glass shelf under the mirror. Then he takes the dead woman's cellphone from her bag, switches it on, and calls the cops, telling them in short what has happened. He waits by the window, pale and focused, smoking one last cigarette. About five minutes later, he hears the sirens in the distance, and he watches the lights of the white-and-blue cars rushing to the scene.

He goes to the door, unlocks it, and steps outside, onto the landing. When he sees the cops darting up the stairs, he takes a step backwards, putting his hands on his head. The first uniformed officer is very young, tall and as thin as a rake, with a sandy-colored mustache. He points his gun at the guy and yells, "NYPD, put your hands up, now! Keep your hands where I can see them and kneel down on the floor, now, now! Don't move! Don't make any move!"

The guy kneels down in the hallway, says, "The body is in the living room," and stretches face down on the floor. I can sense his relief as the young cop thrusts his gun back into the holster and handcuffs him. The officers—there are five or six of them now, plus a couple of paramedics, they're milling all over the place like a swarm of big blue-and-green ants—turn on all the lights in the apartment and start doing their job, mumbling into the walkie-talkies hooked to their shoulders. I know that soon they'll be taking him away in one of their cars, and they'll put the dead woman's body in a rubber sack and take it to the morgue, where she'll be finally reunited with Abraham Hale. But I'll stay here for a while, silent and still, observing all the incredible details I'd never noticed before, like the bumblebee, which is now up on the ceiling, creeping slowly toward the light fitting, in the hope of finding shelter.

# fourteen

## Jack Bertrand's diary (5)

DR. LARRY WALKER, the hospital's chief psychiatrist, had the air of a kid in elementary school who had just solved a really difficult problem and couldn't wait to share the news with the teacher. He'd arranged all his previous notes on the desk, in perfect order, but this time there was no voice recorder.

I leaned against the window frame and looked outside through the knitted wire stretched over the glass pane. There wasn't much to see: the hospital courtyard's pavement, whitewashed by the morning light, the concrete blocks, and the high chain-link walls that encircled the buildings like a trap set for a giant. I'd been gazing at that view many times during my talks with Walker.

His office had recently been redecorated and still smelled of bleach and paint. It was furnished plainly: a desk opposite the door, where he sat during our talks, a couple of shelves filled with heavy books, and a leather-upholstered couch with two twin chairs, their legs bolted in the floor. The walls were adorned with all kinds of drawings and paintings, probably the works of his inmate patients. Most of them were painted in dark colours and depicted landscapes devoid of any human presence, while others were nothing but abstract splotches of paint with no apparent meaning.

"Doc, can I ask you something?"

"Please."

"I heard that a nurse was attacked by a patient this morning, while she was trying to feed him. He ripped her ear off with his teeth."

"Yes, unfortunately it's true."

"Do you really think that I belong here, I mean, to a place like this? I'm obviously not crazy."

"We don't use that word here."

"Whatever."

"Jack, you've been committed to this hospital as a result of an assessment made by three experts and a legal ruling handed down by a judge. It is neither my duty nor my aim to decide if that sentence was right or wrong. I'm sure you understand that."

"Then why are you wasting your time talking to me, if it's not going to change anything?"

"Because I want to figure out *why* you did what you did."

I had the feeling that we understood each other less and less. I'd been trying in vain over the past few weeks to explain to him that maybe I didn't know much about myself and about the real reasons I was there—how could someone claim to know everything about himself, anyway?—but that at least I'd been totally open and sincere with him.

"Please listen to me carefully," he said.

"Sure, doc, I always do."

"Jack, I've carefully read through everything you've given me over the past two months, every single word. Now I want to stress a couple of things that have intrigued me. Where were you born and raised, Jack?"

"Long Branch, Monmouth County, New Jersey. That's down the shore. I thought you already knew that. I presume it's in the file."

"Right, but you've never mentioned your hometown or the names of your parents in your notes or during our talks.

Nobody called you and you didn't call anybody. Do you have any brothers or sisters?"

"No, I'm an only child."

"I see, and what about your parents?"

"What about them? They died, both of them."

"When and how did they die?"

"When and how did they die? Well, mom passed away when I was eight; I barely remember her. And my old man died from a heart attack ten years ago, in eighty-eight, in August. It's all I know, I didn't attend the funeral. Honestly, we weren't all that close. He was a drunk and used to kick the tar out of me when I was a kid. Why do you ask?"

I wanted to smoke, but after begging him a couple of times to bring me some cigarettes, I'd given up trying. Smoking wasn't allowed in the hospital and nobody could break the rules under any circumstances. Apparently, there were some guards who made hay smuggling all kinds of things inside, but my commissary deposit was empty.

"Bear with me ... What were their names?"

"This is really weird. John and Nancy Bertrand."

"And you don't have any other relatives?"

"Maybe I do. What's the catch, doc?"

"You've never mentioned them in your story either. Now, I have a couple of questions regarding that woman, Margaret Lucas."

"That was an assumed name. I'd prefer it if you called her by her real name, Simone Duchamp, if you don't mind."

"You told me that the two of you met when she came to Jackson Heights that Friday afternoon, looking for the guy who had died, Abraham Hale. You described her as an elegant, classy woman, with an attractive French accent and good manners. But during your second meeting, when you went to her place in Woodhaven, it seems that she made a completely different impression on you: she was now a common middle-aged prostitute, and what was more, her accent had almost vanished, along with her manners."

"Well, she was ill that evening, and maybe—"

"No, Jack, it was like you were describing a different person."

"I just told you what I saw and thought. What do you want from me?"

"Margaret Lucas *was* her real name, Jack. She was forty-one, born and raised in Rowan County, Kentucky. Back in the late eighties, she was a minor movie actress here in New York. You met her about a year ago."

At first, I didn't get it. Was that some kind of a test? Sometimes, I felt like he was just messing with my mind for sport.

"No, doc, I met her that Friday, like I told you. I've never lied to you, not once. I've got nothing to lose. Why would I lie to you?"

A nurse entered the office and handed him a file. She was tall, skinny, and stared at me coldly. Her eyes were light blue, almost transparent, like a husky's. I wondered if there was something connected to my case in that blue file. But the doctor just signed a sheet and returned the papers. After she left, he went on.

"I'm not saying that you're lying to me, Jack. It's just … Well, I'm sure we'll put all the pieces together. Now, about the meeting with Mr. Fleischer … What you told me isn't exactly what really happened that evening."

"He told you a different story? I'm not surprised. Do you believe him?"

"I tried to meet him, but I understand he went to Maine for a couple of months. I did manage to speak with Walter, his bodyguard, who was an eyewitness to the whole scene, and he told me what he'd told the police: that one evening you darted in front of the car out of the blue, shouting something about a French woman called Simone. You asked Mr. Fleischer to leave her alone, and then, after he got out of the car to see what was going on, you tried to stab him with a knife. If Walter had managed to immobilize you and to call the police, he'd have saved that woman's life. But he couldn't, and you ran off. Later that same night, you went to Woodhaven, argued with Ms. Lucas, and killed her. You stabbed her five times and watched her die. By the way, Mr. Fleischer recognized you."

"Fleischer is lying and—"

"Jack, I don't need to hear your side anymore, because I know what happened, from beginning to end. What I'm trying to do is to make *you* understand what actually happened, *why* it happened, and *how* it was possible for it to happen. I'm a doctor, not a cop. To me, you're not a violent murderer, but a patient who needs help."

"Thanks, I really appreciate that, but—"

"Listen to me, Jack! Let's go back to the beginning, when you told me about how they found Hale's body in Jackson Heights. You weren't there, so how could you have known so many precise details about the scene? About how he was lying naked on the floor, about the glasses on the coffee table, one of them smeared with lipstick, suggesting that a woman had come over before his death … Do you understand? You couldn't have known these details if you hadn't been there, at the scene."

"Obviously, I wasn't there that morning, but I went by two days later. I must have read a police report at the office or else somebody described the scene to me, I can't remember exactly. Why's that so important?"

"I'll tell you why, Jack: because they didn't find a dead man in that apartment, stuffed with sleeping pills. There's no such case in progress at the office of the Queens County Public Administrator, and there's no corpse in the morgue on Jamaica Avenue with such a name on the tag. That morning, two officers came to *your* apartment, because one of your neighbors had called them. She'd noticed that you'd failed to move your car and obey the parking rules, which had never happened before, and you weren't answering the door. You told them you had the flu, moved your car, and then they left."

I suddenly felt my mouth turn dry, and I had to clear my throat before speaking. In that short interval, I'd remembered a scene, like a flash: I was talking with the super, a man named Mike, about painting the apartment before moving in. He had a stinking cold and kept blowing his nose on some paper tissues. And I'd remembered something else: the daily clutter of the dustcart passing down the street, at eight o'clock in the morning sharp.

I looked out the window again. The sun was up and the sky was streaked with blood-red trails. It had rained during the night and a few puddles were still glinting in the courtyard. A black bird glided soundlessly toward the ground and then soared up.

"So the whole thing was just a charade?" I asked.

"No, Jack, it isn't a charade. It's a delusion."

"But what about Hale, Fleischer, and Simone, all those people and places I hadn't even heard of before? What about the notebooks I told you about?"

"How do you explain that they vanished?"

"I can't be sure, but I'm guessing Simone destroyed them after I made the mistake of telling her about Hale's diary. She probably searched the apartment when I wasn't there, and found them. I hadn't exactly hidden them. They were on the coffee table in the living room."

"Listen to me, these are the facts we know so far. You've lived in that apartment since 1994. You moved there four years ago, when you started working for the Queens County Public Administrator. Before that, you worked for a retail company, and before that, you lived in California for five years. That's as much as the police have been able to piece together so far."

"Never been to California, doc, that's for sure."

"Oh, yes you have. As for the rest, you're a ghost. There was a James L. Bertrand born and raised in Mercer County, New Jersey, the son of John and Nancy Bertrand, but he died in 1968, when he was twelve, from pneumonia. He's buried in Greenwood Cemetery. The police presume that at some point, back in the eighties, or even earlier, you changed your identity and assumed a different name. Whoever forged your papers must have used Jack Bertrand's identity because he died young and had no close relatives.

"The police are still trying to confirm what Mr. Fleischer told us about your real identity. There are no fingerprints, dental records or medical information on file older than ten years, but you've offered me some clues during our discussion. I compared them with what Mr. Fleischer has told us and I think that your real name is Abraham Hale, and you two met a long time ago, at university."

And he proceeded to shove his version of my life down my throat, turning black into white.

According to him, about two years ago I began seeing a doctor by the name of Vincent Roth, complaining of symptoms that suggested paranoid schizophrenia. The doctor prescribed some medication and I was hospitalized for three weeks in Bellevue, on 1st Avenue. I was discharged, but things got worse. I gradually lost all connections with my own life, and I started thinking about it as if it were the existence of a different person, a poor and profoundly disturbed man named Abraham Hale, whose life had been destroyed by one of his friends, someone he'd met at university when he was in his early twenties.

The notebooks weren't real. I probably knew all those details about that story—if they were true—because they were more or less my own fragmented recollections, which had been poured by my disturbed mind into a different mold.

A year ago, after leaving the hospital, I'd met Margaret Lucas and asked her to come to my place once a week and play the role of a French woman named Simone Duchamp. So we'd begun a kind of bizarre relationship. When I ran out of money, she refused to continue. Finally, one night I went to her apartment, stabbed her to death, and watched her die. Earlier that night, I'd had an altercation on the street with Fleischer.

Just in case, the DA's office had gotten in touch with the French authorities and had asked if they had a case in their archives involving a Parisian woman by the name of Simone Duchamp, who had gone missing back in the mid-seventies. Their answer was no.

I have so many questions, but don't want to argue with anybody, because I know it would be useless. Money means power and rich people can get anything they need and do anything they want. Insignificant creatures like me have one single fundamental purpose, to do their bidding, and one single fundamental duty, to stay alive as long as they can in order to serve them. When a member of the master race gets angry, he can swallow you alive, gulping you down in one bite. That's what this is all about.

I don't know how much Fleischer paid to stage the whole thing and how long I'm going to stay locked up in this funny farm. I don't really care. But I'll never let them take my memories from me. I know who I am and what I did and what I didn't. I can remember lots of things: names, places, faces. I have a past, I'm wasting my present within these walls, and I'm still trying to imagine my future. I've walked down hundreds of streets, met thousands of people, and uttered millions of words. And they're trying to do to me what they did to that man, Abraham Hale: to erase me, to nullify me, to take everything I have from me.

I regret losing the notebooks. They would have proven once and for all how intelligent and good hearted was

Abraham Hale, and what a manipulative monster is Joshua Fleischer. So every now and then I try to recall everything I read in those pages, every single word and every single comma. Maybe I've missed something, and the secrets of that time in Paris were hidden somewhere between the lines and now are buried among my recollections. I feel I still have a duty to that man to reveal his real character, even though he intended to make himself obscure while writing those notes: he concealed the mystery inside another mystery, and then inside another, like those Russian dolls. But one day I'll remember everything, I'm sure. There's no need to hurry, because here life itself has lost all shape and consistency and it's been turned into a swarm of echoes, stirring through the caves of time.

# fifteen

MALLORY CALLED ME after a couple of days and asked if I'd read the diary.

"Yes, I have. Did that Bertrand guy die in hospital?"

"Yes, in Kirby Forensic Psychiatric Center, in March 1999. He hanged himself in a toilet."

"Were they sure that he was actually Abraham Hale?"

"Well, that's what they thought, based on what Joshua Fleischer told them and on what was in that diary. But they couldn't find anyone who was able to identify him for sure, because Fleischer didn't want to get involved in this matter and there were no legal means of making him cooperate against his will. Bertrand's parents had already passed away, and there was no next of kin. And just between you and me, I don't think that the police spent too long trying to figure out who the guy really was. He killed that woman, got arrested at the scene, found guilty but insane, and put behind bars in a forensic hospital. The case was closed, so everybody was happy. No one really gave a damn whether he was some nobody from Louisiana or a loser from New Jersey, as long as he was locked up in a nuthouse."

"Yes, you're probably right."

"On the other hand, I talked to my contact in France again. There's no Simone Duchamp filed under Missing Persons either. Could you check whether it's the right name? Maybe

Fleischer lied to you and our girl never even existed."

"I don't think he lied to me, why would he have done that? And he wasn't delusional, either. Listen, I know that Simone lived in Lyon with her parents for many years. Her adoptive father, Lucas Duchamp, was a hero of the Resistance. Oh, yes, she had a younger sister, Laura. Did I mention that?"

"No, you didn't. Okay, I'll keep digging around, but I ought to tell that you might be wasting your money."

"Did you find anything about the period when Josh and Abraham were living in Paris?"

"I think I've tracked down their apartment, on the Rue de Rome. In the mid-eighties, the building was completely renovated and converted into a small hotel. A man named Alain Bizerte worked there as a super at the time, but he died ten years ago. There's no record of the people who rented rooms there before it became a hotel. The foundation that rented the apartment, L'Etoile, ceased operations in eighty-one, and nobody knows where its archives are. So …"

"I really need to know the truth about this case, Ken."

"Well, if wishes were cars, panhandlers would drive Jags. I'm good at what I do, but I'm not a wizard. I was lucky enough when I came across that diary. See me for a coffee on Friday at three p.m., at Starbucks on 80th and York."

"I know a nice restaurant in the area."

"Thanks, but my wife put me on a diet."

That evening I worked until late, and then slept like a log until morning. When I woke up, tired and confused, the dawn was gilding the windowpanes. I took a shower, shaved, and dressed, thinking of Josh.

During our conversations, he'd mostly described himself and Simone as victims of Abraham's complexes and frustrations. But after the first session of hypnosis, he'd also told me that the memories which had risen to the surface made him believe that he was the perpetrator.

Josh had also suggested that Abraham was deeply troubled and possibly quite ill. It also seemed that he'd recognized his former friend that evening, back in ninety-eight, although, for one reason or another, he didn't consider it necessary to share that piece of information with me. However, even though he knew that Abraham was a psychotic and had killed a woman under similar circumstances, he still believed that he rather than his former friend was the one who killed Simone. But why would his mind have invented a world in which he was a murderer? False memories are usually created to protect, to tamper or even to erase tragic recollections, not the other way around.

On the other hand, Abraham's diary indicated that he and Simone had been victims of Josh, who was depicted as an unscrupulous manipulator, and that the killing of Margaret Lucas, twenty-two years later, had somehow reenacted the gruesome murder committed in Paris. But it was obvious that the diary belonged to a paranoid man, whose testimony didn't meet the minimum standard of credibility. In fact, it was highly likely that Abraham had killed Simone too. Schizophrenia often has its outset in late adolescence. Abraham was in his early twenties when he went to Paris, so he was almost certainly a psychotic, harboring a deep-seated delusion, even though his entourage hadn't realized the gravity of the situation. Later on, he did nothing but confirm his diagnosis.

At the same time I had to ask myself whether Josh had been totally sincere during his confession. For example, why hadn't he told me about his encounter with Abraham in 1998? In the course of my clinical research I'd repeatedly proven that a psychotic remains psychotic under hypnosis and that even in an altered state of consciousness he behaves accordingly, that is, differently from a sane individual.

Not even the deepest trance, induced by the most skilled hypnotizer, can completely peel off the thick shell of false perceptions, hallucinatory distortions, and aberrant convictions that such a person has painstakingly constructed for himself, sometimes for decades. Neurotics can be cooperative and sometimes even react positively to posthypnotic suggestion, but psychotics never do. They remain captives in the tangled labyrinth their minds have constructed, often over the course of an entire lifetime.

But nothing had suggested to me that Josh might have had a mental disorder. His career had been successful, without any of the relapses characteristic of psychotic behavior. He'd never undergone professional treatment, and therefore his affliction—if he'd ever suffered from one—would have grown steadily worse, his delusion would have become systemic, and his personality would have gradually disintegrated a long time ago, which was of course what had happened to Abraham. Josh didn't seem to suffer from auditory or visual hallucinations and he was perfectly functional physically, mentally, and emotionally, within the limits of the serious illness he was suffering from.

And the most important question: Why would he have done something like that? Lied? Why would he have spent his precious, limited time just to lead me by the nose?

Abraham had mentioned in his notes a charity called the White Rose, founded by Josh in the late seventies. I searched online and found out that the information was genuine: the NGO did exist and was focused on helping women who were victims of domestic violence. Perhaps the choice of this area, rather than any other, was the key to understanding the entire situation: Josh had thought of himself as guilty right off the bat, at least for triggering the chain of events that finally led to Simone's death. Although the circumstances and some of the details remained unclear, I wondered whether he'd ever really doubted that he'd murdered Simone. Had he expected me to confirm or shatter that belief?

I also questioned whether Josh had really been under hypnosis or whether he'd merely been faking a trance.

A patient must be extremely skilled to playact during a session of hypnosis, but it isn't completely out of the question. And the recording of the sessions had remained in his possession, so I no longer had the option of examining them at length. All I had were my written notes, which weren't enough.

I remembered that Josh had mentioned a woman named Elisabeth Gregory, thanks to whom Abraham had gotten that job offer from France. At that point, with Josh and Abraham Hale dead, she might be my only lead. I sent an email to Thomas Harley, a former colleague who was now a professor at Princeton University.

Dear Tom,

I hope you're well. During a therapy session with a patient, I came across an interesting story that took place at Princeton in the early seventies. I won't bore you with the details, except to say that two young men were involved, both of them students at the time. One was Joshua Fleischer, an English major, and the other was Abraham Hale, a Philosophy major. I also know that they shared a house in their senior year, and that Hale was the protégé of a woman by the name of Elisabeth Gregory, the owner of a small translation company. She must have been in her mid-thirties back then. Would you be so kind as to put me in touch with anybody who might be able to provide me with further details about the two students and Mrs. Gregory?

Regards,
James

In the evening, I found his reply in my inbox.

Dear James,

It must be six months since I last had the pleasure of talking to you, so I was delighted to receive your email. I was about to go to Zurich for a conference, but Amy was ill and I didn't want to leave her on her own. She's here next to me and sends you her best. I don't know whether you're up to date, but I left my position at the university four months ago. I'm now in the research division at Siemens. I've always envied our peers in the sciences for having an alternative to academia, so I was glad to have found something similar for myself.

I promise I'll contact the board about those men, Fleischer and Hale. Maybe they were students at the same time as some of today's professors.

I remember Elisabeth Gregory well. She's retired now, but she's still living in Mercer County, as far as I know. If you like, I can get hold of her address for you.

Yours,
Tom

I thanked him and asked him to send me Ms. Gregory's information as soon as he had it. I received his reply the next day, so I wrote her an email, broadly explaining what I wanted to talk to her about.

On Friday, before meeting Mallory, I conducted three therapy sessions in a row at my practice. When I finished, I told my assistant to go home and I headed for the coffee shop on East 80th Street on foot. It had stopped snowing, but a keen frost had descended upon the city from a deep blue sky and the buildings glittered in the cold sunlight.

I walked inside, got a table, and ordered a coffee. Mallory arrived a few minutes later. He asked for a coffee and carefully scanned my face.

"You look tired. Is everything okay?"

"I had a long day at the practice. Now, tell me what you've got."

"I have two pieces of news for you. First, I got to the bottom of our problem with that girl, Simone. Her family name wasn't Duchamp, but Maillot, let me see, M-a-i-l-l-o-t, with two *l*s in the middle, and she had a middle name, Louise. So her name was actually Simone Louise Maillot. Apparently, Lucas Duchamp never formally adopted her and her sister Laura, so they kept their real father's name. The girls went by Duchamp informally, but officially their name was Maillot. Secondly, yes, there was a case of a missing person under that name, Simone Louise Maillot. It's in the French police archives, dated October 1976. My associate in Paris will send me the full details in a day or two. It seems that the victim, who was twenty-something at the time, disappeared from home one evening and was never found. In charge of the investigation at the time was a detective named Marc Oliveira. Unfortunately, he died in ninety-one."

"Okay …"

"Laura Maillot dropped out of university after her sister's disappearance, and returned to Lyon, to her parents. She's now looking after her stepfather, Lucas Duchamp, who's still alive. He must be over ninety years old now. They live at the same address. The guy had a stroke about ten years ago and he's now in a wheelchair. I tried to contact her, but she's very reclusive. I don't think they even have a phone at home. But my French associate tracked down one of her longtime friends, Claudette Morel, and talked to her. It sounds like she's ready to spill the beans for a fee. I don't how reliable she is, I understand that she has a drinking problem, but there's her number. Good luck."

"Thanks, I'll call her tomorrow."

He took a sip of coffee. "Look, I'm pretty much sure that

Hale's diary answers all your questions," he said. "The guy was already unstable and violent back then in Paris, and he went on to commit a second crime twenty years later, with a similar MO. He probably killed that girl, Simone, fled, went back to the Rue de Rome the next day, took her body while Fleischer was sleeping, and managed to dispose of it somewhere and cover his tracks. He came back to the States and changed his name, but gradually went totally insane and killed the hooker."

I felt tired and sleepy, so I signaled to the waiter to bring me an espresso. "I don't buy this story, Ken, no offense."

"What do you mean?"

"Why did Josh not tell me anything about his showdown with Abraham in 1998? That information was very important, but he intentionally omitted it. He also must have been informed by the police that Abraham killed a woman later that night, the evidence that he was capable of murdering Simone too. And there's another thing: why didn't the French police question Josh and Abraham at the time? I'm not a detective, but it's pretty clear that both of them should have immediately been considered as persons of interest or even suspects when Simone went missing. But no, the police just let them go away, despite everybody knowing they'd been so close to Simone and might have had some information regarding her disappearance. And why did Lucas Duchamp not try to contact them after his stepdaughter disappeared?"

He shook his head. "Maybe he tried, but they'd already left France."

"Come on, a guy like him …"

"Well, the police didn't put those guys on the lamp. So what? These things aren't like in the movies. If the missing person isn't of tender age and if there are no obvious signs of foul play, then a couple of phone calls and the introduction of his or her name into a database is all that's going to happen, even today, depending on the cops' availability and how many open cases they have on their desks. People vanish all the time. Over ninety percent of so-called missing adults, men and women, actually disappear voluntarily, popping back up like a jack-in-a-box after weeks, months or even years. And back in the day, there were no security cameras to check, cellphones to track down, or credit cards to follow their statements."

"Right, but Josh's family was very well known, and it would have been a piece of cake for someone to track him down, even after a few weeks. Another thing: for a while, Josh went to Mexico. Was he thinking of a possible extradition to France, which would have been possible from the States, but not from Mexico, as far as I know? Lucas Duchamp was a famous lawyer, and he'd have been able to pull a lot of strings if he'd wanted to. He could have pressured the French authorities to do their job."

"Okay, what's your point?"

"I believe that we still don't know what really happened that night, not even whether Simone is dead or alive. That story Josh told me, for example, about the suitcase which disappeared the next day, doesn't make sense to me and I don't buy it. Anyway, I could go to France for a couple of days, to talk to those women, Claudette Morel and Simone's sister, Laura."

A man wrapped up in a thick overcoat came inside and sat down at the table next to us. When our eyes met he winked at me and smiled.

"If I were you, I would stop wasting my time and money on this story," Mallory said. "I'm not even sure whether those women know something." He put a twenty on the table and stood up. "This is on me. I'll keep the ball rolling, and if you need anything, call me. I'll be on the West Coast for a couple of weeks."

"Thanks and good luck with your diet."

# sixteen

OVER THE WEEKEND I grabbed a notepad and wrote down the questions that still remained unanswered. I'd read Abraham's diary twice and I'd also made a summary of Mallory's reports. One of the questions was: Had Abraham already been profoundly unstable in Paris, as Josh had described, or did he deteriorate significantly during all those years he spent living in need and fear, his heart broken because of the tragedy he'd experienced? What if he was telling the truth, and back in the nineties Josh had indeed used his money and power to set him up and send him once and for all to a prison for insane criminals? If Abraham had ever tried to reveal the truth to the police, no one would have believed him.

I invoked the Google spirit and discovered the White Rose's website. According to the presentation, the foundation was run using a bequest left by Mr. Salem H. Fleischer, Josh's father. But something grabbed my attention: Josh had told me that his parents had died in a car crash in June 1973, but the foundation had been created about four years later, in February 1977.

I jotted down the number of the president of the board, a man called Lionel J. Carpenter. After a couple of unsuccessful attempts to get him on the phone, a surly assistant finally put me through. I introduced myself and told him that I was calling on behalf of the late Joshua Fleischer. He was immediately interested.

"Dr. Cobb, have you recently spoken to Joshua? In person, I mean ...When?"

"Yes, Mr. Carpenter, I met him in Maine, when I was his guest for a few days, in October last year."

"I hadn't had the pleasure of seeing him over the past forty years or so," he informed me, to my surprise. "I took on the running of the foundation from its inception, at his behest, but then we didn't really keep in touch ... His attorney called me a couple of weeks ago and told me he had passed away."

"Unfortunately, it's true," I told him. "He had leukemia. It was in this context that he called upon my professional services. I'm a psychiatrist and Mr. Fleischer was one of my patients."

"I've heard of you, Dr. Cobb. I saw you recently on TV, I think. You've published a book, haven't you?"

"Yes, that's right. Mr. Carpenter, I'd like to ask you a question, if you don't mind: was the White Rose Foundation set up by Joshua or by his father?"

There was a pause.

"To a certain extent," he said, cautiously, "it was Joshua's idea. But I wouldn't want to discuss such matters over the phone. If your schedule allowed, I could meet you this afternoon. I'm leaving town tomorrow for a few days. Why don't we meet here, at my office, at five o'clock?"

"Sure, thank you, I'll be there."


Carpenter was a man in his seventies, tall, slim, and emaciated. He invited me to take a seat, asked his assistant to bring us coffee, and said, "I joined Salem's law practice in the mid-sixties, eight years before the tragedy. After he passed away, we didn't change the name of the company, Fleischer and Associates, for five years. Later, new partners joined us and we had to change it. Sal was an extraordinary man, loved by all and highly intelligent. His parties were

Manhattan society events back then. He'd been close to the Kennedys and kept in touch with Jackie to the very end."

"Mr. Carpenter, what kind of relationship did Josh have with his parents, if I may be so bold?"

He took off his glasses and began to polish them with a handkerchief.

"To be honest, he was a strange teenager. He was brilliant and all his teachers agreed that he had a wonderful mind, but sometimes he acted … oddly. There were situations when Sal had to exert his influence to keep a lid on certain scandals. The late sixties and early seventies were strange times, and young people used to glory in being rebels and showing the older generation that they were emancipated, but with Josh it wasn't a question of the usual problems—you know, drugs, drinking, or speeding. On the contrary, he was very levelheaded for his age. He didn't even smoke, as far as I can remember."

"And …?"

He finished cleaning his glasses, put them back on his nose, and sipped his coffee.

"Well, Joshua was handsome, rich, and cultured, so the girls were attracted to him," he said, seeming vaguely embarrassed. "As far as I know he had a number of girlfriends. But there was something not quite right about him, and some of the girls talked to their parents, and certain things came to light. It seems that he had some … unusual inclinations. A girl claimed, for example, that he had sadistic tendencies. Obviously, Sal never went into detail with me, and in any case he was convinced that his son's big mouth was to blame, and his desire to provoke by fantasizing, not realizing that his girlfriends didn't have an imagination as fertile as his own and might take seriously stories he'd made up to impress them. It was my understanding that his father was the one who had refused to let him go to Harvard, thereby breaking the family tradition. He was afraid of the talk in a place where his name was so well known."

I got the feeling that he'd been waiting years for an opportunity to talk about the Fleischers. Their story had obviously
preoccupied him more than he was willing to admit. Gradually,
he also revealed how the foundation had come into being.

"After he graduated, Joshua went to Europe—to France,
as far as I can remember. When he came back, a couple
of months later, he called me from a hotel room in New
York. I hadn't seen or heard from him in two years, since I'd
already dealt with the will and he'd come of age. In short,
he told me that he didn't need any of his parents' money,
and that he wanted to take his life into his own hands and
donate the inheritance, everything down to the last cent, to
a foundation, which he asked me to found and administer
with persons of my own choice. I was shocked, as you can
imagine. I tried to make him reconsider, or at least take time
to think it over. I was convinced that something must have
happened while he was in Europe, and I didn't want him to
act on impulse and then come to regret it later."

"What kind of sum are we talking about?"

"Taking into consideration all the assets, including the
house, it was a sum of more than thirty million dollars. It's
still quite a fortune, even by today's standards."

"Yes, it is."

"Joshua assured me that his decision wasn't a passing
whim, but the result of calm and lucid analysis. He gave
me the phone number of a lawyer he'd spoken to and told
me that in the event that I refused to take over the running
of the foundation, there were plenty of other people who
would be willing to do so. I thought of Sal and Sandra, of
our friendship and the possibility that their legacy might
fall into unsuitable hands, and I accepted. So that's how the
White Rose Foundation was born. I retired two years ago,
but I've retained my position as honorary president of the
board. Josh decided that the foundation should devote itself

solely to helping abused women, materially and psychologically. And that's what I've been doing all these years, with very good results, I would say. After the foundation was set up, I didn't hear from Joshua for a while. He'd informed me that he was going to leave the States for a period and I discovered—I no longer recall how—that he'd gone to Mexico. A few years later, I read in the newspaper about a businessman by the name of Joshua Fleischer, who had made a killing on Wall Street. I called him, spoke to him. We kept in touch over the phone, but we never met each other face to face again."

I thanked him and he showed me to the door. Before I left, he tossed his head and said, "Oh, there's one important detail I forgot to tell you about. Sal had changed his will shortly before he died, adding a very curious stipulation: Joshua was to lose his entire inheritance if he was ever mixed up in an incident involving violence against women, with the exception of self-defense."

I was amazed. I'd chosen a profession that had already taught me from way back that if you dig behind a beautiful picture deep enough, more often than not you'll come across a mound of garbage, and probably the Fleischers were no exception. But in their case, the garbage seemed to contain a few unexploded bombs, too.

"But why would Mr. Fleischer have done that? Did something happen which suggested to him that his son might be capable of something like that?"

"I don't know. Maybe you're too young to know, but back in those days lots of things were seen as just unfortunate *incidents*, and nobody talked about them afterwards. A decent family used to keep its *incidents* locked up in a safe place, where even their best friends weren't allowed to enter under any circumstances. Sal and I were very close, as I told you, but he knew well how to protect his privacy and nobody, including myself, would have had the guts to question him on something like that. But to be honest, I've always thought that Joshua's decision regarding his inheritance must have been related to that stipulation in his father's will. I didn't want to dig deeper, because it was none of my business. Have a good day, Dr. Cobb."

I called Claudette Morel the next day, first thing in the morning, and after just two rings a hoarse, smoker's voice answered the phone. I asked her if we could speak in English and she said yes. I introduced myself and she confirmed that she knew the Maillot sisters very well.

"Ms. Morel, I understand that a couple of days ago you spoke with Inspector Henri Solano, from the French police. As he probably told you, I'm very interested in discussing the circumstances under which Simone Maillot, or Duchamp, went missing in October 1976."

"I see ... Have the police found out what happened to her? The inspector refused to give me any details."

"Unfortunately, they haven't, but—"

"He also mentioned your employer, a man named Joshua Fleischer, is that right? I met him a long time ago." Her voice sounded cautious and hostile. "Why is he interested in this story, after so many years? Did he tell you that? Are the police involved?"

"No, they aren't involved, it's a private affair. As for Mr. Fleischer's interest in this story, well, it's a bit more complicated. He was one of my patients, and—"

"I understand, Dr. ..."

"Cobb, James Cobb. Please call me James."

"Well, Dr. Cobb, this whole story sounds very odd. I don't know why I'd agree to talk to you. I don't know who you are and what you really want from me. Do you have a warrant from the authorities, or is there something you'd like to tell me on behalf of Joshua Fleischer?"

"I'm calling because I need your help, Ms. Morel. As far

as I know, you met Mr. Fleischer in seventy-six, and you also met Mr. Abraham Hale, his best friend. And they both were in love with Simone, weren't they?"

She laughed—a snotty, joyless laugh.

"I'm not sure who was in love with whom, Dr. Cobb. It wasn't until many years after Simone disappeared and Laura refused to talk to me again that I put two and two together. Laura and I were very close at the time, but she had her secrets, like all of us. We were university students. Laura had asked Simone to recommend me to the foundation she was working for and she'd helped me get a part-time job there. Then …"

"So you worked with Simone … I didn't know that. For a while, Abraham Hale worked at the foundation too, if I'm not mistaken, so you must have known him quite well."

"Of course I knew him very well. And I knew Fleischer, too."

I heard her lighting a cigarette.

"By the way, how's Fleischer doing? Is he well?"

"I'm afraid I don't have good news. Mr. Fleischer died a couple of months ago from leukemia."

"I'm sorry to hear that."

"Ms. Morel, I'd like to ask you something: after Mr. Fleischer visited Simone in Lyon, he—"

"Sorry for interrupting you, but those boys came to Lyon together, I remember it well. I was there that weekend. Abraham was a very handsome guy, shy, quiet and polite, the exact opposite of Fleischer, who was a strange man. As I've told you, I went out with them a few times, but I eventually stopped joining them mostly because of Fleischer's behavior. Especially when he was drunk, he became unbearable. And he used to drink a lot."

"I understand … Shortly after that weekend in Lyon, Simone disappeared. Do you remember the circumstances? Were you in Paris at the time?"

For a while she said nothing and I could hear her breathing heavily.

"I see you know quite a bit already ... As I said before, Laura used to tell me lots of things about herself and her sister. Yes, I was in Paris when Simone went missing. Laura and I were sharing an apartment. Simone wasn't answering the phone and she didn't go to work, so her parents alerted the police. It was awful. She just vanished ... For years, I thought that she might be alive, living in another country under a false identity, you know, like in films."

"Why would she have done such a thing?"

"I don't know why, but the Duchamps forgot about her very quickly, too quickly. So I said to myself that maybe they knew something. That family had many secrets, Dr. Cobb."

"What about Laura? Are you still in touch with her? I'd like to talk to her too, if possible."

"After Simone disappeared, Laura dropped out of university, went back to Lyon, and completely withdrew from the world. She refused to talk to me or anybody else, as far as I know. I heard that she'd had a nervous breakdown and was hospitalized in a psychiatric clinic in Switzerland for a couple of years. Their parents must have spent a fortune. I've tried to contact her many times, but her father told me to stop calling, and eventually I did. Then my family sold our house and moved to Alsace, so I never went back to Lyon. All I know is that her father is paralyzed and she's looking after him ever since. So I can't help you to get in touch with her, I'm sorry."

Abruptly, she changed the subject and asked me about Abraham's whereabouts.

"It's more bad news, I'm afraid. It seems that he lived in California for a while, and then in New York City. In the fall of 1998, he killed a woman. He was found insane and committed to a forensic psychiatric hospital, where he died a few years later."

There was a long silence.

"Are you sure we're talking about the same person? It must be a mistake."

"Why do you say that?"

"Because Abraham was the kindest person I've ever met and I don't believe he could have done such a thing."

"Unfortunately, what I'm telling you is true, Ms. Morel. He was diagnosed a dangerous paranoid."

"Abraham? Oh my god … Listen, I don't know you, but I want to ask you something: Has it ever crossed your mind that you might be in danger? That your reputation, your career, even your life might be threatened?"

"What do you mean?"

"I mean this story … You say you're a psychologist."

"I'm actually a psychiatrist."

"Well, then you're probably not very good at your job, given that you're rash enough to get mixed up in all this. I remember that Laura had become increasingly pensive and upset during that period of time, after she'd met those boys. It was clear to me that she was anxious about something, probably related to those Americans, something that had nothing to do with love and romance. I think Abraham and Fleischer were involved in something dark and dangerous, but I never found out what. And then Simone disappeared and she ended up in the hospital."

"There's something else I'd like to ask you, Ms. Morel. Do you known by any chance if Mr. Duchamp mentioned Joshua and Abraham to the French police at the time? It looks like you suspected them of being involved in Simone's disappearance and you probably weren't the only one who thought that way. What I don't understand is why the French police didn't even attempt to question them."

"I don't know what the Duchamps told the police, I'm sorry. As for me, nobody ever asked me anything."

Her mood had gradually changed and I realized that she

was getting increasingly nervous. It was becoming harder and harder for her to speak clearly.

"Ms. Morel, I'm truly intrigued by this story. You'd be doing me a huge favor if you agreed to meet with me and talk about the matter. I might be coming to Paris next week and—"

"But you said you're a doctor."

"That's right."

"Don't you have patients and deadlines? How can you just abandon everything and leave? That doesn't sound very normal to me, I'm afraid."

"I have to be in Paris for some other business, and I'd really like to meet you," I lied.

"Your name is James Cobb. C-o-b-b, is that correct?"

"Yes."

I heard the sound of paper rustling.

"It's two p.m. here," she said. "I'd like for us to speak on the phone tomorrow, at the same time. I have to consult my schedule," she emphasized self-importantly, before hanging up.

That evening I found a message from Elisabeth Gregory in my inbox.

Dear Dr. Cobb,

Your message awakened painful memories for me, memories I'd long since buried away. I've heard a lot about you and I appreciate your work, so I'm sure that you must have a strong enough reason to be interested in things that happened so long ago.

I rarely leave the house, so I'd like to invite you to visit me, whenever is convenient for you. We'll talk more when you come.

All the best,
Elisabeth

I replied that I could visit her the next day and gave her my cellphone number. She texted me back right away—she would be expecting me at eleven a.m.

# seventeen

ELISABETH GREGORY LIVED in Bradford Estates, a neighborhood of detached, single family homes, built back in the mid-eighties not far from Princeton Junction. There were about three dozen houses and condos spread around a golf course with a small lake in the middle.

The house itself was a two-story home, with a white façade and a large porch. To the right there was a pond, and on the left there was a garage, in front of which I parked my car. I got out of the car and took in the surroundings.

The property looked as if it had been put on the market the day before, and every single thing seemed to be precisely in its place. The façade had recently been repainted and the water in the pond, despite the weather, was crystal clear. I had the feeling that I was looking at a gigantic version of a dollhouse, abandoned in the middle of the field by a bored, giant toddler, who was now hiding somewhere.

I climbed the steps of the porch and glimpsed an outline at one of the ground-floor windows. Mrs. Gregory opened the door before I could ring the bell.

She was very tall, and despite her age you could tell that she'd once been a rare beauty. Her white hair was held back with a black headband. She wore a Fair Isle sweater and a pair of faded jeans.

I greeted her and she invited me inside.

"You look younger and thinner than you do on TV," she said and smiled.

She closed the door and led me down a passageway covered in framed black-and-white photographs. We entered a spacious living room. The interior gave you the same impression as the exterior—immaculate; each object seemed to have been placed there after long and careful thought. The scent of coffee mingled with smart air freshener and discreet perfume. The chirping of the birds and the faint hiss of an occasional passing car on Vincent Drive were the only sounds that made their way through the windows.

"If you haven't had breakfast yet I can offer you some wonderful croissants," she said, gesturing vaguely in the direction of the kitchen. "They're fresh, I bought them this morning."

"I'm fine," I said. "Thank you for inviting me."

On the table there was a tray with a pot and two china cups and saucers. She poured the coffee and placed one of the cups in front of me. Her gestures were those of a person still firmly in control of her body, calm and measured.

"How did you find out about me, Dr. Cobb? Why did you ask Tom to get you my address?"

"As I wrote in my email, Mr. Fleischer mentioned your name in connection with a man called Abraham Hale. He told me that it was thanks to you that Mr. Hale got a job offer from the foundation in France in his senior year at university. Actually, I'm trying to find out more about their time as students, I thought that you might be able to provide me with some details."

"I see ... Did Fleischer tell you anything else?"

"No. Only that Mr. Hale was your protégé."

"I understand ... Is your curiosity strictly professional?"

"To be honest, there's more to it than that. But it would be very complicated if you asked me to be more specific."

"No, I don't intend to ask you. I only want to assure myself that anything I tell you will never be made public. I hope that your interest doesn't tend in that direction."

"Nothing of the sort, Mrs. Gregory. It's purely personal and won't end up in a magazine or a book. You have my word on that. In any case, Mr. Fleischer imposed a similar condition."

"I'm not surprised … How about you tell me how Joshua Fleischer came to be your patient?"

As we drank our coffees, I told her about how Josh had contacted me, without going into too many details, and about Abraham Hale's diary, but I avoided telling her that before he'd been committed to the hospital, Hale had become a murderer.

She listened to me carefully, without taking her eyes off mine. When I finished my story, she asked, "Both Abe and Joshua are gone now, Dr. Cobb … Then why is something that happened so long ago so important to you?"

"You're quite right to ask me that … Well, what I haven't told you yet is that Mr. Fleischer believed that he or Mr. Hale committed something terrible in Paris. In the meantime I've discovered that events may not have transpired in the way he remembered, but what I'm trying to do now is to discover *why* he created such a false memory."

"Is that possible?"

"Sure. What we call *memory* isn't a video camera *recording* the reality around us, and preserving it as such, unaltered. Distortions occur during the recording process. Other distortions intervene over the course of time, as our perception of things changes. According to research, as much as eighty percent of our recollections are more or less false."

"Has that terrible thing got anything to do with a woman?"

"Yes, with a young French woman he and Mr. Hale met in Paris, in the summer of the year they graduated. Her name was Simone Duchamp and she went missing in the fall of seventy-six."

"Then it may be that I have an explanation, Dr. Cobb.

I have strong reasons to believe that shortly before they graduated, Fleischer was guilty of another terrible deed. Except that Abe covered for him. It had something to do with an inheritance, if I'm not mistaken. Perhaps Abe did the same thing in Paris."

She held her spine very straight, not touching the back of the armchair she was sitting in. She stared into empty space for a time, and then got up and went to a sideboard. She opened the top drawer, searched for a few moments, and then removed a photo. She came back to the coffee table and handed me the photo without a word.

It was quite blurred, having been taken with a cheap Polaroid, and the colors were distorted, but I was able to recognize my host as a young woman, with the body of a goddess, arm in arm with a tall, thin young man wearing a black shirt and a pair of jeans. He was flashing a peace sign at the camera and smiling. They were standing in front of a tall rose bush and in the distance I could see what appeared to be a church spire. I looked at the back of the photo. In the bottom left it was dated June 14, 1976.

"The year Mr. Fleischer and Mr. Hale graduated from college," I observed.

She nodded. "It's the only photograph of us together. And you're the first person I've ever shown it to."

"Forgive me, Mrs. Gregory, but did you have a relationship with Mr. Hale? Mr. Fleischer told me some of it, but he didn't seem very au fait with the details."

"He was very au fait with the *details*, believe me," she said, "sufficiently to blackmail us. This is how it happened ..."

She leaned back in the armchair and closed her eyes, as if it were easier for her to tell her story without looking at me.

"I met Abe after his sophomore year at Princeton, during an internship at my company. He was astonishingly intelligent, shy, and very handsome. For his age, he'd already read enormously. He was far more capable than the other students, and it was difficult not to notice him. Now you told me he was mad. With all due respect, I don't think so, Dr. Cobb. The Abe I knew was the kindest person in the world.

"I had a private talk with him and asked him whether he intended to embark upon an academic career. He confessed that he wanted nothing else. I became a kind of mentor to him, if you like, without having any other intentions.

"The situation remained unchanged until the end of the year. That summer, he lost his scholarship. For months, he'd been very depressed. He was finding it difficult to concentrate, he had all but given up his studies, and for days on end he didn't even leave the house."

"Don't you think that what you describe might have been the onset of his illness, Mrs. Gregory?"

"No, I don't think so, because despite his chronic sadness, he was completely rational. But he didn't get along with his father at all—his mother had died when he was just a child—and he was terrified of the prospect of not finding work here and having to go back to his hometown, to a community where he'd always felt like a stranger. His exam results had been disastrous and, as I said, he lost his scholarship.

"I arranged for him to work for my company again over the summer. I didn't take a summer vacation that year, so we saw each other more often. That's when our relationship began. I didn't feel pity for him, don't get me wrong. I had quite simply fallen in love with him. I think I fell in love with him the first day we met. I was still married merely because I didn't believe in divorce, but my husband, Matt, lived in New York City and I barely ever saw him. He was a notorious womanizer, who in his day had dreamed of becoming a new Arthur Miller, but ended up a tedious drunk, like all alcoholics."

She stood up and opened one of the windows wide. A wave of cold air flooded the room.

"Every spring since I first moved into this place I intend to build a pool and to do all kinds of other things," she said, returning to the coffee table and sitting in the armchair. "And every fall I realize I haven't done anything. Time has a completely different dimension when you're growing old. You probably know lots of things about the relativity of what we call hours, days, and years, don't you, Dr. Cobb?

"Anyway, I don't want to go into details about my relationship with Abe, because it isn't relevant to our discussion. I will merely say that I discovered a young man more wonderful than I ever thought could exist. All the people we hate seem to resemble each other, but the people we love are always different from one another.

"Before I got married I'd never had even so much as a boyfriend, and for me men meant my father—whom I'd adored and who died when I was twenty-one—and Matt, my husband—an arrogant and heartless hypocrite, with whom I'd nevertheless been in love for a few years. Abe was different from them both. He had neither the strength I'd sensed in my father nor the huge talent my husband later drowned in alcohol. But he had something else: an almost infinite tenderness, an angelic gentleness, and a delicacy that I'd previously thought only women were capable of.

"But then two things happened: Abe met Fleischer, who moved into the same house as him. And my husband caught us together one night. Our relationship was destroyed."

She made no gestures as she spoke, and her tone was even, almost monotonous. I'd noticed the pupils of her eyes when she opened the door for me, and I wondered what kind of pills she was on.

"That night was the first night I asked Abe to stay over. We'd gone to my house so that I could change my clothes before going to the motel, and suddenly I asked myself why we had to do that, when we had a house at our disposal, my house. The neighbors across the street were away for the weekend, so there was nobody to see us. I lived in Port Hertford at the time. It was the most unfortunate idea I've ever had.

"Matt had his own key and we didn't even hear him come in. He climbed the stairs into the bedroom and saw us in bed. We were both asleep and he didn't wake us. He left me a note in the living room saying that he was at a nearby motel. He called the next day and asked me to come and meet him.

"He asked me who Abe was and how I'd met him. He used vulgar language, he accused me of all the ills in the world, said that if I didn't break off the relationship he'd destroy me. I wasn't afraid of him—physically, I mean. I knew he was nothing but a coward with a big mouth, but I was afraid of a scandal. So Abe and I agreed not to be seen together in public for a while, until Matt grew bored of playing the wronged husband and cleared off.

"That was when Fleischer made his appearance. Abe enthusiastically introduced me to him almost immediately after they met.

"Up until then Abe hadn't told me about any close friends, only about casual acquaintances. But he seemed fascinated with Fleischer. I could partly understand why—he was very attractive, well dressed, and highly cultivated, a real club panther, as they used to call them back then, self-confident and charming. I knew his type well, because I was born and raised in New York. I knew that behind the glittering exterior there was usually a perverted soul and a mind stuffed with fashionable clichés. But for Abe it was something new to be accepted into the entourage of such a king of the jungle.

"Fleischer had inherited a large fortune and had useful connections in every field. Although they were the same age, he treated Abe like a little brother, with a condescendence that I'd have found insulting. But at the same time it was obvious he cared about Abe a lot.

"Don't get me wrong, Fleischer made a good impression, he was cultivated, and most of the time he was cheerful and relaxed. But behind the appearance you *sensed* something dark and dangerous, even if you couldn't put your finger on what exactly. Maybe it was the feeling that under certain circumstances, he could do you a lot of harm. There are certain people who are incapable of doing any harm, physically I mean, even if their life were in danger, just as others are capable of the darkest cruelty in certain circumstances. Joshua was like a beautiful house, which you can walk around with pleasure, but where you'd inevitably reach a locked room and quickly realize that it's somewhere you should never set foot.

"But I think that Abe was too young and too tired of being alone to realize all that. And then the scandal came.

"Abe and I had spent the evening together, at the motel I told you about. After what happened with my husband, we avoided spending the night together at my house. I'd gone home, ready for a long and absurd phone conversation with Matt, who was in the habit of calling every evening, usually very late. If I took the phone off the hook or didn't answer, he'd come to New Jersey spoiling for a fight, so I preferred to answer and put up with his drunken rants.

"He always began with the same words, which were, *We need to have a serious talk*. As if during our previous talks, which had lasted for hours, we hadn't talked seriously and had only been chatting to pass the time.

"Each time he called he'd be drunk, but the first few minutes of the conversation would go relatively normally. After that, no matter what I said, he'd start to reproach me. Our life together, he claimed, would have been like a paradise if I hadn't committed a series of mistakes and if I hadn't done a number of things that sprang from my innate badness. I'd probably been cheating on him all along, with every man that crossed my path. And lately I'd descended so low that I was *getting it on*—he loved expressions like that—with young students, like a horny bitch. He'd bring up the few male friends we'd had as a couple and interrogate me about my supposedly adulterous relations with each of them.

"That evening—it must have been past midnight—I heard the doorbell ring just as I was trying to bring a 'conversation' to a close, in fact one of his rambling, incoherent monologues that had gone much more badly than usual.

"It took me another ten minutes to get rid of him, and I went to the front door. It was Abe. I invited him to come in, and he told me that a young woman named Lucy had accused Fleischer of raping her. In the meantime, the phone kept ringing and I was sure it was Matt. I asked Abe to wait while I answered. It took another hour before I could get him off the line, and in the meantime Abe kept pacing up and down, signaling at me desperately every minute.

"In short, he was asking me to provide Fleischer with an alibi, for us to make a statement that he'd been with us at the time of the alleged rape. I refused.

"He told me that he knew for sure *where* Fleischer had been at the time—absolutely not at home, where the so-called victim claimed the rape had taken place—but he couldn't tell anybody, not even me, where exactly he'd been or who his friend had been with. So he knew Fleischer wasn't guilty and that the whole thing must be a setup or a mistake.

"We talked all night, with him insisting and me refusing to do what he wanted. I asked him a thousand questions, and he gave vague answers. I realized he knew more than he was saying. He supposed that the so-called victim had probably planned the whole thing, probably out of greed. But who would want to do Fleischer any harm? Who could have paid her to do such a thing? I know who—he told me—but I can't tell you, otherwise you'd think I was mad and it would have dreadful consequences for both of us. I asked him whether Fleischer was capable of blackmailing. He avoided giving me a straightforward answer, but I was convinced that that was the only explanation for Abe's behavior.

"I think I caved more from exhaustion. After two hours of pointless arguing on the phone with Matt and another two hours of tense discussion with Abe, I could no longer reason clearly. I got dressed and we went to the police station where Fleischer was being held. We talked to a detective, who told us that the alleged victim, Miss Lucy Sandler, was at a nearby hotel with a psychologist. Fleischer was going to be brought before the judge the next morning and needed an attorney.

"There followed more nightmarish hours, in a room full of cigarette smoke, bustling with delinquents and police officers. I testified that Fleischer had been at my house, preparing a dissertation. The detective who took my statement kept grinning and asking insinuating questions, and he didn't appear to believe one jot of what I was saying. I hired a lawyer I knew and he looked at the file. He told me that Miss Sandler claimed that the previous day, at around noon, she'd had sexual relations with the accused, at his temporary residence, after they'd both been to a party the night before, which is where they met. After that, Fleischer had left, saying he had things to do, and she'd gone to bed. Late that evening he'd come back drunk, beaten her, raped her, and then fled.

"The tale didn't hold water, as the lawyer pointed out, given that the alleged victim didn't appear to have been subjected to any violence. He concluded that it was probably a case of blackmail.

"Abe admitted that he'd been the one who had introduced Miss Lucy Sandler to Fleischer at the party and that he was shocked at how things had turned out. At one point he whispered to me that if Fleischer were convicted, he'd have lost his entire inheritance, without telling me why.

"In the morning, I went with Fleischer to court, feeling like I was in the middle of a nightmare. The judge agreed to grant him bail, but banned him from leaving town. That same day, at noon, we discovered Miss Sandler had withdrawn the complaint and gone back to New York. Before we parted, Fleischer said, 'Maybe one day I'll pay you back for your help.' I told him that I wasn't expecting any kind of reward: it was the worst thing I'd ever done and I didn't want to think about it ever again. But as a kind of strange coincidence, the tragedy with Matt came shortly after that."

She paused, as if she'd lost the thread of the story. I asked her where the bathroom was, and while I was in there I looked in her medicine cabinet. She had a whole drugstore in there. I went back to the living room, wondering how much I could trust what she was telling me. After I returned, she continued.

"As I was saying, I slept for fourteen hours straight that night. I'd taken the phone off the hook, so my husband had tried in vain to call me the entire night. At around six o'clock in the morning he took the train to New Jersey. He was worse than ever before.

"He ransacked the whole house looking for my supposed lover, convinced that he must be hiding somewhere. In the end, somebody called the police and a patrol car came and took him away to the station, even though I told the two officers that I didn't want to file a complaint.

"I called Abe, but he didn't answer.

"I had to go to work: I had a lot of things to do, and I couldn't postpone them any longer. I had the feeling that everybody was looking at me and that my employees were whispering behind my back. I called the police and they told me that Mr. Matt Gregory had been released a few hours before, after receiving a caution. I called Abe again, but he still wasn't answering.

"The next morning, the doorbell woke me up. Two police officers had come to inform me that Matt had been murdered—stabbed to death, to be precise.

"They told me that his body had been found by some passersby at around four a.m. in a back alley near the railroad station in Princeton Junction. The paramedics declared him dead at the scene. The murderer had probably been a professional—there was a single stab wound, straight to the heart. No money or valuables had been found on his person, so it looked like robbery. Would you like more coffee?"

Her tone of voice didn't change at all when she asked me, so I looked at her in confusion for a few seconds, not understanding what she meant.

"No, I'm fine, thank you. A terrible story … How did Mr. Hale react when he found out?"

"Again, Abe seemed very frightened. He didn't provide me with any plausible explanation about how he'd spent the previous day. He babbled something about helping Fleischer with a paper and that he'd been in the library. It was a lie, because I later checked if they'd signed in on that day and found out that they hadn't."

"Do you suspect either or both of them might have been involved in Matt's death? Did the police catch the perpetrator?"

"No, the murderer was never caught. The theory was that it had probably been a drifter, who left town right after the killing.

"Mr. Cobb, you know how it is when you glimpse something out of the corner of your eye for a fraction of a second and then wonder whether what you saw was real or just a figment of your imagination? I've never forgotten the expression on Fleischer's face when he told me that one day he would pay me back for my help.

"Later, I realized that I'd thought about such a possibility—that he or Abe or both of them might have been involved in Matt's murder—from the very first moment. But at the time I was too frightened and overwhelmed by the way my life had suddenly gone off the tracks to be certain of anything. The world I knew had shattered into pieces, becoming a whirlpool that could suck me under at any moment.

"In any case, I came to an agreement with Abe that it would be better for both of us if we didn't see each other for a while.

"Matt's body had been collected from the morgue by his parents and taken to New York. They didn't even invite me to the funeral. They behaved as if I didn't exist.

"The next few months were confused and I can't remember anything much about them. Abe kept his promise and didn't come looking for me. He was no longer my employee and we never even bumped into each other. He called me in late December to wish me Merry Christmas and I told him I'd be spending the holidays with my parents in Florida. In reality, I stayed at home, alone, but I wanted to make sure he wouldn't turn up at my door. He assured me that his thesis was going well. We didn't see each other the whole winter. I was the one who looked him up, in the end, around the middle of March.

"It was only when I looked into his eyes again that I knew the man I once loved was no longer there. For someone in his twenties, a couple of months is a very long time. No, he hadn't forgotten me and I still meant something to him. But from the very first moment I had the feeling that I'd become a kind of pal, a friend to share memories with.

"Fleischer seemed different too. His humor had evaporated, his answers to questions were curt and unenthusiastic, and most of the time he seemed lost in his own world. I couldn't understand why Abe had insisted on bringing him along when we met.

"Abe had another cause for worry. His exam results had been mediocre and he couldn't see any prospect of a decent job on the horizon. He was afraid of growing old teaching in some out-of-the-way high school, surrounded by bitter failures in the staffroom and hostile students in the classroom. As I told you before, his relationship with his father was poor and he didn't want to go back to Louisiana. I promised to try to find him a job, and he told me to forget it. In any case, we saw each other rarely.

"I think it was May, shortly before his graduation, when he came by and told me about Mexico. It was Fleischer's idea, as far as I could tell. They wanted to go to Mexico—I can't remember where exactly—to buy a small hotel on the beach and make a living from it. He even showed me a flier with some photographs of the property—a dilapidated two-story mansion, with white walls and brown woodwork, somewhere on the shore.

"I asked him where he was going to come up with the money and he reminded me that Fleischer was the heir to a large fortune.

"I decided to do everything I could to prevent him from getting caught up in that adventure. He didn't know anything about running a hotel business. I pictured him as a puffy-faced alcoholic, old before his time, surrounded by lowlifes, sweating on the porch of a crumbling house, a local laughingstock.

"By lucky coincidence, a friend from France had asked me to recommend somebody for a temporary job at a cultural foundation called L'Etoile. The money wasn't great, but for a young man at the start of his career it was an opportunity to work in Europe, and Abe spoke French fluently.

"At first he categorically refused, and I think it was

Fleischer who finally persuaded him to take the job. I didn't know at the time that they'd agreed that Fleischer would join him in France almost immediately.

"In July, I took him to the airport and he left. Looking at him, I had the feeling that I would never see him again."

The sun had broken through the clouds and was blazing. She stood up and gestured for me to follow her. She took a coat from the rack in the hallway, threw it over her shoulders, and we went outside.

On the porch there was a table and a wooden bench, and she invited me to sit. A sparrow landed on the edge of the table and gazed at us with its beady black eyes and then took flight, vanishing into the undergrowth.

"In the first two weeks he called me almost every day. He was happy and enthusiastic. Then he stopped calling. I tried to contact Fleischer and found out he'd gone to Paris too. I had Abe's address and phone number, which he'd given me when he first got to Paris, so I wrote to him and tried to get hold of him, but without success.

"In the end, I went out there. I'd been to Paris before, about fifteen years previously, in the summer after I finished high school, in the days when trips to Europe had started to be a middle-class requisite, along with a three-bed house in the suburbs, two cars in the garage, and a color TV."

"Did you meet Simone?"

She nodded.

"Not directly … In a rare letter, Abe had told me he'd met a woman by that name, who had bowled him over with her beauty and culture, and helped him to acclimatize to Parisian life. He'd talked about her the way you tell something to a mere friend and that made me angry. He probably thought he was doing the decent thing by keeping me up to date with such details, but for me it came like a punch in the face. The presence of that woman in his life was the reason I dropped everything and went there to find him. Have you ever abandoned a woman who was in love with you, Dr. Cobb?"

"Yes, I think so …"

"Well, I don't know what she did or how she reacted, but believe me, she won't have done even a quarter of what she fantasized about doing. I dreamed up all kinds of plans for revenge, each more terrible than the next. I thought about destroying his reputation, accusing him of the death of my husband, telling the foundation that I withdrew my recommendation, finding Simone and telling her Abe was a dangerous maniac and that there was more between him and Fleischer than friendship, if you get my meaning.

"By the time I arrived in Paris, I didn't even know what I wanted anymore. I felt like a middle-aged abandoned mistress, capable of making a scene and humiliating herself in the vain hope of getting back her younger lover. I was aware of being in that regrettable position, but I couldn't stop myself from doing what I had to do.

"I booked a room in a hotel near the street he was living on. The next morning I went to the first beauty salon I found and tidied myself up as best as I could. Trying to look happy and self-confident, I went to the foundation to find him. He wasn't there, so I went to his address, praying to god I wouldn't find him with that woman. He wasn't alone, but he was with Joshua.

"The concierge had called up to say a woman was looking for him, without giving a name, and when he saw me in the entrance hall he froze. He told me that Fleischer was in the apartment, and we left for a nearby café.

"All my self-confidence was gone and I pleaded with him. He'd never been in a situation like that before and was embarrassed and didn't know what to do. He kept asking me to understand, claiming that he thought our relationship had ended before he left for Europe.

"In short, I made a scene. In the end, I managed to calm down and I realized yet again how happy I felt being with him, even under those circumstances. I asked him whether he was in love with that girl, whether they were lovers. He neither denied it nor admitted it, so I still didn't know the nature of their relationship.

"There's no point in my boring you with the details … He continued with his explanations and excuses, I insisted that our separation would be a huge mistake. I lied to him about having some business to settle in Paris, so I stayed there for a few more days and followed him. He met Simone and I was already sure they were head over heels in love with one another. I can't have been in my right mind. I was terribly ashamed of what I was doing, but like I said, I couldn't help myself.

"In any case, I'd dropped everything at my company, handing them some preposterous excuses, and I was wandering through a large foreign city like a ghost, constantly asking myself what I was doing there. I'm not even sure whether I deduced certain things afterwards or whether I merely imagined them. My entire life I'd been a cerebral creature who had obeyed her reason, and all of a sudden I'd turned myself into a lost woman who was behaving in a way demeaning to her status."

I had a strange sense of *déjà vu*. It was as if I were in Maine again, on Joshua Fleischer's estate, listening once again to that long-gone story, told this time from a different angle, by a different character.

"The man who had asked me to recommend somebody for the foundation was Pierre Zolner. He taught at the Poly-technic. I was sure that if Abe lost the foundation job, he would come back to the States. So I wrote a slanderous letter, denouncing Abe and Fleischer, and sent it to Zolner anonymously. Later Zolner called me and informed me that despite his respect and friendship for me, the foundation had been forced to withdraw the initial offer.

"I went home and resumed my life. I refused to think about Abe for a while. He never contacted me again, and I didn't try to get in touch with him. By chance, although the details aren't important, in the late eighties I met somebody from Baton Rouge who knew the Hales well. He told me that Abraham's father had been overcome with grief when he'd happened to see his son walking down the street, in Los Angeles. When he'd called out to him, Abe pretended not to hear. I knew that he'd never loved his father, so I wasn't really surprised that he'd broken off all contact with him.

"What you told me today is very sad, Dr. Cobb. I realize now that out of pure spite, I may have ruined everything and destroyed Abe's life. If I hadn't sent that letter, maybe he'd have lived happily with that woman, instead of coming back here to die alone in a mental hospital."

I understood that she'd come to the end of her story. For a while we just sat there saying nothing. She looked exhausted, and I had the unpleasant feeling that I'd upended an old lady's dresser drawers, rummaging through her lingerie. Then she asked me, "Well, Dr. Cobb, have you found the answers you were looking for?"

"To be honest, no," I said. "I don't know what the nature of the relationship between those two men and Miss Duchamp was, because Mr. Fleischer told me something completely different. And I didn't find out what exactly happened after Mr. Hale lost his job. Mr. Fleischer was adamant that he couldn't remember anything about what happened one particular night. That's why he came to me. And the circumstances surrounding Miss Simone Duchamp's disappearance are still unclear."

"Fleischer probably lied," she said calmly. "Would it be any wonder? That man was a murderer. As time has gone by, I've become more and more convinced that he killed my husband."

"But why then did he hire me and risk everything coming out under hypnosis?"

"Perhaps for credibility, Dr. Cobb. He probably faked the trance. I don't know what conclusion you came to with him, but it was probably one that completely exculpates him. Or else maybe he was looking for a way to confess his sins and ease his conscience before he died. But it was all so predictable, wasn't it? The rich boy, who gets even richer, becomes a respectable member of society, despite his past transgressions. And the poor boy ended up resigned to being a nonentity, forgotten, even insane.

"Abe had a vast mind, which he was hesitant to use because of the thick layer of prejudices and frustrations he carried with him. He was almost a genius but, unlike Fleischer, his self-esteem had been completely destroyed since childhood, probably because of his father's behavior. Abe and that girl paid the price, while Fleischer blithely went on with his life. But it's always the weakest and the kindest who take the fall, isn't it so? I'd have liked to see Abraham happy and fulfilled. Instead, I was as cruel to him as everyone else he met."

We stood up.

The sun had been smothered again by heavy, basalt-colored clouds. I pictured the woman in front of me being eaten away year after year by questions, obsessions, and regrets, frozen in a particular time and place.

"I'm not sure why I agreed to speak to you and tell you what I told you," she said, without looking at me. "As someone once put it, the past is another country. But to be honest, I've always been confused about what really happened back then. A story has a beginning, a middle, and an ending. In this case, I can understand and accept the beginning and even the middle, but the ending has never made sense to me. So probably I was hoping that you'd be able to offer me that ending that I've missed."

"I'm sorry, Mrs. Gregory, I'm not capable of doing that, at least not yet. But I'm pretty sure that Mr. Fleischer wasn't involved in your husband's death. If he'd committed a felony murder in cold blood back then, he wouldn't have been eaten alive by his dilemma about one particular night in Paris. Maybe he did a few bad things in his youth, but nothing of that sort. But I can't say the same thing about Mr. Hale. Unfortunately, I'm not sure he could tell fantasy from reality and right from wrong."

"But I'm sure, Dr. Cobb, because I knew him well, with all due respect. Will you stay for lunch?" she asked politely. There was no trace of warmth in her voice.

"No, thank you, I have to get back to New York. I'm sorry for having taken up so much of your time."

"Then goodbye, Dr. Cobb," she said, extending a hand that was firm and cold. "Thanks for visiting me and take good care of yourself. You give me the impression of a man groping through a crypt."

I shook her hand and got in the car. She remained standing by the bench, clutching her coat around her shoulders. Before I drove away, she called out to me and I cracked the window. "Dr. Cobb, you probably know the answer to a question that torments me: Why do people lie?"

"Out of fear, mostly," I answered. "More often than not, a lie is a means of defense, Mrs. Gregory. Or sometimes they do it in hope of a reward."

"You're right, Dr. Cobb. Never forget the answer you just gave me."

I started the engine and reversed to turn around. She was still standing in the same spot, her white hair fluttering.

# eighteen

THAT AFTERNOON, I struggled to finish writing an article I'd promised to send to a magazine in Chicago. My mind was occupied with that story and my thoughts about Julie's farewell note which Josh had sent me, so it was difficult to concentrate on anything else.

I did a search through my computer and looked through some old files. I nailed together all the information I'd gathered about Julie during our sessions. I listened to a couple of audio files and I read some notes I'd written back then. There was something that made me uneasy while I listened to one of the audio files, but I couldn't quite place it. I listened to the recording one more time, with the same result, and so I gave it up for the moment.

While searching through those files, I came across the name and address of a friend of Julie's. Every patient has to give a contact person in case of emergency. Julie had chosen to give me Susan Dressman's name rather than her parents'. I sat for a long time at my desk, trying to pluck up the courage to call her, both hoping and fearing that her cellphone number was still the same.

She answered straightaway and seemed surprised by my call, but immediately remembered who I was and agreed to meet me in the city, at a café named Gino's on East 38th Street.

When I got there, two hours later, only two tables were

taken: one by Susan, who had already ordered herself a salad, and the other one by an elderly couple. I recognized her immediately, though I'd only ever seen her once, when I'd accompanied her and Julie to the opera. She'd lost weight and changed her hairstyle, but she had the same ironic, self-confident eyes, and the set of her mouth seemed to suggest that life is just a long series of insipid occurrences. She recognized me too, and waved as soon as I entered.

I wasn't hungry, so I just ordered an espresso. As the coffee machine was beginning its loud monotonous buzz behind the counter, she said, "When I saw you in the doorway, I told myself that you haven't aged at all. But now I can see you've got some white hairs, and I'd bet good money you didn't have them when we met—how many years ago was it?"

"Three," I answered. "The year when Julie ..."

"I still can't believe she's gone," she confessed. She spoke quickly and avoided eye contact. "Sometimes I find myself wondering what she's up to and why she hasn't called. For me she was always so full of life ... I was never able to think of Julie as a person ... with problems."

The waiter brought my coffee. I poured in some sugar and stirred. Susan had finished her salad and pushed the plate aside.

"What do you want from me, James?" she asked, looking for something in her purse, which was on the chair next to her. "I assume you didn't call me just to catch up."

"These last few days I've been going through the notes in Julie's file and—"

"That doesn't sound good," she warned. She zipped up her purse and looked me in the eye for the first time. "Julie's file, I mean. Julie wasn't a file. She was one of the most wonderful people I've ever met, and also one of my best friends."

"I didn't mean it to sound like that," I apologized. "She

meant a lot to me too. She wasn't just another patient."

Two red blotches appeared high on her cheekbones. She said slowly, "I was wondering whether you'd bring that up. Julie told me what was going on between you. I thought it was strange, but after all you were both single and it was your business what you were doing. But a shrink is supposed to be ethical and keep a professional distance, not get it on with his patients between sessions. I wondered what kind of man would take advantage of the power he inevitably held over such a vulnerable person to make her take her underwear off."

I was taken aback by her language and the hostility I could read in her gaze.

"And my answer," she went on, "was that such a man must be an utter scumbag. And that he should be prevented from doing the same thing to other female patients. Cliff, her father, called me that night. He showed me her suicide note and asked me if I knew the man the letter was addressed to, because she hadn't mentioned a name. I knew about you, so I told him who you are and urged him to take legal action against you. That was my idea, you know."

I wanted to be anywhere in the world except there with her.

"I found out about the letter she left for me by chance a little while ago," I said. "I thought that perhaps you could answer a couple of questions ... That's why I looked you up."

She signaled to the waiter, "A cappuccino, please. Don't flatter yourself. I'm not even sure she really was in love with you. But what I do know is that you behaved like a jerk."

She sipped her coffee and gazed at me over the rim of the cup.

"I don't want to be here with you, speaking about Julie. I agreed to meet with you because I was very curious about what you wanted from me. Now I know that meeting you was a mistake. I still feel a distinct need to do you harm. Perhaps you, in your wisdom, have a term for what I'm feeling, but I'm not interested. Goodbye. I think it's a terrible thing that you're still practicing and playing with people's minds. But shit happens every day, doesn't it?"

She was so angry she could barely get the words out.

"I was doing my job, Susan. Which is just that, raking through my patients' minds, regardless of how dreadful, dirty, or tragic what I find there might be, regardless of how hidden away things are in the basement closet. I'm trying to help."

"But seducing your patients isn't part of your job, damn you!" she said, raising her voice.

The spoon of the man at the other table froze halfway between his mouth and his bowl of soup.

"I know that and I'll regret what happened my entire life. But about that letter, there's something that …"

She glared at me. "What the hell do you think you're doing? Are you interrogating me now? Do you think I'm one of your patients? Do you want me to lift my skirt up for you too, is that it?"

I placed a twenty on the table and got up. "Goodbye, Susan. Sorry to have bothered you."

"Don't ever dare to call me again."

"I won't."

When I called Claudette Morel back, she answered with a much calmer and friendlier tone of voice and asked me to let her know as soon as I arrived in France. She told me that she was retired and had all the time in the world, abandoning her previous lie about having to consult her busy diary.

I booked a flight for the following week and checked to see whether the Hotel Le Meridien still existed. It was still in business and had recently been renovated. I made an online reservation for three nights. The thought that I was going to be sleeping there gave me a strange feeling, as if I were planning to spend the night in a haunted mansion.

That evening, I took a pen and a pad and sat down at the desk in my apartment, as darkness descended on the city in an icy wave.

This is what I knew. Simone had been murdered that night, and immediately after that, Josh renounced the entire fortune his parents had left him and went to Mexico for a couple of years. Abraham dropped out of sight for a while, and returned to the States under an assumed name. He too renounced everything, including his identity. In Fleischer senior's will there was a clause stipulating that if Josh was involved in any violent act against a woman, he'd have to forfeit his entire inheritance. It was logical to assume that he might have donated his money to the White Rose because he felt guilty, and wanted to respect his father's final wish.

I wrote out ABRAHAM HALE in capital letters, underlined it, and focused on the name.

He began a relationship with Simone Duchamp immediately after he moved to Paris. Most likely, his psychosis was already festering at the time. Josh's arrival in France brought about a major problem in the relationship. Josh's version: he and Simone fell in love with each other. The version suggested by Abraham in his diary and vaguely confirmed by Elisabeth Gregory: Abraham and Simone were deeply in love with each other and Josh tried to destroy their relationship out of pure spite. He never really loved Simone, but he was jealous of their happiness.

But why did he tell me a different story? Why did Abraham change his name and completely abandon his previous life? Neither Josh nor Abraham had been considered suspects by the French authorities, so they had no reason to be afraid of consequences for what had happened in Paris.

On the other hand, it seemed bizarre to me that

Simone's parents had never suggested to the French police that Josh and Abraham might have been involved in their daughter's disappearance. Had they informed the police, the boys would have been treated as persons of interest or suspects, so they'd have been questioned or even taken into custody for a couple of days at least. But it looked like the parents had done next to nothing when it came to Josh and Abraham. Or maybe they had, but the police—God knows why—hadn't followed up on the lead.

While I was rolling all the questions around in my mind, I once again had the distinct feeling that I was ransacking an old manor full of ghosts, the walls of which were ready to come crashing down on me at any moment.

When I was a child, somewhere on the outskirts of my hometown, right by the cemetery, there was a deserted two-story house. It was overrun with weeds, reaching almost as high as the broken roof, which rain and heat had turned black. The front yard was a miniature jungle behind the rotten planks of a ramshackle fence.

Teenagers used the derelict house as a den, holing up there to do pot, to make out, or just to drink beer and get away from the grownups. Tom, a red-haired boy who was two years older than me, claimed that he'd made out with May LaSalle in there and that They Went All The Way; but no one believed the biggest liar in the county, because nobody had been inside the Hogarth house since 1974.

Local legend had it that the three-bedroom house had been the setting for some horrifying and strange events, not long after the family that built it left town. In the late sixties, Caleb Hogarth, his wife, and their three kids left abruptly one night, leaving a note for the sheriff. The note said that they were headed out to California and asked him to keep an eye on the property. No one ever heard from them again after that, and so legally the house and the land couldn't be sold.

It became a haunted house, a place where drunks and hobos took shelter from time to time. But they would never have lingered inside for very long, even if the sheriff and his deputies hadn't chased them away. Old alkies, teenage rebels, thieves trying to scavenge old pieces of furniture or brass light fittings—they all came out of that house scared stiff, claiming to have seen ghosts, bloodstains on the walls, bodies hanging from the rotten roof beams. They heard eerie sounds and felt cold hands touching their faces.

But the most terrifying event was to take place in the fall of seventy-four.

Mrs. Wilbur, an accountant at Rubin and Associates at the time, used to walk her dog in the area. She lived on Crackly Meadow, not far from the derelict house. She also used to visit the cemetery to chat with the late Mr. Wilbur, who had died five years earlier.

One day she was walking her dog by the Hogarth house. The poodle—whose name history hasn't recorded—wriggled out of his collar and jumped through a hole in the fence straight into the yard and disappeared from her sight. She entered the yard and called for him, but he was nowhere to be seen. She thought she heard him whimpering somewhere inside the house, and she went after him.

She was found about half an hour later by a passerby. She was able to speak about what she'd seen and experienced in the house only after the doctors had stitched up fifteen wounds, which were all over her body, given her half a gallon of blood, put a cast on her right leg, which was broken in three places, and tended to her burst lips and black eyes.

Mrs. Wilbur swore that the person who had attacked her was none other than her late husband, Sylvester. When she entered the Hogarth house, he was sitting on a chair at the living room table, with his elbows resting against the wooden tabletop. He was wearing the same blue suit he'd been buried in, and for a couple of seconds he didn't seem to notice the intruder frozen by the door, who was all but having a heart attack.

Then Mr. Wilbur took note of her presence, grinned at her, stood up, and beat her to a pulp. The woman remembered crawling out into the yard, then into the street, where she fainted.

The doctors said that the cuts seemed to have been inflicted with a very sharp object, and it was a miracle that no major artery had been severed.

There had been long debates about post-traumatic shock, about vagrants wandering through our peaceful county, and about the sheriff not doing his job. The local newspaper ran a story on the incident, along with an entire page of messages from readers. Some of them asked that the late Mr. Wilbur should be exhumed to see whether he had become a zombie or whether he'd turned himself into a vampire.

That's the place I went to one August evening, when I was fourteen and in love with a girl named Marsha Johnson. She was eager to check out the haunted house, so I didn't want to miss an opportunity to prove my guts.

So that evening, at around nine, we were in front of the Hogarth house and, honestly, I almost wet my underwear. I'd always been afraid of the dark, and the ghost stories were giving me goose bumps. Once, after I'd read some short stories by Edgar Allan Poe, I'd had nightmares for weeks. Had Marsha asked me to jump from a three-story building, it would have been easier to do it.

We sneaked inside through the planks of the ruined fence and tiptoed across the front yard up to the cracked front door, which wasn't locked. I was covered in sweat and my throat turned dry immediately.

What happened next still isn't clear to me. I remember that we walked into an almost completely dark living room and turned on the flashlight I had brought along, and which almost instantaneously went off. I opened it up and wiggled the batteries, unscrewed the casing and wound the bulb. Nothing—it was completely useless. In those few moments we managed to glimpse a few pieces of furniture with coverings on them that seemed like a dead body's shroud, and the large cracks in the floorboards.

We groped our way to what turned out to be a door leading to a staircase that looked like the spine of one of those huge dinosaur fossils you see in the natural science museums. The only good part was that Marsha was holding my hand for the first time so we wouldn't get separated. The floorboards creaked deeply with each step, and the remains of a curtain fluttered over the missing shutters. There was a wooden table in the middle of the living room, its legs sunken halfway into the rotten floor. It smelled like rats and mold, like old clothing and spoiled pickles. I knocked down an empty bottle with my foot and it rolled over into the wall. We were stepping on broken glass, carton waste, splinters of wood, and empty cans.

We reached the stairs and I was getting ready to climb the first step, wondering whether it was solid enough to carry my weight, when I saw something. Not on the stairs, but somewhere to the left, where there was a hallway leading to the basement.

I've never really been able to recall what I saw in that moment. I couldn't describe it or, better said, I forgot it the very next second. My mind had probably been unable to process what my eyes had seen.

People divide time into seconds, minutes, hours, days, weeks, months, years, centuries, and millennia. But there are minuscule intervals, so small that they practically don't even exist to us. Such a time "particle" can't be seen with the eyes, perceived with the mind or placed somewhere in the stamp catalogue of our senses.

It would have been easy to tell you that I saw a ghost clattering in its chains or a zombie with an axe shoved in his head or a one-eyed hairy giant. But what I saw was a million times worse, more horrific and dreadful than all those things put together—that's why it has no name and can't be captured in words. Not even in nightmares.

I only know that I completely froze. I tried in vain to scream, and then I ran away, not even caring about Marsha anymore. I remember tripping like a ball over a step and falling down on the dirty floor. I tumbled over and the cuffs of my pants got tangled up in the bushes. I only stopped running when I reached the park, in front of the city hall. It took over an hour before I was able to stand up from that wooden bench and go home. I mumbled an excuse to my parents, went up to my room, and slept for weeks with the lights on and a folding knife under my pillow.

I don't know whether Marsha had seen something or not, because we didn't see each other afterwards. And I never tried to remember precisely what I saw that evening, because I knew it would have been in vain. I only know that I asked myself for years why I had to go inside the Hogarth house and what kind of sick curiosity prompted me to do it, apart from my great love for Dan Johnson's daughter. Or, more exactly, why, once inside, did I become aware of that thing that was lurking in the darkness, as if it was waiting for me and only for me. I may not remember what I saw that night. But from then on, I knew that there are things far worse than death, and that each of us has their own one-of-a-kind nightmare.

I remembered what Julie had once told me: "You've picked the most dangerous profession in the world. One day, while you're raking through those dark places, you'll come upon a monster that will gobble you up in the blink of an eye, before you even realize what's going on. If I were a ghost hunter like you, I'd be more careful."

I went to the bathroom, took a shower, and then fell back asleep, leaving the bedside lamp on.

In the morning, I switched on my laptop and checked my emails. In my inbox I found a new message from Mallory. One of his researchers had come across some new information about Abraham Hale. It was a story that ran in a local newspaper in Louisiana back in the early sixties. The scan was attached and read like this:

*The Mirror*, September 4, 1962

## Recent murder case possibly connected to five-year-old kidnapping

by Randal Cormier and Olima Landry

According to a source close to the police, the murder that recently shattered the quiet community of Credence Creek might be related to a kidnapping case. Three years ago, a local boy named Abraham Hale, aged five at the time, was kidnapped and held for more than two weeks at an unknown location.

Abraham was born in Credence Creek, a township about twenty miles from Baton Rouge. His father is a salesman and during the fall fishing season works on a shrimp boat. His mother is a housewife. Abraham is the couple's only child.

At around seven o'clock on August 14, 1959, Mrs. Hale realized that her son had vanished from their front porch, where he'd been playing just minutes before. Mr. Hale was out of town on business and after looking for her son in the surrounding area, she called the police. It was as if the ground had swallowed him up.

The authorities carried out an extensive operation for several days and nights—the Sheriff's Office in Albert

County, Louisiana State Police, and even federal agents were involved in the search—but there was no trace of the child. Kidnapping for ransom was deemed unlikely given the family's financial circumstances, and detectives concluded that the boy had probably wandered into the swamp, about three hundred yards from the Hales' home, and either drowned or been eaten by gators. After a week, the search was called off. Pictures of little Abraham remained pasted up all over town. Neighbors and acquaintances described the Hales as a quiet, reclusive family, with no known problems.

Two weeks later, on September 4th, Abraham was found wandering in Mulberry Park by some passersby who alerted the police.

The boy was wearing new clothes, the labels of which had been carefully removed. A medical examination concluded that he showed no traces of physical violence, nor had he been abused in any way. He had been well fed. The authorities stated that somebody had been looking after him during the missing period.

For days, the police, his parents, and a psychologist from the county general hospital tried to get the boy to speak, but all he would say was that he remembered somebody had come up to him on the porch while he was playing and that he couldn't recall anything else.

Four days ago, the body of a white adult male was discovered in the swamp a short walk from the Hales' house. He was wearing a black leather jacket and jeans, and had drowned two days before, a suspicious occurrence, given that the county has been experiencing a severe drought and the water level is very low. "It's like the guy drowned in a puddle," Sheriff Donoghue said.

At the autopsy, the medical examiner discovered that the victim had been hit over the back of his head with a blunt object. Detectives suspect that he may have gone to the edge of the swamp to relieve himself, before being hit from behind by an unknown aggressor. He lost consciousness, fell, and drowned in just a couple of inches of water. The man still had fifty-five dollars in his pocket, ruling out robbery as a motive.

The victim, in what has now become a murder investigation, turned out to be Eloi Lafarge, a vagrant who spent most of his life in and out of prison, with a long list of convictions including sexual assaults against minors. He recently moved to the area from New Orleans and was living in a caravan on the other side of the town.

The police think that there might be a connection between Abraham's disappearance, three years ago, and the death of the man near the Hales' home. A source confirmed that Mr. Hale was brought in for questioning. "It was a simple interview rather than an interrogation," our source stressed, "and Mr. Hale was cooperative and responded to all our questions. He does not have an alibi for the evening of the murder."

We'll be bringing you news of further developments as the investigation continues.

Mallory had added a postscript:

I don't know whether this piece of information is important or not, but it looks like Hale Sr. didn't believe his son. He thought that Abraham was lying and remembered everything that had happened. The guy was a violent alcoholic, who abused his family. He put pressure on his son to get him to tell the truth. Eventually, Mrs. Hale filed a complaint with the police and they gave him a caution. The police never found out who killed Lafarge and whether the guy had been involved in the kidnapping.

I also found something very interesting about the old man, Lucas Duchamp. I'll try to call you later today.

Mallory

He called me at about ten, told me about the information he'd uncovered, and gave me the phone number of a man named François Garnier, who back in the seventies had worked for the DGSE, the French secret service.

I phoned Garnier that evening and had a long talk with him. After a rambling introduction, he told me what he knew about Lucas Duchamp. He kept insisting that none of what he told me should be made public, and I assured him yet again that I intended nothing of the sort.

I spent the rest of the evening checking online a few details about the piece of information Garnier had given to me, and the next day I left for France.

# nineteen

I LANDED IN PARIS at 8:35 a.m., having finished the last fifty pages of an entirely predictable crime novel, watched two movies, and eaten a terrible meal. The weather was dreadful: a cold rain and biting wind whipped across the city. After I passed through passport control and collected my luggage, I had to wait for fifteen minutes in a long line before I finally got a cab.

I'd visited the city a few times before, the last time being a year and a half previously. There were few places I liked at first sight as much as I did Paris, and I can still remember the impression the bridges over the Seine, the large plazas, and the historic monuments had on me the first time. On the journey from the airport, I looked out the window of the metallic green Renault Scenic, trying to relive the sensation of that first encounter.

But all I saw were the streams of water furiously lashing the wide boulevards, through which people and cars darted like fugitives. I didn't even realize when we arrived at the hotel. We pulled up in front of a tall building and the driver turned and said, "Le Meridien, monsieur."

The reception desk was at the left of the entrance and I had to wait another ten minutes for my turn. I went up to my room and stored my things in the closet by the bed. I took a shower, changed my clothes, and went down to the bar on the ground floor, which was just opening. The breakfast room opposite was crowded, and it looked like the hotel, although huge, was probably almost fully booked.

In my imagination, the hotel from Josh and Abraham's story looked more like an old mansion on a mysterious street, covered in ivy and crammed with secrets. Instead, I found myself in a modern building fitted with dark marble and stainless steel, and I wondered whether I might have come to the wrong place.

I ordered a coffee and drank it slowly, chatting with a young bartender with a golden ring in his right earlobe. The hotel first opened in the early seventies and had gone through a couple of renovations, he told me. It was always full, thanks to the fact that it was near the Palais des Congrès, where there were conferences almost every day. I asked him whether he knew of any dark tales connected with the building's past, and he asked me if I was a journalist.

"I'm a psychiatrist," I said.

"Oh, I see ... You Americans have an interesting term for people in that trade—*shrimp*?"

"The word you're looking for is *shrink*."

"Right, shrink. Well, I've been in the business for eight years now and I've worked in a number of hotels. Every place has its own story. Two years ago, a woman committed suicide here. Her lover, who was a famous singer from Spain, had left her, so she booked herself into a suite and jumped out the window. Management kept it quiet, because stories like that can drive customers away. But people quickly forget unpleasant things. We have short memories, don't we? And of course there was also the story of those twin girls who were murdered with an axe by their crazy father ..."

I looked at him in amazement. "What twins?"

He laughed. "I'm joking. I remembered an old movie with Jack Nicholson, *The Shining*, about a big hotel up in the mountains."

"I've seen it, it's a very good movie," I replied, and signed the bill. "See you later, take care."

★

I called Claudette Morel and told her I'd arrived in Paris. She gave me the address of a café and invited me to meet her there at twelve o'clock.

I had two hours to kill, so I left the hotel for a walk. I went right, passed a pub called the James Joyce, which wasn't open yet, and arrived in a small plaza with heated sidewalk cafés covered with awnings. The rain turned to bone-chilling sleet. I headed toward the Champs-Elysées, and stopped in front of a café with a front terrace called Le Madrigal. The place was heated and I sat down at a table.

It was full of people laden with shopping bags, many of them with that dazed, contented air of people on vacation, a stream of passersby flowing along the pavement and gazing at the window displays. Not far away, the Arc de Triomphe looked like a large gray hound crouching ready to pounce.

I ordered a coffee and thought about Simone, Josh, and Abraham.

I imagined them meeting in a place like the one I was in and pictured Abraham's reaction when he read for the first time in Josh's eyes that he had more than a friendly interest in the woman he'd fallen in love with. Cain's motive for killing Abel was jealousy—Abel's offerings were more pleasing to the Lord than his own. But in that case, who had fallen in love with whom, and who had been jealous of whom? Somewhere, in a big city shining like a diamond, three destinies had intersected and mingled forever. Whether in pain or love wasn't important—too often the two words mean one and the same thing.

A blonde girl dressed in a burgundy-and-blue school uniform bent down, picked up something from the pavement, and walked away, absorbed in her cellphone. I finished my coffee, stood up, and headed for the cabstand across the boulevard.

\*

I was quickly able to pick Ms. Morel out. She was sitting alone at a table on the pavement, dressed in a green raincoat which she hadn't taken off, her frizzy hair pushed back with a couple of bobby pins. Although she was wearing a lot of makeup, it was obvious that the passing years hadn't been forgiving.

"Ms. Morel?" I asked, and she gave a nod. "I'm Dr. James Cobb, pleased to meet you."

I sat down at the table, on a chair upholstered in red artificial leather, while she studied me carefully, sizing me up with her light brown eyes.

"Pleased to meet you too. You must be very interested in this story to have come all this way for it," she said and then pointed at the menu. "Your first time in France?"

"No, I've been here a few times. Thank you once again for agreeing to meet with me, Ms. Morel."

"Please call me Claudette. May I call you James?"

"Thank you, Claudette. Of course you can."

"Are you married, James? Do you have any children?"

"No, I'm not married."

She already had a glass of amber-colored liquid in front of her. I asked her what she was drinking, and she said, "Calvados, apple brandy. It's a suitable drink in France. If I were ten years younger, I'd show you the Paris that only the real locals know. We'd have hot tea and red wine, a stroll down the Champs-Elysées, and stay up until dawn in a café in Montmartre. But for me those days have long since passed."

I ordered a Calvados, thanking God that she wasn't ten years younger.

"Santé," she said theatrically and half-drained her glass.

I tasted the liquid. It was as strong as whiskey but more aromatic. A blackbird landed near the table and gazed at us with its beady black eyes and then took flight, vanishing into the sky. An ambulance siren could be heard in the distance, like a bad omen.

"Well, James, you haven't told me yet why you're so interested in this," she said.

"The whole affair's very intriguing. I'm sure that Laura and her parents did everything they could in order to find out what happened to Simone, didn't they?"

Her face suddenly darkened and her mood changed, as often happens with drunks. She finished her drink and then fumbled through her handbag, which was on the chair next to her, took out a pack of cigarettes and lit one of them, smearing its filter with lipstick.

"Laura and I weren't just schoolmates, but the best of friends," she said, while looking at the waiter and pointing at her glass. "We always kept each other warm, because in our lives it was always winter."

She suddenly went silent, as if she'd forgotten what she meant to say, drank her second drink in a single go, and looked around her primly. The table was very close to a heater and it was warm, but she didn't seem to notice, wrapped up in her shabby coat.

"I'm desperate, James. Two years ago, a friend of mine persuaded me to mortgage my apartment and invest the money in a business that came to nothing. He vanished after that, and now I barely have enough to get by. My husband died fifteen years ago, I don't have children, brothers or sisters, and so I'm all by myself. I live hand to mouth and it won't be long before I will be thrown out onto the street. I couldn't bear such a thing. I don't deserve to spend the last years of my life in a cheap old people's home because I was stupid enough to trust a friend."

Her accent was getting thicker the more she drank, and it was harder and harder to understand her. She ordered another drink and I realized that I'd have to work fast: at the rate she was going, in another half hour or so she'd be stone drunk. I noticed that she was wearing an old gold watch on her left wrist, probably a family heirloom.

"Do you know what happened to Mrs. Claudia Duchamp, Simone's mother?"

"She died in the late eighties, from peritonitis. I found out later from my mother, who had been in touch with one of the Duchamps' neighbors. We weren't even invited to attend the funeral. I understood that she'd been feeling sick, but refused to see the doctor. When she eventually did, it was too late, she already had septicemia. I don't know why Laura refused to talk to me all these years. We were like sisters."

She lit another cigarette and asked me, "Now, might you be willing to offer some money for the information I have, James? Are you rich, like Fleischer? You probably don't know this, but a few months ago I called him and sent him a letter. I must admit: I asked him for money, I knew he had plenty of it. And I was sure that he didn't want anybody else to find out what I know."

I told myself that she must have sent the letter around the same time Josh hired me, so her call must have been the catalyst for his last desperate attempt to remember what happened that night.

"When precisely did you call him?"

"Four or five months back, in the fall ... I think it was in September. He probably thought I was just an old woman who wasn't worth paying any attention to. We talked on the phone once, but after that he refused to speak to me. A man called Walter, who was very rude, told me to stop calling."

"Mr. Fleischer was very ill."

"I know, you told me, but if he'd wanted to help me, it would have been very simple for a wealthy man like him. If I hadn't been so desperate, I'd never have asked him for help. Not him, never, because ... So, what do you think? Are you willing to pay?"

"I'd like to know what you have to say first."

She grinned and winked at me. "Do you think that's how it works? Do you think I'm some stupid old woman you can ply with drinks so that she'll talk?"

"No, I don't think that. But I have to know how important and valuable what you have to tell me is, before we discuss anything else."

"Do you think I'm afraid of you?" she snapped. "You look like a hitman, not like a real doctor. Have you come here to intimidate me, to tell me to keep my mouth shut?"

"Not at all. I just want you to tell me what you know, and then we can discuss the money."

For a few seconds she seemed to be bracing herself. A beam of sunlight bashed her face; beneath her makeup, her nose and cheeks were covered by a scribbly pattern of tiny red-blue veins, like a small-scale, clumsy reproduction of a Jackson Pollock painting.

She looked around her, as if afraid that somebody might overhear us, waved her cigarette at me, and said, "Well, it's about those boys, Abraham Hale and Joshua Fleischer."

"Alright …"

"Do you think that one of them was involved in Simone's disappearance or that maybe they did whatever they did together?"

"I don't know, Claudette. I'm here to find out what happened that night."

"Abraham wouldn't have hurt a fly, but Fleischer … Did he confess to anything before he died?"

"He claimed he didn't remember much about what happened on that night."

"He lied to you!"

She'd raised her voice, and she cautiously looked around her again.

"I'm sure he knew exactly what happened and—"

I interrupted her, "Before we go on, I'd like to ask you

something: which of the two was Simone's lover?"

"What do you mean? Neither of them, they were just friends, nothing more than friends. The boys had fallen for Simone, that's true, because she was very beautiful, but she didn't encourage them in any way."

"Mr. Fleischer said that he and Simone were lovers."

"No way, James, I'm sure about that. For Simone it was nothing but a game. You know, two tall and handsome American boys, head over heels in love with her, who were sending her flowers and courting her ... She enjoyed it, but there was nothing more than a flirt."

"Mr. Fleischer also claimed that Abraham was drinking heavily during that period."

"That's another lie. I never saw Abraham so much as tipsy, but I saw Fleischer potted a couple of times."

"Why did the foundation withdraw Abraham's job offer? Do you remember that episode?"

"Yes, of course I do, I was working there, as I told you ... As far as I remember, they had received an anonymous letter full of compromising information about him. Simone was upset and hinted that Abraham had told her who had sent the letter: an ex-girlfriend of Abraham's from America. She told me that Abraham didn't think he stood to lose very much and decided to go off to Mexico."

"Was the letter only about Abraham?"

"It was about both of them, I guess. I'm not positive that Simone knew what exactly was in the letter, because she refused to speak to me about it, so I found out all this mostly in snatches from Laura. She liked Fleischer and told me that while I was in Lyon for my mother's birthday, he'd given her a very nice present, a jewel, I guess. And then everything blew up: Simone disappeared and Laura went to that hospital in Switzerland."

She whined like a sick animal, in a way that gave me goose bumps.

"I knew they were bad news, those boys! I knew that something bad was going to happen, James! May I have another drink, please? You haven't finished yours, don't you like it?"

I finished my drink and called the waiter. Her mood had changed yet again, and she smiled. "Now let me tell you a couple of things about that family ..."

Claudia Duchamp, Simone and Laura's mother, was born in Paris and got married at a very young age to a charming con man by the name of Antonio Maillot. That was back in the early fifties, when life was still very hard in France in the aftermath of the war. Claudia had numerous siblings and her family wasn't very well off. Antonio had promised her the moon and had asked her to move to Marseille. After she did, he squandered the little money she'd received from her parents and vanished four years later, abandoning her and their two little children. She went back home, not having anywhere else to go, but she received a cold welcome. I understand that Simone's grandma suffered from severe neurosis, and living with her wasn't easy at all.

Then Prince Charming turned up, in the form of a lawyer by the name of Lucas Duchamp.

He was eleven years her senior and considerably wealthy. He'd managed to keep his fortune almost intact during the war. While in college, he'd become a member of the Resistance and had been captured and tortured by Klaus Barbie himself, the famous war criminal known all over the world as "the Butcher of Lyon."

Even though he was very young at the time, he refused to speak. So in the end, more dead than alive, he'd been handed over to the local authorities to be trialed as a traitor. The sentence was death, but he managed to escape with the help of a French police officer who had sensed which way the wind was blowing. He remained in hiding until the Allies were approaching Paris and the Nazis were on the retreat. His parents had been deported to a concentration camp in Poland and died before the end of the war. In the summer of 1944, after the liberation, he was hailed as a national hero. In those days, people weren't as cynical, and deeds like that impressed them. Such heroes restored France's honor after its humiliation at the hands of the Nazis, and doors were opened for them.

As a young man, Lucas Duchamp was handsome, tall, and impeccably attired. He finished his studies and began practicing as an attorney in Paris. A relative looked after his estate in Lyon, which he visited about once a month.

He seemed to be the answer to all the poor woman's troubles. He was kind, rich, and self-assured. What's more, he was head over heels in love with her, courting her the old-fashioned way, with flowers, romantic dinners, and discreet gifts. Claudia, who married her first husband just two months after she'd met him, had never experienced anything like it.

Lucas Duchamp had offered to pay the rent on the apartment where she'd been living with her daughters, and also to hire a nanny to take care of the girls so that she could go back to work as a nurse.

A few months after that, Duchamp asked for Claudia's hand in marriage and she accepted.

Moreover, he'd even proposed to adopt her two daughters.

After the wedding, there was an embarrassing episode with Antonio Maillot, like something straight out of *Les Misérables*. Duchamp legally needed the real father's consent in order to formally adopt the girls. He pulled some strings, and the police tracked the guy down somewhere in Provence, where he'd been bleeding some other woman dry. When he realized what was at stake, he milked the situation for all it was worth. He claimed that he was about to look for Claudia, whom, naturally, he still loved, and that he intended to bring up their children. He said he had proof that he'd been corresponding with his daughters' mother and that he frequently sent her money.

Obviously, these were blatant lies, but the man had a talent for that sort of thing and the adoption procedure could have dragged on for months or even years. In the end, Duchamp decided to pay him a large sum of money in order to get his signature for the adoption papers. After grabbing the cash, the loving father vanished and was never seen again.

The girls lived in a wonderful mansion and had everything they needed, because Duchamp proved to be a very generous man. Both of them attended an elite private high school, and later a prestigious university.

But after Simone's disappearance, everything went downhill. Claudia Duchamp died, and five years later Lucas Duchamp had a stroke that put him in a wheelchair for life.

The waiter brought us fresh drinks and Claudette lit another cigarette. She looked drunk and was barely able to speak.

"You know, James, I'm not exactly sure when the rumors began, but I remember that the girls were in high school. We were neighbors at the time and visited each other. People can be mean and envious of others' happiness. To cut a long story short, some of them claimed that Lucas Duchamp's love for his stepdaughters was more than a normal attachment, if you get my meaning. They went as far as to claim that Claudia Duchamp knew about the whole thing, but that she was unwilling to do anything about it, or that she didn't dare, because she was afraid of her husband.

"The sisters weren't really bothered by the stories at the beginning, but the allegations hovered over them like a dark cloud. At one point, people were saying that Laura tried to commit suicide. Later, she told me it wasn't true. She was shy and withdrawn, distrustful of others, and she didn't really have any friends, except for me.

"The truth is that Lucas Duchamp was obsessed with them, especially with Simone. He personally drove her to school every day. If she wanted to go out with friends, the girls had to come pick her up at the house and would be subjected to a thorough interrogation. Sometimes, he'd get in his car and come and check whether she really was where she said she would be. Of course, there were also times when an outdoor bistro she wanted to go to was too crowded or it was raining so she'd go somewhere else. As Laura told me, such incidents were treated like catastrophes and the outcome would be interminable discussions about loyalty and truthfulness.

"You know how children think: whatever adults do is automatically right, because in the mind of a child, grownups are never wrong. So they just thought that their stepfather loved them and took care of them, probably in an exaggerated way sometimes, yes, but with the best intentions."

Things got worse after the girls were offered places at university and went to live in Paris, Claudette stressed.

Every Friday, Lucas Duchamp would be waiting by the door of the lecture hall to take them back home. They weren't allowed to spend a single weekend in Paris, not under any circumstances. And they obeyed. Their mother didn't intervene.

In her senior year, Laura took on a part-time job and shared an apartment with Claudette. Simone had graduated a year previously and was making her way in her career.

"When Abraham and Fleischer arrived in Paris, everything changed," Claudette went on. "They both fell in love with Simone and were arguing with each other all the time. Simone didn't fall for either of them, not really, but she was amused and flattered by the situation. At one point, Simone and Laura invited them to Lyon. The atmosphere was tense, and on top of that, Fleischer did everything he could to transform those days into a living hell. He complained about the room and the food, left the estate in the middle of the night and checked into a hotel in the city, and got drunk every day. Simone was very upset, but Laura strangely accepted his behavior, inventing all kinds of excuses for his blunders. Eventually, Abraham had an argument with Fleischer and left for Paris, but Fleischer spent another couple of days in Lyon with the girls."

She stopped talking and sipped her drink. For a moment, I thought she'd fallen asleep with the cigarette dangling between her fingers.

"You don't get it, do you?" she suddenly asked me, raising her eyebrows.

"I'm not sure I do."

"Simone didn't particularly care about those boys, James. She had other cats to whip, as we say in this country. I mean she was all about her career. It was Laura who was trying to get under Fleischer's skin, God knows why. She and Simone were very different from each other, you know … Simone had taken ballet and piano classes, was always confident, and used to spend a lot of money on clothes and trifles. Laura was as beautiful as Simone, but she was an introverted frump with two left feet, plainly dressed, shy and reclusive.

"On top of that, something happened to Laura in that spring. It must have been connected to her father, I think, because suddenly she refused to submit any longer. Each time he'd come to see her or to take her home for the weekend, she'd either avoid him or simply ignore him. She seldom returned to Lyon, and when she did, it was only to see her mother. I asked her what had happened, but she just shrugged and told me that some people pretend to be someone they aren't. She borrowed from the library a pile of books about the Resistance and read them. I told myself it was just a caprice and I minded my own business. I remember that on a Sunday evening she came home with an elderly, one-legged man whom I'd never seen before, and they spent the whole evening together in the kitchen, whispering to each other. When Laura showed him out, she had tears in her eyes. The situation was strange, because up until then we hadn't kept secrets from each other. I didn't have time to resume the discussion, though, because shortly after that she came home one evening very agitated and asked me for help in a crucial matter. I had a very bad feeling from the start, but she was my best friend and I didn't want to let her down, so I accepted."

"What kind of help?"

"I was there that night, James, at the hotel. Let me tell you what happened …"

She told me that both Abraham and Fleischer were putting pressure on Simone. Abraham, who had lost his job at the foundation, was planning to go to Mexico, and he asked Simone to come with him. Fleischer intended to buy an apartment and settle in Paris for a while, so that he and Simone could live together. The game Simone had been playing up until then, flirting with both of them, wasn't a game anymore. Laura and Claudette were following Josh and Simone to see what she was up to. For Claudette it was a kind of adventure: she wasn't sure what was going on, but she was playing detective with her best friend.

When Laura found out that Simone had checked into Le Meriden, she thought her sister was secretly planning something with Joshua. But she was sure that Abraham, who had started behaving increasingly strangely, wouldn't accept such a situation and something bad would happen. By chance, one of the suites next to the one Simone had rented was vacant, so Claudette took it under her name.

The suites were linked by a locked connecting door and Laura bribed the maid so she'd give her the key, in case things took a turn for the worse.

They got there at around five o'clock in the evening and began to wait. Claudette wanted to leave almost immediately, but Laura begged her to stay. They drank some wine from the minibar and smoked a few cigarettes. Three hours later, they heard voices in the room next door and pressed their ears against the connecting door. Fleischer was angry and Simone tried to calm him down. Then Abraham arrived; Laura and Claudette heard his voice, but they couldn't make out the words. Ten minutes later, the doorbell to the other suite rang; it was room service. They couldn't make out what was happening in there for the next two hours or so, but from time to time they could hear snatches of conversation. The door kept opening and closing. Abraham and Joshua must have gotten drunk, because their voices grew increasingly louder. They were arguing with each other.

Claudette didn't look drunk anymore, but exhausted and ill, as if she regretted that she was giving me, a stranger, an all-access-tour ticket for the darkest byways of her life.

"They must have been sitting near the door, because suddenly we heard Simone's voice clearly," she went on. "She laughed and sarcastically mentioned something about her going to Mexico. Fleischer said that Abraham was nothing but a loser, incapable of taking care of himself, let alone Simone."

"I don't know … I looked around me, and the whole situation seemed suddenly grotesque. We stood there, two ridiculous girls, lurking by a hotel room door. Laura was furious and told me to unlock the door between the suites, because she wanted to talk to her sister straightaway. But I refused and left. I went home and tried to sleep. Laura didn't come home the next day or attend any of her classes. I called her mother and she told me that Laura was home, in Lyon, because she had had a nervous breakdown. She refused to put her on the phone. A couple of days later, when I called again, she told me that Simone had disappeared, and Laura had left the country for medical treatment."

"So you don't know what actually happened after you left?"

"No, but those men must have known. I never forgot that night and later, as time went by, I sought information about Abraham and Fleischer. I couldn't find anything about Abraham, but I discovered a lot about Fleischer. That's why I told him in my letter that I'd been there that night and I know what he did. In a way, I've always been angry with myself because I let Laura down when I left her in that hotel room. Probably she never forgave me, because she refused to talk to me after she came back to France. If I had stayed with her, maybe I could have done something to avoid the tragedy."

"After you heard that Simone had disappeared, did you try to contact the police, to tell them what you knew?"

"No, I didn't, and nobody asked me anything."

"Was Laura interviewed by the police? She's not even mentioned in the case file."

"Probably she'd already left the country when Simone was officially reported missing, I don't know ..."

"How much money did you ask Mr. Fleischer for?"

"I asked for a hundred thousand dollars. It hardly meant much to him. Perhaps you regard me as a despicable person, eager to take advantage of a tragedy in order to make money. But don't be quick to judge me too harshly. In my life too many people have done so already. I'm not a bad person, please believe me, and I was totally sincere with you today."

"I promise I'll try to send you some money after I get back to the States," I told her and signaled for the waiter to bring the bill.

She looked at me in amazement and said, "Is that all? Are you leaving? Aren't we going to talk seriously about money?"

She'd raised her voice, and faces from the adjacent tables had turned toward us.

"You've been leading me on, haven't you?"

The waiter brought the bill. I paid with my card, and then I placed a few coins next to the receipt. He thanked me and left, while Claudette was staring at me.

"I don't even know whether you're telling me the truth," I told her and stood up. I put a business card on the table. "That's my email address and phone numbers."

She took the card, gazed at it with her blurry eyes, and thrust it in her purse. "I'll never see you again, right?"

"You never know."

"Can you leave me some money? I'd like to stay here a little longer. I rarely get out."

I took all the euro bills I'd exchanged at the hotel and laid them on the table.

"I'm sorry that this is what I've become," she said and looked away. "I don't know where I went wrong. I lived a good life, but then everything went downhill. You won't think badly of me for trying to get hold of some money, will you?"

"No, I won't. Take care of yourself, Claudette."

"I didn't lie to you. Every single word I've said today is true, please believe me. Maybe I could remember more things …"

"I believe you."

I left, sensing her eyes on the back of my neck. There was a cabstand nearby and I had to wait a few minutes before I was able to hail one. Before getting into the car, I looked back at the terrace, but she'd already gone.

I went to the hotel and stayed in my room the whole evening, skipping dinner. I listened to the unfamiliar noises, closing my eyes and thinking about what had happened in that place forty years ago, almost seeing the outlines of the three players, as young as they were back then, almost teenagers.

It was already clear to me that Josh had told me his side of the story, which was neither true nor entirely false, just as Abraham's jottings were merely some figments of his own delusion rather than a proper diary. But beyond those things, beyond the inherent distortion of facts brought about by the time passing, beyond lies and confusions and errors and subjective perceptions and delusions, there was at least one fact, as solid as a rock: Simone had vanished without a trace that night.

Josh had probably had a violent past in his adolescence, and he'd punished himself by giving up his entire inheritance. Abraham had possibly already been ill in Paris, and he was fighting against the disease that was later to crash his mind completely, turning him into a murderer. Did Mrs. Gregory really leave Paris, as she claimed, after realizing that Abraham was head over heels in love with another woman? Or did she decide, overwhelmed with jealousy and despair, to do something more than send a slanderous letter? Was Lucas Duchamp frightened that Simone, his favorite, would leave the country with one of those American boys who were courting her, even though Claudette had told me that for her it was nothing but an innocent flirtation?

And there was another crucial question: why didn't Lucas Duchamp use his connections to chase down Josh and Abraham? He was obsessed with Simone, so he should have done everything in his power to find out what really happened to her. Did he know something else right off the bat, something that had stopped him from acting as he should have? Did Laura witness something that night, something horrible enough to make her drop out of university and lock herself up for years in a mental clinic?

Gradually, the room became pitch dark and so quiet that I could hear my own breathing. Time and space ceased to exist. While the answers were still hiding from me, I remembered a story from my childhood.

One day, after he got home from work, dad told me to get in the car and we headed out to a kennel on the outskirts of town, next to the Kansas Turnpike. He proudly told me that I was about to witness with my own eyes the secret method dog breeders used when they wanted to pick out the best of a litter of newborn puppies. We were in Kansas, back in the early eighties. I'm not sure whether people still do this nowadays. Probably not.

Dad parked his car under an oak tree, and we walked into a large, grassy enclosure, encircled by a high wooden fence. He smoked a cigarette and talked briefly to an old man—or maybe he just looked old to me at the time. I waited by a barn, examining my surroundings. A strong smell hung in the air, and from inside the barn I could hear dogs barking and whining. Up ahead in the distance, I could see a small pond, its surface glinting in the sunset. About twenty yards from the barn, there was an old camper without wheels, its axles resting on logs.

The man went into the barn and dad said to me, "Come closer, J., he's gonna bring out those puppies."

I walked over to him, but when I was halfway there, I stopped and turned on my heel to see what was happening: one of the dogs inside the barn was whining loudly, in a way I'd never heard before; it was the bitch, whose puppies were being taken away.

There were four of them, each no bigger than a clenched fist, their eyes still closed, and their small heads trembling. Dad's friend walked to the middle of the yard and put them down on the grass. Then I saw him grab a canister of gasoline and I froze.

He poured the liquid around the puppies in a large circle, around five or six yards in diameter, and then he went back into the barn and brought out the bitch, holding her up by the collar. She was a German shepherd, trying hard to escape from his grasp. "Now, Don!" the guy shouted, and dad lit a match and threw it on the grass. In an instant, two things happened: a ring of fire about one foot high shot up around the puppies, and the breeder released the mom.

Without any hesitation, she darted inside the burning ring. She nosed around for two or three seconds, and then grabbed one of the puppies in her teeth by the scruff of its neck and jumped back through the fire.

The breeder put the fire out with an extinguisher, picked up the other puppies, and laid them beside their mom. She worried over them, almost smothering them in her panic. Then the breeder took a small paint sprayer out of his pocket and marked the first puppy with a small red mark.

"That's our champ," dad said. "Would you like to have her? I'll buy her for you, if you want. We can take her home in a couple of weeks, after she's been weaned and had her shots."

I'd never had a dog before and I wasn't really sure whether I wanted one. But I said yes, thinking I'd be protecting the puppy from any other potential cruel experiments, maybe even crueler than the one I'd witnessed.

We took the puppy home a month later. Mom named her Erin, a strange way of paying respect to that environmental activist from Lawrence. She was a good, intelligent dog, and passed away long after I'd left home to go to university.

And just then, surrounded by darkness, in a suite of the very hotel where that young woman died long ago, while all the details of that story were rolling in my mind, I finally saw the big picture and knew what had really happened that night.

Houdini once said that the best magician isn't the one who's capable of producing an elephant from a hat—no man could ever do that—but one who knows how to divert the public's attention as the elephant enters the stage.

This whole time I'd been looking for the elephant rather than the magician.

# twenty

I LEFT FOR LYON in the morning, and it took me over two hours to get there by train, traveling through a monotonous, gray-tinged landscape. It had been raining for a while, but by the time I arrived at the railway station, the sky had cleared. A pale sun and a cluster of clouds lent the surroundings a heavy, sad atmosphere. I took a cab and headed for the Duchamp estate.

When I saw the mansion, I remembered the feeling I'd had in the Hogarth house. The mansion was painted light yellow and lay in a cul-de-sac at the edge of a pine forest. It consisted of a two-story-high central corpus and two adjoining twin smaller buildings of the same color. A large porch at the top of a flight of steps led to the main door, which had a brass mailbox in the middle.

The façade was partially covered in ivy and the white frame windows peered at you through the snaking brown branches like some huge eyes. To the right there was an old barn, and on the left I could see a garden with rose bushes and a few apple trees. The whole property had a gloomy air, an impression which was heightened by the somber sky swathing the place like an old blanket. The silence was as heavy as concrete.

I climbed the steps and rang the doorbell, but nobody answered. As I was getting ready to press the button again, I spied a small blue Renault Clio approaching the house on the dirt road. The car made a turn and stopped by the barn.

An elderly woman stepped out and opened the doors, then parked the car inside. She reemerged from the barn and headed for the house, carrying a transparent plastic bag full of groceries in her left hand.

She noticed me on the porch and came to a halt at the bottom of the steps, looking up at me. She seemed to be around the same age as Claudette Morel, but much better looking, despite her age.

"Hello there," I said, "and sorry to bother you. Are you Ms. Maillot? My name is James Cobb, and I've come from the States with a personal message for you from Mr. Joshua Fleischer."

For a few seconds she didn't say anything, as if she hadn't understood what I'd said, and then she asked me, "Am I supposed to know this gentleman?"

"I know that you and your sister, Simone, met him and his friend, Abraham Hale, in Paris, back in the mid-seventies. Simone and Abraham actually worked together for a few months at a foundation called L'Etoile, as far as I know."

She didn't answer, but started climbing the steps to the entrance. I descended to help her with her groceries. When we arrived in front of the door, she took her bag back and said, "I don't have time to talk to you right now, Mr. Cobb, I'm sorry. My father is ill and I have to look after him. It's not a good time, I'm sure you understand."

She took a complicated brass key from the pocket of her raincoat and unlocked the door.

"Joshua Fleischer died from leukemia, Ms. Maillot," I said. "Abraham is dead too. He passed away in a psychiatric hospital, after he killed a prostitute he was paying to play the role of your sister."

She looked ashen but said nothing, and after a moment's hesitation gestured for me to follow. I went inside and closed the door behind me. I found myself in a spacious hallway, with a marble floor and wood paneling.

"Papa, j'arrive," she yelled. "Nous avons un visiteur! Tout va bien?"

She took off her coat, hung it on a rack, and invited me to do the same with mine. I left my parka and briefcase in the hallway and followed her upstairs.

We crossed a large kitchen and entered a huge living room with a long table in the middle. To the right there was a marble fireplace, and a mahogany buffet to the left. The place was clean, well lit, and looked like a museum, stuffed with antique furniture, paintings, etchings, and panoplies with edged weapons. A man was sitting in a wheelchair close to the fireplace, swathed in a woolen blanket like a mummy.

She rushed over to the man, searched the blanket, and sighed.

"Please wait here for a minute," she told me. "I'm sorry, but I have to change him."

She released the safety catch, pushed the wheelchair into the next room, and closed the tall doors behind her. I sat down on a chair at the table. The floor had been recently polished, and the walls repainted. A large chandelier hung from the ceiling. In one corner there was a small pillow and a half-drunk bowl of water, a cat's nest without a cat. In another corner, I saw a strange shrine: on several wooden shelves there were icons, crucifixes, and a couple of small statuettes, laid out in some mysterious order. In the middle of them, there was a framed photo of a young woman, next to a small oil lamp.

It was very warm and the air was sultry. I stood up and checked the radiators; they were burning hot. From the other side of the doors, I could hear the woman's voice buzzing monotonously, like a bee trapped in a jar.

When she came back, after ten minutes or so, I noticed she'd changed her clothes and was now wearing corduroy trousers and a light woolen sweater. The old man in the wheelchair was tall and round-shouldered and looked so aged you would have sworn he was over a hundred. Despite the heat, he wore a thick calf-length smock, beneath which I could see a pair of pants of the same color. His hair was completely white and covered his skull in long disheveled locks. In the bright light, his face looked like vintage parchment, his eyes sunken deep in his head, staring into empty space.

"We're good now, aren't we, Papa?" she asked him, running her fingers through his hair. "Perhaps we should offer our visitor a glass of wine, what do you think?"

I told her not to bother, but she hurried off to the kitchen, leaving me alone with Lucas Duchamp. I moved my hand up and down in front of his face, but he seemed not to notice, and his eyes didn't follow the movement. His cheeks were covered in dark blotches, and his face was furrowed with deep wrinkles.

She returned carrying a silver tray with two glasses and a carafe of red wine. She put the tray on the table, poured the liquor, and half-drained her glass without waiting for me.

"Would you like to join us for lunch, Mr. Cobb?" she asked me. "We have andouillette, one of Papa's favorites."

I told her that I wasn't hungry, and she said, "Well, actually I'm not hungry either, but my father is probably starving. We can talk while I feed him." I took a sip of wine and waited once more, watching Lucas Duchamp, who remained motionless in his black wheelchair.

She laid the table with sweeping gestures, as if performing a long-established ritual, and brought out some sausages and fries. She started feeding her stepfather, dabbing his lips with a kitchen towel after each morsel. I said nothing, waiting for her to talk again.

"He was the best father in the world," she said. "When my sister and I were little, he never laid a finger on us, ever, under any circumstances. I hired a nurse, who comes twice a week, but I enjoy looking after him, for me it's not a chore or a hassle."

She sipped her wine and smacked her lips, searching my face.

"Now please tell me, Mr. Cobb, how do you know Abraham and Joshua, and how do you know so much about their past?"

"I'm a psychiatrist, Ms. Maillot, and Josh was one of my patients. He told me about the period of time they had spent in Paris in the mid-seventies. After he died I came across a diary that belonged to Mr. Abraham Hale."

"You told me that you had a personal message for me from Joshua. What could it be?"

I told her as briefly as I could what I knew about Josh and Abraham and she listened to me carefully, without comment. Finally, I mentioned that before coming to see her, I'd met with Claudette Morel in Paris.

"I've learned from one of our mutual acquaintances that she hasn't been exactly sound in the head these last few years," she stressed. "If I were you, I'd take what she says with a big grain of salt."

"She told me that you were best friends back then and shared an apartment."

"Well, I wouldn't say that. We were friends, yes, and we shared an apartment, but—"

"She also said that you asked her to come with you to the hotel where Simone had arranged a meeting with Joshua. It was the night when your sister disappeared."

She'd finished feeding her stepfather, and cleared the table, coming back from the kitchen with an ashtray and a pack of Vogue. She produced a lighter from her pocket, lit a cigarette, and said, "I can't remember many details, Mr. Cobb, it was so long ago. And it doesn't really matter anymore, don't you think? What was Joshua's message? I don't have much time, I'm very sorry. I know you've made such a long trip to come here."

"Before we get to that, I'd like to ask you something, Ms. Maillot, if I might be so bold. Do you think that Josh or Abraham, or maybe both of them, were involved in your sister's disappearance?"

"I beg your pardon? No, I don't think so. Why?"

I took from my pocket the gold pendant that Josh had sent me and put it on the table, in front of her.

"Josh asked me to give you this."

She glanced at the jewel, but didn't touch it.

"Well, I don't have a clue why he did this, but thank you, Mr. Cobb. I'll keep it and treasure it. Is there something else you would like to tell me?"

"What happened that night, Ms. Maillot? You were right there, in the next room. What happened to your sister after Claudette left the hotel?"

She stubbed out the butt of her cigarette and looked me straight in the eye.

"I don't think that's any of your concern, Mr. Cobb. I don't know what Claudette told you exactly and I don't think it matters anymore. Now—"

"But you know exactly what happened, don't you?"

She stood up and pushed the wheelchair to the fireplace. Lucas Duchamp's eyes were now closed, as if he'd fallen asleep. She sat back down on her chair, lit another cigarette, and said, "Are you insinuating that I had something to do with my sister's disappearance?"

"No, I'm not insinuating anything. I'm certain."

"And I suppose that you want me to confirm whatever Joshua's imagination has conjured up. I can't and won't. I think you'd better leave. At the end of the day, I don't know who you are, why you came here, and what you want from me. If you don't leave immediately, I'll have to call the police."

I decided to play my ace up my sleeve. "Ms. Maillot, have you ever heard about a man named Perrin, Nicolas Perrin? Does this name ring a bell?"

Her face turned red, and for a moment I thought she was going to suffer a stroke. Her hands were shaking, and she almost dropped her cigarette from between her fingers. I heard a choked, gurgling sound coming from Lucas Duchamp's throat, as if he was struggling to say something, but the words drowned before reaching his lips. His eyes were now wide open and focused on me.

She made an effort to pull herself together, cast a glance at her stepfather, and asked, "Would you like to go outside? There's a nice place by the garden in which we can stay and talk."

We stood up and went downstairs. She took her coat from the rack and threw it over her shoulders, then exchanged her slippers for a pair of boots. She ushered me along a paved path around the side of the mansion. There was a large sunhouse and we walked inside. The place was full of old things—clothing, garden tools, broken pottery, empty bottles, watering cans—but by the entrance there was a fold-up table and four chairs.

The smell of damp and dust hung in the air. A black and white cat appeared out of the blue and rubbed against her legs. She bent over and fondled the scruff of its neck, then searched her surroundings and fetched a mug to use as an ashtray.

We sat down and she lit a cigarette. "Now tell me how you came across that name you mentioned," she asked.

"Before that, I want you to know something about Josh. He never knew the truth about that night and spent the rest of his life suspecting himself of being a murderer. The sense of guilt ate him up inside. When your friend, Claudette, sent him a letter a few months ago, accusing him of having been involved in your sister's disappearance, he tried to get to the truth one last time. He hired me to help him, but I couldn't do anything. For him, over the years it became less about what really happened that night, and more about what might have happened and what he might have been capable of doing under certain circumstances."

She lifted her shoulders.

"And am I supposed to feel guilty about that, Mr. Cobb? How on earth could I have known all this? I'm not sure what Joshua told you about us, but the truth is that we barely knew each other. He was just a nice and handsome young man who was courting my sister. Then the tragedy happened, he left the country, and that was that. I never heard from him again."

In the dim light filtered through the dusty glass panels, her pale face, surrounded by tiny clouds of cigarette smoke, looked almost ghostly.

"You know, Ms. Maillot, I kept asking myself questions about Josh, trying to understand why he would have hurt your sister. I examined his possible motives, his past, and his character. What I didn't realize until yesterday was that the story was never about him, but about you, your sister, and your father. About the Duchamps. In the real story, Josh and Abraham were just minor characters, who had nothing to do with what was really going on backstage. For you, at least, there has always been just one leading character: your stepfather. And now we come to the name I've mentioned, Nicolas Perrin."

She was listening to me carefully. I imagined her sitting there, year after year, decade after decade, surrounded by her secrets and no other sound than the moaning of the wind.

"After the war," I went on, "your stepfather was considered a hero. He was one of the few members of the local Resistance who had escaped the Gestapo's clutches. Although he'd been tortured for weeks, he didn't betray his comrades' whereabouts. Or this was the official story.

"In the late forties, the French authorities began to chase Klaus Barbie, the former chief of the Gestapo here in Lyon. Finally, in seventy-one, he was identified somewhere in Peru, where he was hiding under an assumed name, Klaus Alttmann. It was a scandal, because the American secret agencies were suspected of having helped him avoid extradition in exchange for what he knew about the network of Soviet sleeper spies in France. Immediately after that, he fled to Bolivia and managed to escape again.

"Under those circumstances, the stories directly related to Klaus Barbie all of a sudden came back into the spotlight. A couple of important newspapers ran articles on that subject and your stepfather's name was mentioned repeatedly on TV and radio. Had Barbie been extradited to France, your father would have been a key witness at the trial, because he'd been interrogated a couple of times by Barbie in person.

"Well, to cut a long story short, Barbie was finally extradited in eighty-three and sentenced to life. He died in prison in 1991. But your father never testified against him in court. Why?"

She stubbed out her half-smoked cigarette, got up, and threw back her shoulders. "What do you want from me?" she asked me. Her voice had turned aggressive. "And why do you care?"

"I came here because I simply wanted to know what really happened to your sister, and because this story needs an ending. I'm now sure that neither Josh nor Abraham, despite their troubled past, had anything to do with what happened that night. It's none of my concern whether your stepfather was a hero who withstood torture and refused to betray his comrades, or whether he was a traitor, as Perrin claimed after he saw his name all over the news."

"Perrin was a madman, a liar, and a coward!" she

exclaimed, bending toward me. She slapped her palms down on the table and a small cloud of dust rose into the air. "Before he came here and tried to blackmail my father, he'd been in jail for a hit-and-run, did you know that? He was old, desperate, and paranoid. After my father sent him away, he tried to sell his story to the press, but nobody believed him."

"Maybe, but the authorities considered his story reliable enough to carry out a discreet inquiry, the result of which was ambiguous. Perrin had been a member of the Resistance too, and he'd been arrested by the Gestapo shortly after your stepfather. He'd been told during his interrogation that Lucas Duchamp was the one who had betrayed him. Coincidentally or not, nine members of the local Resistance's cell had been caught after your stepfather's imprisonment. All of them, except for Perrin, had been executed."

"Lies ..."

"Eventually, the authorities decided to drop the inquiry, because it might have been used by Klaus Barbie's defenders and by far-right revisionists. Perrin died from a heart attack in March 1978, and so the whole affair was buried."

Her eyes were glued to mine and her lower jaw was moving, like she was chewing gum. "What kind of man are you?" she hissed at me. "Do you have any idea what they did to him? He told me that they carved his skin and tore his nails off! I never gave a damn what that lunatic was claiming, whether it was true or not. Back in the day nobody cared anymore about what really happened during the war. There were endless discussions about who did what and to whom in those years, about who was a hero and who was a collaborator and why. It was fashionable to rewrite the entire history sitting in an armchair with a pipe in your mouth and to blame the former generation, good and bad people all together. All nonsense."

"You got me wrong, I'm not judging him."

She didn't seem to hear me.

"Alright, maybe he couldn't withstand the tortures and did what anyone would have done. But who are you to question his integrity? Do you know what it's like being tortured? Did you experience something even close to what he went through? I don't think so, Mr. Cobb! But I do know that he saved us and was like an angel to us."

"Is that why you did what you did, Simone? Did you try to protect him?"

For a while she just looked at me blinking rapidly, her lips quivering. Then she sat down on her chair and asked, "Why would you call me that?"

"Because you're Simone, not Laura, isn't that right? One of the things that puzzled me the most was: why didn't Lucas Duchamp do more to find out the truth about her disappearance? She might have still been alive somewhere, kidnapped, waiting for help. But after just a couple of days, when nobody could have known for sure what had happened to her, Laura left the country and went to that hospital. Your stepfather had money and power, he knew the right people, and he was a lawyer. He knew how to put pressure on the police. At the same time he'd have been able to track those boys all the way to Alaska, if he'd really wanted to. But no, he didn't do much, did he? I carefully read the case file, Simone. Honestly, what the police did was next to nothing. And then I figured out the only pertinent answer: Lucas Duchamp didn't do anything because he wanted to protect someone. And whose reputation and freedom could be on the line? Laura's? No way. She'd rebelled against him, and she'd never been his favorite. Had Laura hurt Simone, Lucas Duchamp would never have helped her to get away with that. By the way, you didn't recognize the pendant. It was a gift for your sister from Josh."

"I recognized it," she said. Her voice was dry. "She was wearing it that night."

"Are you sure?"

"Yes."

"But why didn't Josh recognize it? … He'd have realized it was Laura's body, not yours … He told me he'd found the pendant in a drawer later on, along with Abraham's passport."

Suddenly, I figured out the answer. Abraham had woken up first. He'd seen the body, and arranged the crime scene in order to protect Simone. He must have realized what had really happened and that Simone had made the mistake of leaving that pendant around her sister's neck, so he'd removed it and taken it with him.

Did he try, the next day, to set up Josh, leaving the pendant in his apartment on the Rue de Rome? Did he try to draw the attention of the police by throwing that suitcase on the street? Unlike Josh, he must have known all along that Simone didn't die that night. It's probably why, much later, when he was already deeply shattered by madness, he'd staged that masquerade with the actress, scraping together an imaginary world in which he and Simone were finally lovers. But then his troubled mind had turned his imaginary Elysium into a nightmare, where Josh was trying once again to take her from him.

"I was sure you did it, Simone," I said, "but I couldn't figure out why. Initially, I thought that it must have been something connected to Josh, because you'd arranged the meeting with him that evening."

"It had nothing to do with him or with Abraham."

I knew she was ready to tell the truth and I didn't want to push her harder. She lit a cigarette and just smoked for a while, absently, avoiding my gaze.

"That man, Perrin, came here on a Saturday afternoon, when Laura and I were both home," she said. "Purely by chance, we'd come home for the weekend. Laura and I were together, looking up a book in the library, on the first floor. We heard voices coming from my father's office, and so we eavesdropped. That man was accusing my father of being a traitor and a liar. My father never knew that we were there that afternoon. Later on, when he asked me why I did what I did, like you today, I told him that I was jealous, because Laura and I had fallen for one of those American boys. I'd have rather died than tell him that Laura was thinking of betraying him.

"I didn't mean to hurt her. She was my little sister and I loved her. When she burst into my suite that night, crying, screaming at me, insulting me, I was afraid that the boys would wake up and hear what she was saying about our father. I asked her to leave me alone, but she attacked me. I couldn't immobilize her hands and stop her, because she was stronger than I'd thought. I must have lost my temper, grabbed something near at hand from the nightstand, and hit her over the head. When I eventually came to my senses I found myself holding the lamp, which was covered in blood. Laura was lying on the carpet motionless, battered. I dragged her to the bathroom, undressed her, and heaved her into the tub. I tried to resuscitate her for a time, but I realized that she was dead. Despite my efforts, she had no pulse and wasn't breathing. When I went back into the room, Abraham opened his eyes for a moment and gazed at me, apparently without even seeing me. I went into the adjoining room—the door was still open—washed myself, gathered Laura's clothes, and left. I didn't know that Claudette had been with her that night."

She was crying. No grimaces or sobs, just tears trickling down her face, heavy and shiny like two minuscule creeks of molten lead. I'd desperately wished to know the true about what had happened, for reasons which I myself couldn't entirely understand. But at that moment, when I finally got to the bottom of the story, I felt as if I'd traveled to the ends of the earth to assemble something important, only to end up collecting another person's bad blood. What's the point of absorbing somebody else's nightmare, when you've got yours? Perhaps Josh had been right, and sometimes facts can simultaneously be true and false, because in real life there's no such thing as the truth, the whole truth, and nothing but the truth.

The cat gave a sudden start and left. Outside in the garden, the shadows of the apple trees traced twisted patterns between the dark puddles.

"But why did Laura come to the hotel?" I asked her. "What's the connection to the story about your stepfather?"

She shrugged and stubbed out the cigarette.

"I didn't care about what that man, Perrin, had insinuated, but Laura acted differently. She carried out her own research and jumped to the conclusion that Perrin was telling the truth: our father had been a traitor. We argued for days. I tried to convince her that she was wrong: If our father were a traitor, the Nazis wouldn't have deported his parents, who had died in a concentration camp. But she wouldn't listen to me, and her so-called arguments against our father were totally irrational. I never knew whether she really believed them or she was just trying to punish our father because I had always been his favorite and not her.

"That was in May. Shortly after that, in the summer, we met Abraham and Joshua, and she came up with a bizarre plan. I don't know if she really liked Joshua or just wanted to leave the country. She had had this fantasy about America since childhood. My father is a good person, Mr. Cobb. He never did anything to hurt us, despite the rumors spread by mean people. He was just overprotective, worried that something bad could happen to us, probably because he'd lost his family during the war and was afraid that it could happen again. I understood and accepted it, but Laura didn't. That summer, as I told you, she came up with the crazy idea that Joshua should help her and take her with him to New York, at all costs, because she could no longer bear our father's behavior, and if she'd stayed in France, he'd have never left her alone. So she wanted to go abroad, to a place where he couldn't have tracked her down. Joshua was rich, so he could help her.

"In short, she blackmailed me: if I didn't convince Joshua to help her, she'd reveal the whole story to the press. It was a lousy plan, of course. I told her that Joshua intended to stay in Paris for a while, but she didn't care: I had to convince him to take her to the States, or everything would go in the newspapers. So I lied to her and I arranged that meeting at the hotel with Joshua. I was trying to buy time, pretending that I was going to convince him to help her. But Abraham had followed me and showed up there uninvited. He and Joshua got drunk and started arguing, as usual. I had no idea that Laura was in the next room, trying to make sure that I'd fulfil my promise. At one point, after she realized that I had no intention of talking to Joshua about her so-called plan, she burst inside. You know the rest."

"Was it your stepfather or Abraham who removed her body the next day?"

"I don't know and I didn't want to know. I called my father from a payphone and told him I was in trouble. He came by car, rented a room for me in his name at another hotel, and instructed me to stay there and wait for him. He returned the following day, in the evening, and gave me Laura's passport, some cash, and a one-way ticket to Switzerland. The next day, at the airport, while I was waiting for my flight, I saw Joshua sitting at a table in a café. For a moment I wanted to go over there and tell him everything, but then he walked away and vanished into the crowd."

"Are you sure it was him?"

"Of course I'm sure. It was the last time I ever saw him."

"What happened to Laura's body?"

"I don't know. We never discussed it. My father handled the matter, that's all I know."

"He handled the matter … Isn't that what he did all his life? He handled the matters and cleaned up the trash."

We got up and left the sunhouse. She clutched her coat around her body and asked me, "Why did you *really* come here, Mr. Cobb?"

"I wanted to know the truth. The truth Josh never knew. It could have set him free."

"Truth is a very heavy word. You know what it's like when you have a nightmare, wake up, and then you see details and images from your bad dream in reality? After a while, you can no longer tell the difference between what you dreamed and real life."

"I know what you mean."

"No, you don't, you just think you do. I'm not even sure whether I truly remember what really happened or whether my memories are just snatches of bad dreams."

A soft breeze ruffled her hair. I thought about Lucas Duchamp in his wheelchair, trapped inside that house with her like they were two prehistoric insects in the same lump of amber.

We were close to the main entrance. She took a deep breath, tossed her chin toward the mansion, and said, "This place hasn't been a shelter. I had to lock myself up and throw away the key. I've lived like a ghost almost my entire life. After I came back from Switzerland, I stayed locked away in my room for over three years. Can you imagine what it's like? My mother was eaten alive by what happened and never really forgave me … I've had my share of punishment, you can be sure of that. But I'm glad I've been able to look after my father. It wouldn't have been fair if a man like him had ended his life in an old people's home, surrounded by strangers."

"Have you never been interested in knowing the truth about him?"

"I've always known the truth about him, Mr. Cobb. What happens now?"

"Nothing. I guess everybody's had enough."

"Are you going to talk to the police?"

"I don't work for the police."

"So everything ends here?"

"No, I don't think so. Things like that never really end. But I fulfilled my promise."

I don't know how long we kept talking for. At one point, I went back inside, took my parka and my briefcase, said goodbye to her, and set off on foot. She remained standing by the entrance, frozen. In the faint light of the noon sun, she looked like a broken toy.

I was in the middle of nowhere, so I walked for around twenty minutes along the cobbled road before I came to a gas station from where I called a cab. It started raining and the sky darkened. That story hung round my neck like a millstone.

I remembered the dog choosing one of her puppies in the ring of fire. And I imagined old wheelchair-bound Lucas Duchamp, who was still strong and able at the time, listening to his precious stepdaughter, and deciding to do what he had to do, because all he wanted was to save his favorite.

We all have to make choices and live with the consequences for the rest of our lives. Josh had chosen to run away in order to survive, because he was too young to know that surviving and living aren't the same thing, and that there are no walls thick enough and locks strong enough to protect you from your own consciousness.

I recalled too the moment when an unknown voice told me on the phone what had happened to Julie. "Dr. Cobb? Good morning, sir, sorry for disturbing you, it's about one of your former patients …" and I instantly knew that it was about her and that what I was about to hear over the next few seconds would break my heart forever.

They say that time heals. They're wrong. When something truly bad happens to you, time just splits into two different streams. In one of them, you go on living, at least apparently. But in the other one, there's only that moment, crashing down on you over and over again.

# twenty-one

New York, New York, five months ago

**A FEW DAYS LATER,** while I was still trying to get back on track, I suddenly remembered the detail that had eluded me while listening to Julie's audio-files: "(…) he gave me that book, *The Waves*. Virginia Woolf was his favorite author and he was always quoting her. I think he knew all her books by heart …"

And I read again the last paragraph of her goodbye letter: "Remember that quote from that book you love so much? 'I'm not one and simple, but complex and many.'"

I checked online: the quote she'd mentioned was from *The Waves*. I've never been a big fan of Woolf's and I'd never discussed books with Julie, except for *The Divine Comedy*.

She hadn't given me too many details about that man, one of her ex-boyfriends. She'd only mentioned his first name, David, two or three times during our conversations, and told me that they'd had a casual relationship shortly before we met. Nothing notable, nothing important. Just an impulsive thing, she said.

Susan Dressman called me a couple of days later, after St. Patrick's Day. I'd spent that weekend all by myself at home, thinking about what had happened and writing a long report addressed to the Office of Professional Medical Conduct.

After a few pleasantries she got to the point.

"I couldn't stop thinking about our last meeting ... I was absolutely livid with you, but afterwards I realized that maybe I made a mistake. I was looking into your eyes that day, watching you talk about Julie, and I couldn't help but think you really did care about her."

"I didn't *care* about her. I *loved* her. But you're right, I was wrong and now I know what I have to do."

"Yes, maybe you do, but ..."

There was a brief pause while we both waited for the other to speak again. She eventually went on.

"I lied to you that day. There's something you should know about Julie and her goodbye letter. It wasn't for you, but for a man named David Heaslet, who now lives in Detroit. They were lovers, but he broke up with her before moving to Michigan. I knew the truth, but I was outraged because you'd taken advantage of her, or that's what I was thinking at the time, and I wanted to punish you. So I suggested to her parents that the letter was addressed to you so they could use it as evidence in the future inquiry carried out by the police ... That's what I wanted to tell you. Well, I wrote you a note today and sent it to your office. It was easier that way. I wanted to make sure that you still practice at the same address and that you'll get it."

I confirmed that I had the same address and thanked her, bringing the conversation to a close.

I received her note on Wednesday, but I didn't open the envelope. Instead, I sent the report I'd written over the weekend to the OPMC. Professor Atkins, who was the vice-chairman of the board, called me after two days, first thing in the morning. He was stunned and confused. After my graduation, we'd made a point of getting together every now and then, but over the past few months we hadn't seen each other.

"It's the first time I've ever heard of a doctor who files an ethics charge against himself," he said. "What do you think you're doing?"

I told him that I'd been thinking a lot over the last few months and I'd come to the conclusion that there was no other way. We met for a drink that very afternoon and had a long talk.

"Why are you doing this to yourself?" he asked me. "Have you had a breakdown? You could lose your license for life, do you realize that? Having sexual relations with a patient is automatically considered malpractice, whether the treatment had something to do with her decision to commit suicide or not. Yes, you were deeply wrong, and I wonder how on earth you could do something like that. But if I were you, I'd try to find another way to punish myself."

"George, with all due respect, I don't think you understand. I'm not punishing myself, I'm trying to save myself. If I don't do this now, if I don't take responsibility for what I've done, this thing is going to destroy me, as it has already done to some extent. I met some people who spent their entire lives alone, hiding from themselves, because at a certain moment they hadn't been capable of assuming the responsibility for something they'd done or just thought they'd done. And I don't want to make the same mistake."

It was a warm Friday evening and we were sitting at a terrace in Tribeca, not far from the Rockefeller Center. The sky was the color of latte coffee and the sun was about to set behind the skyscrapers. Endless streams of people were pouring down the streets, like a secret procession.

"You're the best psychiatrist I've ever met," Atkins said. "You're intuitive, cultured, and you like healing people, you care about them, and this must be the first quality of a doctor, in my opinion. I was hoping that sooner or later you'd consider a career in academia and come join me at Columbia. Believe me, they'll crucify you. Are you sure you really deserve to go through something like this? Is there no other way?"

"Yes, there's no other way. I should have been there, with her, to help her out of the ring of fire, no matter what. But I wasn't, nobody was, and she just sat there and burnt, because everybody had left her behind."

"What ring of fire are you talking about?"

"It's a long story. I'll tell it you someday."

We kept talking for another half hour. In the end, he walked me to a cabstand, shook my hand goodbye, and promised me that he'd summon a review board of peers as soon and as discreetly as possible. That evening, I had a long discussion on Skype with my parents in Kansas, trying to explain to them what was going to happen over the next few weeks. It was one of the hardest things I've ever done—it's always excruciatingly painful to hurt the people you love.

I didn't know Julie's stepparents' address, but I'd included Susan Dressman's contact information in my statement. To my surprise, the Mitchells refused to file a lawsuit against me. However, the DA's office reopened the case, given the new information that had come to light, in order to determine whether I'd breached the duty of reasonable care or whether I'd failed to conduct a proper suicide risk assessment, with lethal consequences for my ex-patient.

Somebody leaked the information to the press and another nightmare began. The malpractice attorneys started hounding Julie's parents and a number of my female ex-patients, offering their services pro bono and promising them multi-million-dollar compensations if they agreed to sue me.

The reporters pursued me around the clock for a couple of weeks. Mrs. Kellerman, my sixty-five-year-old assistant, was asked by one of them if she'd had sexual intercourse with me. Some friends stopped returning my calls and one of my ex-girlfriends was interviewed by a popular blogger, describing my sexual preferences in small detail. A magazine nicknamed me "Dr. Strangelove." I had to close my Twitter account and my website was hacked and stuffed with porn.

My life was gradually falling apart, peeling off layer after layer, but I experienced a strange sense of relief. Fortunately, there's something named "the pain principle": our brains are designed in such a way that we can't feel two or more pains simultaneously.

But then one million other things happened and the reporters forgot about me. For the press, there's always a bigger fish to fry in this city.

As the first step, the review board decided to suspend my license for ninety days, so I had to transfer my clients to other doctors and close down my practice. Suddenly, I had a lot of time on my hands, which I didn't know how to kill. In the meantime, the spring slowly turned into summer and the dog days descended on the streets.

The board concluded that I'd acted unethically and I'd violated the boundaries between doctor and patient, but I was found not guilty of failure to warn. Julie had committed suicide a year after we'd stopped seeing each other and the medical treatment she'd received was considered proper and necessary. The prosecutor stood by that view, so the legal action for malpractice went on without that count. Eventually, my license was suspended for three years, and there were no other legal charges. During the suspension, I was allowed to practice on modified qualification only, as a medical assistant. So I called New York Harm Reduction Educators and at the end of June I started working as a part-time assistant at a small rehab facility in Hunts Point, Bronx.

On the 7th of July—Julie's birthday—I woke up early. Out of the window, the sky was like an immense swath of blue cotton. I got dressed and went to a nearby florist's, where I bought twenty-nine yellow tulips, arranged in a bouquet.

I caught a cab and headed for Queens, slicing through

the serene morning air, amid the hundreds of cars crossing the bridge. The cab took me along Queens Boulevard and then onto 58th Street, before dropping me at the Calvary Cemetery. I paid the driver and lingered for a few moments in front of the wrought iron gates before entering.

I walked down the central lane and turned left at the Johnstone Mausoleum. It was sprinkling, and my shoes left dark wounds in the flesh of the grass. The screech of a stray bird shattered the silence with its tidings.

Julie's grave was plain—a small stone inscribed with her name, date of birth, and date of death. In front of it there was a bench. I laid the bouquet by the headstone and sat down. The light raindrops settled down one by one on the flowers, like diamonds.

I took Susan's letter out of my pocket and placed it next to the grave. It was Julie's secret and she had the right to keep it. I lit up a lighter, fired the paper, and watched it burn. Josh was right: some long-gone stories should never come to light, because once they do, they shrivel up like flowers. Their shapes have changed, and their meanings have vanished. But you always have to take responsibility for what you've done; there's no other possible ending to such stories. That was what I'd forgotten, lugging a briefcase stuffed with books around the city, rummaging in strangers' haunted attics.

I left the cemetery and took a cab back downtown. It had stopped raining. The deep blue sky was like a window to another world, and steam rose from the river. I lingered for a while in Central Park, looking at the passersby and wondering about their hidden stories, which seemed to vibrate in the air, mysterious and untold. And later still, when the light had become so faint that I could no longer make out the people's eyes, and the shadows that followed them were those of giants, I went away.

In heaven and earth, Horatio.

New York, New York, today

I framed the photograph Josh sent me and now it hangs on a hallway in the rehab facility where I've been working for two months now. Almost all the patients notice it and ask me who those people are. I tell them that it's an old memory from Paris, but that I can't remember either the people's names or their stories, and that maybe it's no longer important. I ask them to use their imagination, to make up their own story about them, to study their attitudes, their postures, and their expressions.

And without realizing it, almost all of them begin to unfold their own stories, hidden among the patches of light and shadow.

# acknowledgements

Well, this one was tough.

I wrote the first draft five years ago, while living twenty-four miles northwest of London, in Hemel Hempstead. I wasn't happy with the result, so I wrote a second draft a year later, in Reading, Berkshire, where I had moved house in the meantime. I finished it within three months, but kept it stashed away in my computer for another two years or so. During that period, I published two non-fiction books and continued to polish *The Book of Mirrors*, the novel that was to change my writing career, turning me almost overnight into an international writer published in over forty countries. A whole cluster of projects was rolling in my mind at the time, but this one particular book was like a nine-inch nail lodged in my head. I felt that unless I managed to squeeze the best I could out of this story, it would continue to lour over me like a dark cloud. So I decided to give it another shot, eventually doing so in the summer of 2016. Ten months later, *Bad Blood* was finally done and ready for submission.

My thanks go to Marilia Savvides, my agent; her advice was priceless, as usual. To Cecily Gayford, my editor, who believed in this project from the very start and helped me to see it through to the end. To the wonderful people of Serpent's Tail, who didn't march me to the gallows for splitting infinitives or starting the occasional sentence with a preposition. Thank you, guys. To my good friend Alistair Ian Blyth; he kept an eye on me, so as not to injure myself too seriously while swinging with the English language. Finally, to my wife, Mihaela, the main (or perhaps the only) reason why I haven't picked up sticks and gone back down the rabbit hole yet.